THE TRIBE

THE TRIBE

Valerie Bloom

MACMILLAN CHILDREN'S BOOKS

First published 2007 by Macmillan Children's Books
a division of Macmillan Publishers Limited
20 New Wharf Road, London N1 9RR
Basingstoke and Oxford
www.panmacmillan.com

Associated companies throughout the world

ISBN: 978-1-4050-4782-1

1 3 5 7 9 8 6 4 2

A CIP catalogue record for this book is available from
the British Library.

Typeset by Nigel Hazle
Printed and bound in Great Britain by Mackays of Chatham plc, Kent

In loving memory of my mother, Edna Wright

With special thanks to Tracy Clark for the time,
Lorna Barden for the space, Rachel Denwood
for her tireless assistance and unlimited patience,
and to my family for not giving up. I would
also like to thank Tamara and Richard Mansell
for help with Spanish translations, the Arts Council
of Great Britain, Amaru and the many other friends,
family and acquaintances who contributed to
the realization of this project.

Kiskeya

1
Omens

The birds should have told us. They should have been silent in the trees, not singing and squabbling as if it was just an ordinary day. The sky should have worn his angry face and the sea should have been boiling with rage. There should have been a flash flood, forcing the river behind the village to mount its banks, or a hurricane, uprooting the trees in the forest, on the day that such a change overtook us. But none of these things happened, so we had no warning. And we were not prepared.

I was planning to go hunting, so I got up just as the birds started singing the spirits to bed. I was going through the doorway of our *caney* when I heard my name.

'Maruka! Wait!'

1

I turned to see my sister scrambling from her hammock and I forced my lips to smile a morning greeting, but my heart sank. I thought of the work I was hoping to do before everyone else was awake, and searched for a way to get my sister to go back to her hammock.

Guabonito had lived five dry seasons already, seven less than I, and, since she had started to walk, had decided I should be her teacher and constant companion.

'Nito! I hope I did not wake you.'

'I was ready to wake.' She yawned and rubbed the sleep from her eyes. 'May I come to wash with you?'

'Wouldn't you rather sleep a little longer? The cocks have barely started their morning songs.'

The coral black hair danced against her round cheeks as she shook her head. 'I have had enough sleep. I want to go with you.'

Her voice rose to emphasize her wish and I glanced anxiously at the other hammocks in the *caney*. My father's swayed and squeaked as he turned on his side, but then there was quiet again. I sighed in defeat, stretched out my hand to Nito and led her towards the doorway.

'Very well. But you must promise not to spend the whole day in the water. I am going hunting.'

'I promise. May I go with you?'

I laughed, softly, so as not to wake the others. 'You will have to ask your mother.' I held her as she turned to run back inside. 'Not now. Let her sleep. You may ask her when we return.'

I had a favourite place where the river met the sea. It reminded me of the place in my old home on Iyanola where Caicihu had taught me how to fish. But I did not want to think about my brother today. He belonged to a time when I was someone else. Anani. No one had called me that for two dry seasons and I did not want to remember her now.

A shy breeze stroked the leaves in the genip trees, and caressed my cheeks; the smell of ripe guavas drifted to me from the plantation above the village and a gentle light touched the dew on the grass so that it sparkled like ciba stones. My spirits were light. There was no room in me for sad thoughts.

The sun had painted the rippling waves with gold, but the water was not yet warm, and for a couple of breaths my whole body tensed against the sudden shock of the cold. Guabonito squealed, and ran back on to the sand. She was not used to washing so early and was not prepared for the cold. I ran after her, laughing, lifted her and dropped her into the sea. She screamed, and splashed about, but soon her body adjusted to the temperature.

'Look at me, Maruka! I am a manatee.' She was swimming slowly and clumsily in the shallow water, a stupid expression on her face.

I laughed. Then I screwed up my face like a lizard's and croaked in my throat.

'An iguana!' Nito clapped her hands.

I opened my eyes wide, pursed my lips and whistled. An answering whistle came from the trees a little distance away. Nito's eyes grew round.

'A parakeet! More! More!'

'Very well. Who is this?' I made small squeaking noises, wrinkled my nose, and sniffed around her as if looking for food. Nito was shaking, covering her mouth, her eyes almost completely closed with her laughter. Then she stopped, eyes wide.

'That was even better than the first one! How did you do it?'

I shook my head. 'That was not me. Look.'

Her gaze followed my pointing finger to the lowest branch of the tree which drooped over the water. A *hutia* was clinging to the branch, gazing at us, its expression puzzled and a little frightened.

I squeaked again. The mouse-like head tilted to one side and the small brown eyes focused on me before it turned and disappeared into the foliage, squeaking indignantly to itself.

Nito had a wistful look on her face. 'I wish I could talk animal like that.'

'Perhaps the hunters will teach you as they taught Caicihu and me.' But I knew Nito's mother would never allow her to hunt. I quickly changed the topic.

'Race you to that boulder over there.'

*

4

We swam for a while in the sea and then waded up the river to wash the salt and the paints from our skin. The digo plant grew on the banks of the river and I picked some leaves and scrubbed the *roucou* from Guabonito's body, watching the red dye stain the water for an instant before it disappeared. Then I scrubbed myself.

While we waited for the sun to dry us, I hunted along the shore. Guabonito searched with me, her brows furrowed in concentration. After a while she stopped and turned to me.

'What are we looking for?'

I could not help laughing. 'I need a new head for my axe,' I told her. 'My old one is getting blunt.'

I noticed a boulder at the mouth of the river, covered with seaweed and swarming with flies. That meant there were shellfish trapped in the weeds from the last high tide.

I waded across to the rock. There was a heap of shells and stones at its base and some of the clams were still shut tight. They were piled up high, a gift from the sea. The water grumbled around my feet and the flies rose, buzzing indignantly as I approached. I found a shell that would make a good scraper, smooth and unbroken, just what I needed. My fingers closed over it and I glanced towards Nito. She was busy digging among a pile of broken stones. She had not noticed me taking the shell.

'Will this do?' Guabonito was holding up a sharp stone of hard flint, tapered at one end.

I took it, turning it in my hand so that the sunlight found the shiny pieces of the stone and winked at me.

'That is perfect, Nito. You are so clever.'

She beamed with pride, her tongue poking through the gap where she had lost a tooth. The sun kissed her then, and her face shone under the dark circle of her hair. Now, after all that has happened, that is the picture of Guabonito that I still remember.

'Good,' she said. 'May I go and ask Bibi about the hunting now?'

I smiled. She was never patient when she set her mind on something. I turned to follow her and a flash of red caught the corner of my eye. I bent back towards the pile and lifted it from where it was nestling, half buried in the sand.

It was hard, smooth and cool against my palm, and the corners ended in three sharp points. The sea growled around my feet as if telling me to leave it alone, but as I wiped the sand from it, it sparkled at me and I knew I was meant to have it. It was hard as flint, thin at the edges but heavy and strong in the middle. As I twisted it, it caught the light of the sun and flashed fire. Red fire. A good omen. I turned it over and my heart stopped for the space of a breath.

In the centre were two holes, two sightless eyes

staring at me. I took the *zemi,* the image I was wearing, from around my neck and held it beside the red stone. Each was like the other, the image of Atebeyra, goddess of fertility and mother of the sea; except that the stone I had found was smooth below the eyes. It had no hole for a mouth.

The goddess has sent a message, I thought. The likeness from the sea was sent to tell me that she approved of what I was doing.

'Thank you, Atebeyra.' I said it quietly so that Guabonito could not hear.

I turned towards the sea in gratitude. Far out on the water I thought I saw a shape, large and white against the mist-shrouded outline of the island. I strained my eyes, but through the thin white morning mist I could see nothing. I must have been mistaken.

'Hurry, Maruka. The sun is up and the midges are starting to bite. We must get ourselves painted.'

With an inward shrug I turned away and followed Guabonito up the track to the village.

2
Secrets

The morning fires were lit in the compound when we returned and our *caney* was empty. All the men had gone to wash and the women were preparing the morning meal. My mouth filled with water at the smell of the fresh cassava bread.

'Good morning, Karaya. Shall I help you with the meal?'

Nito's mother's face was an older version of hers, round like the moon after which she was named, and my heart warmed as she beamed at me.

'Thank you, Maruka.' She looked at my naked body. 'But you should go and get painted. The mosquitoes must be having a feast.'

*

I was carefully drawing three straight red lines across Guabonito's forehead with the *roucou* dye when she said, 'What will you do with the shell?'

I started, and the perfect line zigzagged across her brow, so that she looked as if someone had just surprised her.

'What shell?' I stalled for time.

She raised her eyebrows in scorn. 'I am not blind, you know. Why did you hide it from me?'

I bit my lip. I could not think of a way to avoid telling her. It was a dishonourable thing for a Taino to lie.

I dipped my finger into the calabash of *roucou* and made a zigzag line across Guabonito's left eye to match the one on her right. Then I took clay from the other calabash and drew six short diagonal lines on her cheeks, three on either side. Her eyes never left my face as she waited for my answer.

'Nito,' I said at last. 'What I am going to tell you is a big secret. You must promise not to tell anyone.'

Her eyes gleamed with pleasure.

'I promise.'

I thought for a few breaths. It was difficult to find the right words. 'I am making a canoe. I need the shell to smooth the inside. I have almost finished.'

Her eyes were round pools of disbelief.

'Does Baba know?'

'Nito, I have just told you it is a secret. We do not

tell secrets to Father.' I held her chin so that our eyes were talking to each other. 'No one else must know. Do you understand?'

Guabonito nodded, and then her forehead creased into a frown so that the lines zigzagged even more across her face.

'But everyone will know when you put it on the water.'

'No, they will not.' I smiled to myself. I had planned it all. 'I will wait until the feast of maize. When everyone is busy dancing, I will go.'

'Go? Where will you go?'

I bit my lip. I had not meant to tell her this much. The words had left my lips before the thought had reached my head. I sighed. 'I am going to rescue my mother.'

Guabonito's eyes grew to the size of our *casabi* griddle. Her mouth dropped open and forgot to close again for some time. When she spoke there was great fear in her voice.

'Maruka, you cannot mean . . . you are not going back?'

I nodded.

'But the Kalinago will catch you. They will eat you!'

'I will not get eaten.' I tried to sound confident, but I could see from her expression that I had not convinced her. 'I will be careful not to get caught, I promise.'

I turned her round so that she had her back to me and I daubed the *roucou* around her shoulder blades.

She was silent for a while and I began to regret telling her so much. It was a big secret for her to keep, but I knew she would not tell anyone. She had given her word and even at her age she knew that a Taino did not break a promise.

When I had almost finished painting her back Guabonito started fidgeting.

'Maruka,' she said tentatively.

'Nito?'

She was silent for a breath, perhaps choosing and discarding words in her head. When she spoke I felt my heart flutter and then race like a hunted coney to its den.

'What if your mother is already eaten? It is such a long time since she was taken.'

'Bibi has not been eaten.'

Without knowing, I had been pressing my fingers hard into her skin.

'Ouch!' Guabonito wriggled away and turned accusing eyes on me.

'I am sorry, Nito. I did not mean to hurt you. My mind had gone hunting.' I took the calabash of clay from her, laid it on the floor and reached for the *roucou*. 'Go get some dead coals from the fire. You need some black to accompany all this red and white.'

I tried to smile, but I do not think she was fooled.

When she had gone, I sat on the floor of the *caney*, cradling the calabash between my thighs. I dipped my fingers into the *roucou* and drew lines and circles across my chest and thighs, but my mind was not on what I was doing and I did not take as much care with the designs as I normally did. Guabonito's words had stirred a fear in me which I had buried deep, a fear that I was running out of time. She was only repeating what the whole village had been saying for a long time. They all thought my mother had been eaten. But I knew differently. And I knew I had to save her before it was too late.

3
A Promise

'Maruka, can I ask you something?'

'What would you like to know?'

Nito stuck her tongue through the gap in her front teeth and thought for a moment. I continued to carve the manatee bone.

'That looks difficult.'

I nodded, but said nothing. She would find the words to ask me her question in time.

'Why do you put your mark on the tips of your arrows? Everyone else just marks the wood. That's easier.'

I was silent for a moment, remembering. 'Caicihu showed me how to do this,' I said at last. 'He was the most skilful young carver in the tribe. Not many people can carve on such a small surface.'

'Will you teach me?'

I smiled. 'One day. But you did not want to ask me about my arrowheads.'

'No.'

Nito took a deep breath, and the words tumbled from her mouth in a rush.

'Can I see the canoe you are making to rescue your mother?'

I glanced round in alarm.

Azzacca was chipping at a stone, making an axe head, just out of range of Nito's words. He glanced up as I looked at him and our gazes held for a breath before I looked away hastily.

'It's all right,' Nito said. 'I made sure no one was listening. I will keep your secret. Have I not promised?'

I smiled. 'Yes, you have promised. And yes, you may see the canoe. After the second meal. Karaya says we do not need any fresh meat today, so I will not go hunting.'

'She does not like you hunting like the boys. She says you should be cooking and weaving or you might never get a mate.'

I pursed my lips. Nito was right. Her mother had tried to be a mother to me since mine was lost, but she was not like my mother.

'I know Karaya would like me to stop,' I said. 'But I would rather hunt than find a mate.'

Our heads were close together and we were whispering.

14

'Would she be really angry if she found out about the canoe?'

I nodded vigorously. 'Very, very angry, Nito, and so would everyone else, so do not breathe a word.'

'I will not. But why will they be so cross? I know only the men make canoes, but you hunt, and only the men do that.'

'What do you two talk about?'

We jumped. We had not heard Azzacca approach.

'Nothing you would find interesting,' I said. Nito giggled behind her hand.

'Tell me. I will decide if it interests me.' I raised my brows. The trouble with Azzacca was that he thought he was more important than others knew he was. Did he think he could order me to tell him what we were talking about? Before I could say anything, Nito piped up.

'Do you really want to know?'

I looked at her in alarm, trying to warn her with my eyes to be quiet, but she was staring innocently up at Azzacca.

'I have already said so.'

'Really? I did not think Maruka's mate would interest you.' Nito giggled again, this time clamping both hands over her mouth. Azzacca gave us a disdainful look and walked away. I did not bother to cover my mouth as I laughed.

15

'When will your canoe be finished?' Guabonito turned from watching Azzacca as he continued his chipping, and carried on as if we had not been interrupted. I glanced at the sky. It was cloudless and vivid blue. There would be no rain for a while.

'Very soon now,' I told her. I looked at her from the corners of my eyes. 'Perhaps if I had help I could finish it sooner.'

Her eyes widened with pleasure and surprise. 'I will go and get the scraper and axe you made me.' She was gone before I could remind her we had not yet had our second meal.

4

Alarm

'Are you building this canoe at the end of the world?'

I stopped and waited for Nito, and laughed at the way she stuck her tongue out and panted like a dog left too long in the sun.

'We are nearly there now, but we can rest here if you like. I could not build it too close to the compound or someone might have heard the sound of the axe and seen the smoke from my fire.'

Nito sank heavily to the ground and I sat beside her.

'You move too fast, Maruka. It is because you have so little flesh on your bones.'

'Perhaps I am skinny because I move fast.' I glanced at her chubby body and shook my head. 'I would not

17

catch many iguanas if I could not move fast. A hunter has to be quick.'

Nito looked sceptical. 'You never catch iguanas.'

She was right. I had tried to catch an iguana only once, and after that ill-fated attempt I could not look at one of the lizards without remembering, but my pride was stung.

'I could if I wanted to.'

'Could you? We have not eaten iguana for ages. The men say there are no more on Kiskeya.'

I thought of the large lizards I had glimpsed while working on my canoe. I had watched them going towards the sacred caves and thought they must sleep inside at night. Here, where the caciques and behiques held secret ceremonies, was the most important place on Kiskeya. No one else was permitted to touch the floor of the caves where the spirits of the ancestors lived.

But I had touched it once.

I had not meant to enter the cave. It was while I had been searching for a tree for my canoe. I had climbed up the hill, my eyes on the large ceiba tree I could see from the valley, but halfway up I had caught sight of a large coney and my hand dropped to the axe at my waist. It would be a good addition to the pepperpot.

I crept up behind it, as silent as a shadow, but when I was almost within striking distance, a family of parrots started a racket in the blue mahoe tree up

18

ahead. The coney stopped snuffling and raised itself on its hind legs. Its nose trembled as it sniffed the air and then it was speeding away from me. I had flown after it, and when it disappeared into the opening in the rock, I followed. I stopped just inside the cave to let my eyes adjust to the dark. My breath caught in my throat. I turned and catapulted from the place quicker than an arrow from a bow, feeling the accusing eyes of the *zemis* carved into the walls, watching as I fled.

I had only been inside for a breath or two. But I knew that was long enough for the wrath of the *zemis* to fall on the Taino. It had been almost a day before the trembling had left my body, and for many nights afterwards I lay awake wondering how the gods would punish me. I had not dared tell anyone what I had done. Even now I did not like to remember.

Now I glanced at Nito, hoping the fear I still felt was not written on my face. 'The men do not know where to look for lizards,' I said. 'Come on, you must be rested now.'

The path sloped down into a small valley and Nito stopped, a worried look clouding her face.

'I do not like it here, Maruka. It is too dark.'

I scanned the place I had started to think of as my own, and saw it as Nito must have been seeing it. The trees stood around the cleared space like guards, their heads close together, blotting out the light and

19

looking as if they shared secrets and plotted together above us. Their roots snaked into the stream, slowing its journey to the sea, forcing it to grumble unhappily as it climbed over or swirled around them. Mangoes had fallen into the water and the skins had rotted away, leaving the hairs of the fruit to float and bob like drowned spirits in the foaming water. And through the trees, we could see the wide waters of the ocean spread out in an azure sheet.

I had forgotten how this place could seem frightening at first. I too had been disturbed by it until I thought how it reminded me of a place I had known on my old home, Iyanola. I hugged my sister close to me.

'Do not be alarmed, Nito. The spirits who live here are good ones.'

'How do you know? Have you spoken to them?' The wary look had not left her eyes.

'I knew somewhere like this on Iyanola. Caicihu and I fished there and the spirits were good to us.'

Nito nodded and was silent, but when I went on down the path she did not follow. She was still not happy. I came back and sat on a log by the side of the path. I patted the space beside me and she sat gingerly on the edge.

'I felt just as you do now, the first time I saw that place.'

'Tell me.'

So I told her about the growling waters of Iyanola.

We were going fishing but too many people fished where the river met the sea, and the fish were beginning to leave. We had to find another place if we were to have a big catch for the harvest feast. I hugged the jar of powdered dogwood bark to my chest.

'We will go to the pool by the growling waters,' Caicihu said.

My eyes grew large with disbelief.

'No one fishes in the home of the spirits.'

A light danced in Caicihu's eyes and I felt a snake of fear slither up my back. I knew that look.

We had not been forbidden to visit the place where the waters fell from huge rocks into the pool below, but we had grown up hearing about the spirits who lived in the shadows where the tall guangu trees bowed their heads over the still waters. The trees blocked out the sun, so that even in the brightest, hottest part of the day, the place was dark and cold.

'The spirits will not harm you if you are respectful to them, you know that. Come on, do not be a ground lizard.'

He knew how to get me to agree. Striped green, blue, red and yellow, the ground lizards looked like tiny rainbows as they scuttled between the rocks. But they were not very brave. At the slightest movement they would panic and head for the nearest hole.

21

I lifted my head and stuck out my chest.

'I am not scared. And you will see if I do not catch more fish than you do.'

I ran ahead of Caicihu, wanting to show him I was not afraid; wanting to hide from him the loud pounding of my heart and the way the beads of sweat decorated my forehead. Sometimes I thought Caicihu was mad. He tempted the gods as if they were only the dead stones and wood we made their images from. But the zemis were powerful. I knew that. I touched the one that hung around my neck. 'Atebeyra, goddess of love,' I prayed silently. 'Please do not be angry with us. Do not harm us. We mean no discourtesy.'

Caicihu was close behind me and suddenly I felt a cold wind climbing my spine. I had the strangest feeling that it was not Caicihu but an evil spirit that was chasing hard behind me.

Fear breathed new life into my feet and I ran as I had never run before. There was a surprised shout behind me, but the blood pounding in my ears stopped me from hearing the words. The fishing basket I carried banged against my side as I ran, but I did not feel anything except the urge to outrun whatever was behind me. The path sloped steeply as we neared the place. I heard the roaring of the waters before I saw them, and it joined with the roaring in my head. The ground stopped, fell away to a field of sharp rocks and boulders far below.

The path turned sharply at the edge of the land and

wormed its way down the side of the pool so that it was possible to see the angry foam and spray as the water tumbled down the rocks into the pool below.

I knew all this, but I was being driven straight ahead by the evil spirit behind me. I was going so fast that I felt I could fly across the boulders below, across the calm waters, to the steep rocks opposite.

My senses returned just before I leaped, but even though I tried to stop, my speed was carrying me towards the lip of the land. Frantic, I flung myself on the ground, grabbing hold of one of the pineapple plants that were growing there. I heard the jar of dogwood bark splintering on the rocks below, and a soft sigh as my fishing basket landed beside it.

A searing pain cut through my side as Caicihu's foot made contact. Then he was falling over me and sliding down to the rocks below. His basket joined mine.

My hand shot out and I held on to his foot just as it was following the rest of his body over the edge.

The jagged edges of the pineapple leaves were cutting into my palm and the extra weight was pulling the roots from the earth, so that I felt Caicihu slipping and taking me with him over the edge.

I looked around desperately for something else to hold on to. There was a small custard apple tree two toes' length from my foot. If I could just reach it.

Caicihu dug his fingers into the clay and tried to push himself backwards. It was enough. I stretched my foot

23

towards the tree and hooked it round the trunk. I pulled myself back and hooked the other leg around the tree.

Then I let go of the pineapple plant and grabbed Caicihu's ankle with my freed hand.

'Push, Caicihu.'

He pushed. I pulled. Slowly he crawled from the edge of the ground and collapsed beside me. When we had recovered our breaths, I turned to look at him. His stomach was scraped and red where the ground had rubbed his skin. The beautiful circles painted in red roucou and white clay were smudged to an untidy mess. Streaks of soil mingled with the white paint on his face. I wiped a smudge from beneath his eye, and left a trail of red instead. Puzzled, I looked at my hand. It was chewed from clutching the sharp leaves.

My thighs, my belly, my chest were stinging. They were scraped and bruised, the thin film of blood mixing with the paint I had spent so much time putting on earlier.

'I am sorry I almost sent you to Coyaba. I did not mean to put you in danger.' My voice was hoarse as I thought that I had almost killed him.

'I know. But our mother is right. You should learn to walk like the rest of us. One day you will run right into some serious trouble and I might not be there to rescue you.'

'You *rescue* me!' I spluttered. 'Who was hanging helpless upside down? And who was it who hauled you by your foot from the door of Coyaba?'

But Caicihu was on his feet, laughing. I guessed he had used these words to chase away my guilt and sorrow.

'Come on, the fish are waiting.'

I paused as I rose. 'We are still going fishing then?'

'Is that not why we came?'

I searched for words to tell him that the spirits might have been warning us away. It was not the first time I had felt this way. I had had the knowledge of something dreadful happening before. Just before my grandparents had gone to be with the ancestors, I had seen them lying without the breath moving their chests. And I had known. But when I told Bibi she had warned me to say nothing to anyone, not even to Caicihu. I did not know how to warn him that the spirits were telling us something dreadful was about to happen. Now more than ever, I did not want to go to fish in their pool. I scrabbled about in my mind for a reason that would allow me to keep my secret but convince Caicihu to turn back. A light went on in my head.

'We cannot fish today. I have lost the dogwood bark.'

'Then we will find it. Where do you think you dropped it?'

I shook my head. I might have known it would not be easy to discourage him.

'It is in splinters on the rocks. All the powder is gone. I am sorry, Caicihu.'

He went to peer down over the land's edge and my heart thudded a warning.

'Be careful, it is slippery there.'

He came back with a smile folding the corners of his eyes. 'It is not all gone. The jar is broken, but I think we can save enough powder to get a few fish. I promised Bibi some fish for the pepperpot and I will not disappoint her.'

My feet were heavy as I followed him down the track. He was right, of course. I sometimes think the zemis were pleased by Caicihu's daring and blessed him more than the rest of us.

As we approached, a large turtle waddled towards the water and a couple of iguanas slithered into the pool and swam for the other side. A flock of parrots squabbled in the branches overhead, and I could see a hutia clinging to a branch above us. I frowned. Hutias were early-morning or night animals and this did not seem the place for iguanas — it was too cold. I turned to Caicihu, suspicious.

'Is this not a strange place to find iguanas?'

Caicihu shook his head. 'They are not spirits, Anani.'

He always knew what I was thinking. That was what came from being born together.

'They come to eat the fruit, then go back to warm themselves on the beach.'

I looked at the mangoes and guavas covering the ground. Flies hummed and bees sawed the air above them. The smell of ripe fruit filled my nostrils. Caicihu was right, of course. He was always right.

The jar could not be repaired, but there was enough dogwood powder to stun more than a few fish.

After the noise and anger of its journey down the rocks, it was unsettling to see the stream so still, as if it was waiting for something. I waded into the water after Caicihu, and felt my skin pimpling from the cold. I shivered as the water lapped against my ankles.

Caicihu reached into the water and lifted a large stone. He took it to the edge of the pool where the water flowed towards the sea.

I followed his example and together we stacked enough stones to form a dam across the end of the pool. That should keep the powder in the water long enough for the fish to be stunned by the poison.

When we had finished we sat on the bank and waited. It seemed an age before anything happened and I was anxious to leave the place. It felt wrong to be there. The deep darkness of the pool made me nervous. And the falling waters seemed to be roaring especially at us.

'I do not think it is working,' I said after a while. 'Perhaps we should forget about fishing today.'

'That would be a shame when we have such a catch.'

I followed his gaze towards the centre of the pool and gasped. The fish were rising, lifeless, to the surface. And what fish they were! They had been undisturbed for so long that they had grown fat and long. It would take both of us to lift some of them.

'How will we get them home?'

Caicihu grinned. 'We will have to make several trips. Think of the praise songs they will sing in our honour tonight.'

Suddenly I felt free of the cloud that was pressing on my spirit. I laughed with Caicihu as we plunged into the cold black water to gather the fish.

We were still laughing as we approached the village with our laden fishing baskets on our heads. My fear of the growling waters was gone. I was grateful to the place for the large catch it had given us for the feast.

Nito's eyes were as round as calabashes when I had finished. 'Do you think the spirits of this place would give us fish like that?'

I smiled and shook my head. 'The waters do not run as deep here.' I put my hand on her arm. 'Nito, what I said about me seeing things before they happen . . . You must tell no one. It is another secret between us.'

Nito nodded solemnly.

'Now, I thought we had come to work on my canoe,' I said, changing the subject.

Nito looked around, puzzled. 'Where is it?'

I pointed to the mound of leaves and branches in front of us.

'You have hidden it well,' she said, pulling a dead branch from the top of the mound.

It took us a while to get all the branches and leaves off and then Nito gasped.

'Ja, Maruka, it is beautiful. How long have you been making this?'

My face was one big smile of pride. 'It took me two dry seasons and three full moons to get this far. But there is still a lot to be done. Help me to turn it over.'

Together we turned the canoe on its bottom. I took a handful of dried leaves and rubbed the earth from around its rim.

The hard ceiba wood gleamed pale in the sunlight, streaked dark in places by the shadows of the branches overhead. I ran my hand across the insides, feeling the rough wood cool against my palm. My hand came away black from the charred wood where I had lit a fire to burn out the inside.

I had watched the men making boats on Iyanola, and although as a female I was not allowed to touch them before they were finished, I could sit and watch. Canoe-building was the only thing I was not allowed to do with Caicihu, but away from the men I pestered him until he secretly showed me how it was done.

'Where do you want me to start?'

I looked at Nito and then at my canoe. It was the length of her twice over. We could fit inside together if we were not both wielding axes.

'Would you like to cut or scrape?'

She held her chin and cocked her head to one side, considering. I waited, trying not to laugh. She was so much like our father when she did that.

'I would not like to cut off a part you want to keep,' she said eventually. 'Perhaps I should scrape.'

We worked until the sun was going home to bed. Except for the scrape of Nito's shell on the bottom of the canoe and the thud of the stone head of my axe against the wood it was quiet. Only the chattering of the blue tits preparing to sleep and the song of the river disturbed the silence.

I got up, stretched my arms above my head and bent backwards, trying to dislodge the ache in my back and shoulders. My thighs felt as if they were being stabbed by broken shells.

Guabonito straightened too, rubbing the small part of her back with her fist.

'We should go soon,' she said. 'It is almost time for the dead to walk.'

'Yes.'

I gave my canoe one last loving look for the day. There was more to do than I had thought. But we had worked well. The charred wood had all been scraped back to bare whiteness and the inside was almost completely smooth.

'I could not have done so much without you, Nito.'

'I liked it. I know now why the men want to keep

this work to themselves. Perhaps I shall make a canoe of my own.'

I smiled. Looking at her expectant face, I felt a tightness in my throat. She was waiting for me to say I would help her, but I could not make such a promise. I would soon be far away and I did not know when I would be back.

'We need to cover it again. If we hurry, we could have a quick bath before it gets dark.' I turned to look out to sea; turned from the disappointment in Guabonito's eyes.

A flock of sea birds were returning home to the land to roost, their squawking loud in the still evening.

The sun slipped hastily over the edge of the water in a blaze of orange red. The light spread across the darkening waters, turning it into a sea of blood. Dusk fell, sudden and heavy like a rotting mamey apple from a tree.

It would not do to be caught in the darkness when the dead left their beds. A shiver made its swift journey down my spine. The breeze moving its way through the trees was warm, but I was suddenly cold.

I turned to pick up a branch then stopped abruptly. My gaze darted back to the sea. I straightened, heart pounding, eyes large in disbelief. Once before I had stood like that with a black cloud smothering my insides. For a moment, I felt the same cloud stifling me, keeping my feet fastened to the ground when my mind was yelling at them to move. In my mind I journeyed back to Iyanola, back to the day when I lost so much.

And I screamed.

'Nito! Nito! Run!'

Iyanola

5

Attack

I was hunting the day my mother was stolen. My father and the men had gone on a trade visit to another island, and my twin brother, Caicihu, was ill in his hammock.

I had told Caicihu many times not to eat the unripe star-apples, but would he listen? Now he was paying for his hard ears with a stomach ache. My mother had given him a drink of guanabana leaves and told him to rest in his hammock. He was not happy. He wanted to be with the men, not left in the village with the women and children.

Time was dragging heavy like the zemi I wore round my neck. I tied my arrow pouch around my waist, stuck my axe into it and took the bow and arrows from their place near the door of the hut. I beckoned to my dog, Cico. He rose from the spot where he was lying under the roof of the hut, and Daha, my brother's dog, rose as well.

'No, Daha. You stay.'

Daha gave me a sorrowful look and I almost let him come. He was used to going hunting with Caicihu and me and could not understand why I would not let him come today. I took him over to my brother's hammock. Caicihu's forehead was hot and sticky. He opened his eyes when he felt my hand on him, and tried to smile as he saw the bow in my hand.

'Going hunting, Anani?' he asked, and I could see he wished he was coming with me.

'I will not be long,' I said. 'I am going to get a nice fat iguana to make your stomach better.'

He sighed, pretending to be distressed. 'Ah, then I shall be ill for a long time.'

'If you were not already at death's door, I would send you to him.' I turned to the opening of the hut.

'Where is your respect?' Caicihu pretended to be shocked at my words. 'Remember I will be cacique one day. You should not talk to a future chief like that.'

I smiled. 'And a future chief should show appreciation when someone is trying to help him. Where are your manners? Look, Daha will keep you company.'

And I left.

I had to get used to being on my own more often. Soon Caicihu would be leaving to go and live with our mother's brother who was cacique on the island of Boriken. I would miss him terribly when he went. When my uncle died Caicihu would inherit his chiefdom and be in charge of his own cacigazgo.

My mother and Karaya, my father's second wife, were coming towards the caney from the direction of the cassava fields. They had baskets of maize and cassava on their heads and Karaya had my sister Guabonito on her hip. They stopped when they saw me and studied my bow and arrow, but with different expressions. Nito's almost black eyes sparkled and she tried to wriggle out of her mother's arms.

'Going hunting?' my mother asked.

'Caicihu is still poorly, Bibi. I am going to find an iguana to make him better.'

'That is a kind thought.'

My mother smiled but my second mother's face wore a resigned expression.

'I was hoping you would go with me to collect some clams from Bird Island,' she said. 'But your brother needs you more than I do.'

I knew she would prefer if I did not go hunting and concentrated on cooking, planting and weaving baskets, but she had long ago accepted that I was not like the other Taino girls. My mother said it was because I had shared a womb with my brother. His spirit had subdued mine and now I had the spirit of a boy. Her gaze shifted from my weapons and went to rest on Cico.

'If you are going on a proper hunt, you should take a proper hunting dog with you. The only way Cico will kill anything is if he does it with kindness. Why do you not take one of the other dogs?'

I bent to pat Cico's head. I had picked him from the dog pen soon after he was born.

'I do not want another dog,' I said. 'Cico and I understand each other.'

It was true that instead of killing the animals we hunted, Cico tried to play with them. But he was still only a puppy and while he was trying to coax the coneys and hutias to play, their attention was turned from me and my arrows.

In the centre of the village a group of boys was standing in a circle playing guamajico. I stopped to watch them for a while. It was a game I loved to play when I was younger. Now I preferred to hunt and fish like my brother and the rest of the men.

The boys' faces were creased in concentration as they clutched their jico, the cord that was tied to their guama seeds to make the guamajico. They laid their seeds on the ground in the middle of the circle and my cousin Azzacca stood over them and prepared to hit them. I thought he should have grown out of such play by now. He was two dry seasons older than I was.

'I do not think that is going to win you the game, Azzacca,' I said. His guama seed was not as large as some of the others and I did not think it would break many of them.

36

Azzacca held out his guamajico to me. 'Would you like a go?' There was a challenge in his eyes.

I was tempted, but shook my head. 'No, you go ahead. Let me see what you can do with that pebble.'

'Oh, forgive me, Anani. I did not know you were a coward.'

I could not ignore such an insult.

I laid my bow and arrows carefully on the ground behind me and rubbed my hands together. His guama seed was heavier than I expected. I weighed it in my hand to decide the best angle to bring it down. Thwack! A large guama seed splintered beneath it and one of the boys in the circle groaned.

'I had not even had a go yet,' he complained as he dragged his broken guamajico from the circle.

I played some more, and by the time I remembered that I was supposed to be hunting, the sun was already so high in the sky that the trees in the compound made no shadows, and people were moving towards their bohios for the midday rest. I thrust the gaumajico towards Azzacca and looked around for my bow and arrows. He was not pleased. There were only five boys still left in the circle.

'I take back my words, Azzacca,' I said soothingly. 'It is a champion guamajico. Thank you for letting me use it.'

I looked around for Cico, but he must have got tired of waiting for me and gone back to lie in the caney out *of the sun. I did not bother to find him. I could not let Caicihu see I had not even left the compound yet.*

I followed the path down to the beach and looked longingly at the water, so blue that it almost hurt my eyes. It would be good to swim for a while, but first I wanted to bring back the iguana for Caicihu. I wanted to watch him eating his words along with the meat.

Once upon a time the iguana was plentiful on Iyanola, but now they were harder to find, so only the nitainos, *those of noble birth, were allowed to eat them. Sometimes, when the village expected me to set an example for the rest of my age group, I wished that I was born a* naboria, *just an ordinary Taino instead of the child of the cacique; but when the iguana was cooking then I was glad of the privilege. The great lizard's meat was succulent and tasty, whether it was roasted over the coals or cooked in the pepperpot.*

If I had not stopped to play with Azzacca and his friends I would not have been in such a hurry. That is my excuse. I have no other for being such a bad hunter that day. The youngest boy in the tribe would have noticed the signs and been more alert. He would have heard the silence of the forest, felt the stillness in the air and noticed how the trees themselves appeared to whisper as he passed. And I, who had been taught to hunt by Caicihu himself, the greatest young hunter in the five tribes, walked that day as if blindfolded, and noticed nothing.

If I had not stopped to play, I would have met the canoes as I rounded the headland and then I would be telling a different story. But I did not even see the wash from their oars, even though they could not have passed long before I came to the bay.

I walked lightly, not crushing the twigs. My feet automatically found the places where they would make the least noise. I came to a clearing where the trees had been cut for building and found a large branch left on the ground, one that would not snap easily. With my axe I chopped off a piece, the length of my arm. Large boulders dotted the ground and I climbed up on to one of these, sat, and waited.

The stone was hot against my bare skin and the top of my head was roasting, but I sat as still as a zemi, *only my eyes skimming the rocks for any sign of movement. I stayed like this for a long time before an iguana poked its head from behind one of the boulders. Its green skin glistened in the midday sun, and the sharp frill on its back stood upright in challenge as its red eyes swivelled towards me.*

I was not as short as most of my age-mates. I reached almost to my father's cheek when I stood beside him. But this lizard was longer than I was when I was stretched in my hammock. From the slow way he bobbed his head and the way his tail twitched from side to side, I could tell he was not pleased to see me and was getting ready to attack. Keeping my eye on him, I nodded my head rapidly, like a submissive female iguana.

I had not intended to try and capture this one. He

was too big even for one of the men to take on his own, so I had meant to wait for a young iguana. But as I watched the sharp plume on his back slowly settle down, I suddenly had a picture of Caicihu's face as I walked into the caney with this monster. And I became a fool.

The lizard turned and headed for the group of cocoa trees on the other side of the clearing. If I waited until he started to climb I would not have a chance to catch him. In the time it takes to blink twice I was off the rock and crawling like a hunting snake towards him, the bow and arrow in one hand, and the branch I had found in the other.

When I was within two hands' length of him, I opened my mouth and made the harsh mating cry of the iguanas. The monster stopped and stretched his jaws wide to reply. He swung his head from side to side, trying to find the female who had called. I croaked again and he swivelled his head towards me, mouth open in response. For a moment I hesitated at the sight of the sharp rows of teeth in the bright red mouth. Then I shoved the branch between the jaws. They snapped shut around it. Now I could concentrate on avoiding the huge thrashing tail.

I was not going to be able to capture this one alive. I jumped back, out of reach of a vicious lash, positioned an arrow into my bow and took aim. I kept my eyes on the soft spot under the neck, waiting for him to rear his head again. I pulled the bow as far back as it would go, until the bone arrow tip bit into my left first finger. With the branch still clamped firmly in his jaws he lunged at me, death in his red-rimmed eyes.

I let go of the arrow and it lodged in the fold at the side of his head, but he did not seem to feel it. I turned and ran, stringing another arrow as I went. My heart was pounding so hard that each breath hurt. I knew I had to get above him, but it was useless trying to climb a tree. An iguana could climb faster than any Taino and I could not shoot if I was clutching a branch to steady myself. I looked around, desperate for high ground, but the land was flat all around, except for the boulders.

The boulders! The first one I came to was too small but the next was large enough to give me a platform high above the iguana. I scrambled up the rock as if all the demons from the land of the dead were after me. I could hear him crashing through the undergrowth but I dared not waste time to look back. Only when I was standing on top of the rock did I allow myself to look and see what the iguana was doing.

He had managed to fling the branch from his mouth and his plume was now pointing straight towards the sky. In one breath he would be below the rock. With sweaty palms I fitted an arrow and let it fly. It sailed over his head and landed harmlessly in the earth behind him. My hands were shaking as I took out another arrow from the pouch. There were only three left now. I had to make

41

them count. I blinked to get the sweat out of my eyes and licked my lips. I wished I had gone to get Cico. He would have been useful in distracting the lizard while I attacked.

By the time I looked up from arming my bow, the iguana was standing on his hind legs below my rock, his front claws making grooves in the stone as he started to haul himself up, his head swaying from side to side. This time the arrow found his open throat and he fell back with a strangled bellow of rage. I fitted another arrow, but it remained unshot.

A scream ripped the air as I raised my bow. My heart stopped pounding for the space of a breath, then raced like a hunting dog after a coney. I remained unmoving, with my bow raised and my eyes fixed on the iguana. My gaze followed him as he turned and thrashed into the trees, still snorting and bellowing in anger, and my brain tried to tell my fingers to let go of the arrow, but the message could not get through.

Another scream split the air, and another, then several in quick succession. A flock of parrots rose from the canopy around the village and flew screeching into the forest on the other side of the island. Thick black smoke rose to meet the clouds and through the leaves I caught a glimpse of orange and red.

All this my brain registered in a few breaths, but it seemed I was unable to move for a whole dry season. Then

I ran. At the edge of the trees, where they gave way to the compound, I stopped, unable to believe what my eyes were telling me. The village was swarming with demons, and all the bohios *were on fire.*

6
The Raid

The demons were dragging the women and girls towards the sea. Fire was swallowing the bohios *and children were running like scattered chickens in all directions, screaming for their mothers.*

I told my feet to keep running, to find my mother and my brother, but they were deaf with fear and stayed rooted to the ground. My heart had been pounding like the ceremonial drum while I ran, but now it seemed to have stopped. I was having to catch quick, sharp gulps of air, but the breaths were thick with smoke and dust. My eyes streamed and my throat ached. There was something in the smoke which bit into the eyes and throat.

Then there she was. A demon had her by the waist. She was kicking and yelling and trying to scratch at his enormous black eyes. He threw his head back and laughed.

The bone threaded through his bottom lip jiggled and the necklace of bones around his neck rattled in time to his laughter. The grinning white skull on his chest danced as he moved.

I opened my mouth to shout at him; to tell him to leave my mother alone. A feeble croak was all that came out. But it was enough for my mother. Bibi looked up as if she had heard, though she could not have above the noise. She screamed my name.

'Anani!'

The demon's head jerked in my direction. For a moment his terrible gaze held mine captive. Then he shouted something to another demon who was bending over the body of an old man on the ground.

The second demon looked up, his black eyes terrifying in his bone-white face. That is when my feet received the message from my brain. My mother screamed my name again and I ran.

Not in all the races against Caicihu; not in all the contests in the village had I run so fast. I ran until my heart threatened to burst from my mouth. Until my feet buckled under the strain and I crumpled, exhausted, at the foot of a large kapok tree.

I slumped, gasping, my chest burning as if a pot of boiling water had been emptied inside. I listened for following footsteps, but heard only the silence. The birds were too shocked by what they had seen to move in their secret places. The cicadas were dumb with fright. The wind did not tickle the leaves or caress the branches, but kept its arms for once to itself.

The only sounds were the rasping of my breath rushing from my mouth, and the pounding of my heart in my ears.

I did not have the energy to move. Not until I heard the harsh call of the parrots above me in the top of the trees.

I leaped to my feet, staring wildly around me. I could see nothing, but I knew a demon was there. I could feel his presence. I knew I should run, but I did not know in which direction. He could be in front of me, beside me, or behind.

'Oh, Atebeyra, help me,' I prayed.

The parrots rose and flew towards the sun's resting place and I followed. This time the demon did not try to hide. I heard his feet pounding behind me as I ran.

Where could I run to? How could I get rid of him? My thoughts were jumbled in my head, confused by panic. And then, in the middle of my despair a thought came, clear as a dry-season sky.

I had done this before. I had been chased by demons. And I knew how to outwit them.

My feet found the path as if I had travelled it that morning. I risked a glance behind me. His blackened mouth opened like a cavern in a grin, revealing sharpened teeth. I realized that he was just playing with me. He could have caught me before. But he was enjoying the chase. That is why he had not used the axe in his hand.

I willed every bit of energy into my legs. The spurt caught him unprepared. I left him far behind. But only for a while. I prayed to all the gods of my ancestors, 'Please do not let him catch me before we get there.'

They answered immediately. I heard the growl of the waters and gave one last spurt. Even so I felt his hand reaching for me as I threw myself to the ground at the edge of the land. His scream went soaring above me as he fell, and then there was a sickening crunch and silence.

I could not move.

If he came crawling up the path now, I would not be able to do anything to save myself. My legs felt lifeless. My arms hung limply over the edge. My breath came in painful gasps from my heaving chest.

I lay like that for a long time, partly expecting him to come striding up from the rocks below. I did not know if demons could be killed. Was he dead, or just injured?

I rose on shaky legs and peered over the edge.

He was lying on a boulder, sprawled like a dead hutia put out to dry in the sun, his head turned towards the pool.

The path down to the rocks was steep and my knees shook so that I had to hold on to the bushes by the side as I went down. Even so, I slipped twice and almost turned back. What I was doing was stupid. I should leave him

47

there for the vultures to eat. But I had to make sure he was dead.

Even closed, his eyes were still hideous. The lids were black circled with white and were painted with teeth, sharp and pointed like a shark's. Three scars ran from below the eyes to his ears. A trickle of blood seeped from the corner of his mouth on to the rock. He looked so young and helpless that pity sprang to life inside me.

I reached out to touch him. I had never touched a demon before. But my hand remained hanging above his face. I was too scared to touch him. I was straightening, about to return to the village, when his eyes suddenly flew open. I screamed and leaped back.

'Help me.'

The words stopped me as I was about to sprint back up the track.

'Help me.'

I knew my face showed how astonished I was. How did a demon know my language? Or had I suddenly learned how to understand demon?

I bent towards him, careful to stay just out of reach of his long arms. I was ready to run if I had to.

'What did you say?'

'Water.'

I did not think. Instinctively I ran to pick an eddo leaf and bent it into a cup. Not until I was standing beside him with the water from the pool did I wonder what I was doing. I was getting water for the demon who tried to kill me. I must be mad.

His eyes begged me to give it to him and his lips parted, ready to drink. I held the water closer.

'Who are you?' I asked. 'And why have you come here?'

He groaned and closed his eyes for a breath. When he opened them, his gaze fastened on the water in my hands.

'Maruka, My name is Maruka.' His words were faint and I had to lean towards him in order to hear them.

'Are you from Coyaba?'

I knew the land of the dead was the home of the spirits. Perhaps it was the home of demons as well. He tried to shake his head and winced at the pain that caused.

'No, Kalinago,' It was only a whisper but I heard it.

I gasped and the eddo leaf fell from my hands. He groaned and his hand moved feebly towards the water already drying on the stones.

'You are Kalinago,' I said. 'You are not a demon.'

'Water, please.'

Anger bubbled inside me like a pot on the fire. I had heard of the Kalinago. They had attacked the Taino before I was born, and the stories of their cruelty were told to us from the moment we could understand. When we were small, we were warned not to go too far from the compound or we would be kidnapped by the Kalinago and eaten.

I was confused. It was right to destroy a demon, but a Taino should not take the life of another human. On the other hand, revenge was allowed. And this boy had taken the life of other Taino. I looked around and saw his axe on the sand. It was stained black with the drying blood of the Taino. I could not feel pity for him.

'I will not give you water,' I said. 'But I will ease your burden so you do not have so much to carry on your journey to Coyaba. I will take your name. From now on I will be called Maruka, and you will go nameless to Coyaba. That will be your punishment for what you have done to my people. In Coyaba you will be nameless and despised.'

I waited for him to say something. A fly settled on the blood drying on the corner of his mouth. He did not move. He had already started for Coyaba. I turned, feet heavy like an old woman's, and made my way up the track.

I could not just enter the village from the normal approach. The demons were bound to see me. Why was I going back anyway? What could I do?

At the back of my mind I knew I was going to rescue my mother. But how? I could not fight all those demons on my own. Even though I knew they were Kalinago, their actions were those of demons in my mind. If only my father had not left the village on his trading trip. If only Caicihu had not been ill.

Caicihu! What had happened to him? My heart

started another frantic race. If Caicihu had been well, they could not have taken my mother. There was no one like him with the axe and bow and arrow.

But ill as he was, he would have been no match for the demons. I bit my lip.

'Please, Atebeyra, Yucahu and Opiyelguaobiran, take care of Caicihu. Do not let the Kalinago demons eat him.'

I wanted to run to the caney to see for myself that no harm had come to my brother, but a coldness was wrapping itself round my heart. It travelled up my chest and into my head. It slowed my heartbeat, and my feet, but cleared my head enough to let me see that it would be madness to go rushing to the village.

I could go for help, but I knew it would take too long to get to the nearest settlement and back. It would take me at least half a day to get there. By then my mother, my brother and the rest of the village would be dead.

I hurried down the path to where it branched off to the right. Here the ground rose gently for some distance until it became a small hill which overlooked the village.

Halfway up the hill a movement caught the corner of my eye and drew my gaze out to sea. I shaded my eyes against the glare of the sun and watched the canoes paddling away from Iyanola. I was too late.

As I watched, two other canoes came round the bay and headed out to the open sea. The first held many Kalinago and five Taino women, one with her hands tied behind her back. She wore a beautiful *nagua*. The short skirt, which married women wore, was decorated with shells, red beads and pressed gold to show her rank. I would know that *nagua* anywhere. I stretched my hand out to her, and the scream seemed to echo in my head long after it left my mouth. The wind carried it towards her, and she looked up at me.

As the wind had carried my scream to her, it carried her answer to me.

'*Anani! Please save. . .*' And the cruel wind whipped her last words away before they could reach my ears. Without hearing it, I knew what she had said. But I could not save her. I wanted to run across the water to her, but my feet stayed glued to the ground, my hand outstretched, frozen in horror at what happened next. I stood like that, unable to move, long after Bibi disappeared from my sight.

The smoke from the burning *bohios* formed a thick cloud over the clearing, so that I could see nothing for some time. I strained my ears for any sound that more Kalinago were around, but all I could hear were the waves slapping against the rocks like a *behique's* palm on the funeral drum.

Even this far away, the smoke found my nostrils, stinging my eyes and throat. I coughed. The sound was loud in the stillness, and I held my breath but nothing moved. I started down the side of the hill towards the village. All my senses were numb and my feet dragged as if I walked through thick mud.

At the trees separating the village from the hill I slowed and peered into the clearing. I clamped my hand to my lips to stop my stomach climbing through my mouth, and closed my eyes, hoping if I could shut out the sight, it would go away.

But when I opened them nothing had changed. There were the heaps of smouldering ashes where the bohios had been. And there, littered across the ground like overripe fruit in the height of the mango season, were the bodies of the Taino, old men and young boys, their headless necks gaping at the sky. There was no sign of the Kalinago.

My head felt as if it was being squeezed between two large rocks. A volcano erupted from my stomach. I opened my mouth, gasping for air, and the morning's meal catapulted on to the ground in front of me.

For what seemed like a whole dry season I bent over, retching and moaning, my face washed with tears. My insides were empty, but my stomach continued to heave. I did not care if the demons heard now. My life was worthless.

I remembered my father's words as he had left. 'I need you to stay here and look after the village, my little warrior, and take care of your brother.'

My brother! I straightened. My feet devoured the ground to where my father's caney now sat, a pile of smouldering ashes.

The wail started deep in my belly and by the time it

leaped from my mouth it was like the cry of a tortured spirit. I flung my head back, and howled at the sky. It was a cry demanding an explanation from the gods. If they heard me they must have been too busy to answer. The sky looked back, unconcerned, its face partly hidden by a covering of smoke.

I fell to my knees and scrabbled among the ashes. If Caicihu had been burned in the caney, perhaps there was still a part of him I could rescue. A part of him I could keep as a zemi.

I yelped and sprang up, flapping my hands. They were red and raw from the embers. I rubbed the back of my hands against my bare belly and thighs where the scattered hot ashes had left their marks.

Looking around frantically for something to ease the pain, my eyes fell on the large jar lying on its side by the cooking place. I ran towards it, trying not to look at the bodies as I ran past and around them. I wanted to look. I wanted to see if Caicihu was among them. But I was afraid.

I could see the jar was empty, but I turned it upside down, holding it with the tips of my fingers and grimacing at the pain of the hard clay against my sore skin. It was as if the jar had never heard of water.

I threw it to the ground and ran. The river was not far away. The thought of all that cooling water lent wings to my feet.

The water soothed the burns on my stomach and

thighs, and cooled the stinging of my hands. I waded in up to my neck and let its coolness wash over me. Then I thought about the Taino lying in the village.

I had to get help, I knew that. I could not stay in the village. Our caney *had gone and there were no* bohios *left. Besides, I would not be safe once night came and the spirits started walking.*

I thought of all the people who were gone. My mother and Caicihu, my baby sister Guabonito and her mother, my father's second wife. I felt a warm stream bathing my face. Beautiful, funny Nito. It was too hard to think I would never see her again. My cousin Azzacca was gone too. And the children I had played guamajico with only that day. It seemed many dry seasons away now, that game of guamajico.

I sat like that for a long time, my tears seasoning the fresh water of the river. I sat until my eye pools dried and only dry sobs and hiccups disturbed the evening prayers of the birds and the crickets. When the tree frogs cleared their throats for the night's song service and the midges started to bite, I hauled my wrinkled body from the water and crawled like an old woman to the bank.

With the rest of the Taino gone, the midges and mosquitoes trained their attack on me. I swatted at my arms and legs but it did not make much difference. The assault lifted the numbness from my heart so that I began to notice my surroundings again.

The sun had almost fallen off the edge of the world

and I knew that I needed to make a fire quickly. I looked around for a good piece of dry wood, and a sturdy stick. I would make the fire by the side of the river. I collected dry wood and made a pile, ready for lighting.

Fire making was something every Taino learned to do as soon as they could run and work in the fields. But rubbing the sticks together was not easy with sore palms. The sweat was pouring down my face and neck before I decided the pain was too much. I would have to go back to the village after all.

I straightened and glanced towards the sea, hoping I would see my father and the men returning. But it was calm and undisturbed.

I glanced at the path that wound under the trees to the village. The shadows were already taking on their night-time shapes. I closed my eyes, clutched the zemi *around my neck and prayed to Atebeyra to keep me safe. Then I took a deep breath and sprinted up the track.*

It was not hard to find fire. The bohios *and father's* caney *were only heaps of smouldering ashes now.*

I found the broken jar I had thrown away before, and a piece of stick to collect the embers with.

I felt slightly better once the fire was singing. I tried not to look at the ocean, but my gaze kept reaching for the pool of darkness where now and then lights flickered in the distance. I knew what those lights were – the spirits of people who had died at sea and had not had the prayers for the journey to Coyaba said over them. They were forced to remain homeless, travelling the waters forever, unless someone released them by saying the prayers for them where they had died.

A cicada chirped two hands' length away from my head and another answered. A tree frog sang to the small fires in the sky. Others joined its chorus and the air was filled with the sounds of the night creatures. These were the sounds which had sent me to sleep every night as I swayed in my hammock. They belonged to Iyanola, and were as comforting as the soft snores of my family coming from the other hammocks in the caney. But here in the open they were not such a comfort. My mother's face swam before my mind's eye and I swallowed the lump of pain that threatened to choke me.

Each new sound sent a finger of fear to scratch at my mind. Every rustle of hutia or mouse in the dried leaves left my heart banging against my ribs. I knew I would not sleep. Outside the light, the night-people waited. Those spirits who had lost their way to Coyaba, or who had been so bad in life that they were not allowed to enter the land of the dead, were waiting in the shadows for the flames to die down.

I shivered and poked at the fire. As long as it was singing, the spirits would stay away from me. But that meant I could not risk falling asleep. It was going to be a long night.

7
After the Raid

The sun was yawning, stretching into wakefulness when I leaped from my bed of leaves and grasses. Something had woken me. There it was again. A long, low wail. I clutched my chest to still my heart. My first thought was that the Kalinago had returned.

As I listened I realized that the voice was female and my reason returned. My feet flew over the ground, devouring the distance to the village. I burst through the clearing, then stopped, trying to take in what I was seeing.

Karaya was kneeling by the body of an old man, her face raised to the skies, her mouth open. He was her father. A long, low wail of pain and anger climbed from her throat and went speeding to the ancestors in the sky.

Nito was bending beside her mother, sobbing softly,

clinging to her nagua. My cousin Azzacca was walking among the fallen Taino as if he was still asleep.

I felt the life leave my legs and I sank to the cool earth, which was still damp from the dew. The relief was more than I could carry all at once. They were not dead. They had not been captured. I was not alone. I did not have to face the horror on my own any more. Karaya would know what to do.

Nito looked up as I hit the ground and a cry sprang from her lips.

'Anani! Anani!'

She launched herself into my arms and we were laughing and sobbing on the ground together. Then her mother was there, hugging us both, her tears mingling with ours.

'Thank Yucahu! Thank Atebeyra! Thank Huracan!'

A shadow blocked the sunlight from my face. Azzacca stood over us. His eyes looked at me but I did not think they saw me.

'You have not been taken.' He said it without feeling. I could see he was in deep shock and my spirit went out to him.

'We thought you had been taken, Anani,' Nito said.

I hugged her closer. 'Atebeyra watched over me and I escaped. But how were you not taken? And where were you in the night?'

'We stayed on Bird Island,' Karaya said. I had forgotten they were going there. She wiped the back of

her hand across her cheeks and sniffed, trying to stop the tears, but the dam behind her eyes had broken and the river could not be halted.

'We heard the noise and saw the smoke. I wanted to come back and find you, but Azzaca said it was best if we stayed on the island.' Nito rubbed her eyes and hiccuped.

I turned my gaze on Azzacca. So he had preferred to stay in safety while the rest of the Taino died. My lips curled, but Karaya squeezed my shoulder.

'If we had not listened to Azzacca we would have been taken too. He saved our lives. There was nothing we could do against people who could do – this.' She gestured towards the ground behind us and, rising, moved back towards her father's body.

I rose, pulling Nito up with me, and brushed the damp earth from my skin. I turned to Azzacca.

'What are we going to do?'

He looked at me as if I had asked him to carry the sky on his head. I felt sorry for him. He had only had his manhood ceremony that dry season. Now he was the only man on the island and with my father absent he had to decide what we should do.

'We must prepare for the burials.' But he did not move. His eyes were fixed on the dead. None of us knew where to start. I looked at Karaya. She would not be much help. She was too broken by the death of her father.

Azzacca's head suddenly jerked upwards and life crept

back into his gaze as he turned towards the sea. I heard it then, the sound of the guamo telling us the men had returned.

Azzacca ran towards the sound of the conch and we followed. Wave after wave of relief flooded my body. Baba was back. He would know what to do.

'And your mother, was she taken too?'

I swallowed. 'All the women and girls who were not on Bird Island, Baba.'

'No, not all.' He was looking over my head and his face lightened with hope. I spun round to see Taino emerging from the forest. Women, children and a few men. All had bowed heads and sad faces. I knew who my father was hoping to see and I too searched the faces, but inside I felt sure Caicihu would not be with them. I could not feel his spirit. And I knew Caicihu would not have run away to hide from the Kalinago. He would have stayed to fight, even though he was sick.

I turned to tell Baba I did not think that Caicihu had escaped but my words remained unsaid. Baba's face had crumpled like a folded fishing net. His jaw went slack and the light fled from his eyes. A moan gurgled in his throat and his face hardened, like stone.

'Baba!'

But he did not hear me. His gaze went walking above my head, and I knew. I turned, slowly, not wanting to see, but knowing I had to.

61

He was carried by four Taino boys, not much older than I was. His face was turned towards the forest, but I did not need to see his face to know who it was, or to know there was no life in him.

8

Burial

The days had changed. The Taino walked and worked with bowed heads and silent lips. The songs and laughter had gone back to the gods who gave them. People kept glancing fearfully towards the sea and the men who were rebuilding the caney *and the* bohios *worked as if their spirits were sleeping with the dead Taino. Even so, by the second day after the raid, almost all the houses had been rebuilt.*

Under Baba's direction, the village had been cleared of the dead, but they still waited for the prayers to be said to release their spirits for their final journey. Because of the repairs to the compound and the number of the dead, the arrangements for the funerals took longer than normal. I wanted to help the women with the preparation for Caicihu's farewell ceremony, but a part of me died whenever I thought of him lying lifeless in the cave where he had been placed, waiting to start his journey to Coyaba.

I longed to talk to Baba. I wanted to ask him what to do about the hole that seemed to open in my chest whenever I thought of my brother and my mother. I needed to talk to him about Bibi. Once or twice I started to tell him but the words were pushed aside by tears clamouring to be released and I said nothing.

Besides, my father would not stay still long enough to have a conversation with me. He was busy assigning duties, or hunting, cutting palm branches to thatch the bohios or comforting those who had lost members of their families. I had never seen him as busy as he was now.

The women wailed and the men moaned, rocking themselves from side to side. My father and I were silent, the pain too deep for tears. At last I could share with him the loss I felt. But it was not the time for words. We held hands and stared at Bamako, the chief behique, as he chanted the prayers for a safe journey to Coyaba. Then he beckoned to Baba.

Baba placed the bow and arrows on the ground and the spear in Caicihu's right hand.

'Here are your spear, your bow and arrows, Caicihu. May you have good hunting in Coyaba.' His lips trembled and his voice sounded like a canoe being dragged across the sand, but his eyes remained dry.

Nito's mother brought the bowls of pepperpot, and

two other women brought the cassava bread, fish and hutia *meat*.

'Here is food for your journey,' the behique chanted. 'So you will not go hungry to Coyaba.' He laid the food by Caicihu's head, so he would not have far to look when he was hungry.

One of the elders stepped forward, a lifeless Daha in his arms. The priest took the dog and placed him at Caicihu's feet.

'A companion to help you hunt and protect you from loneliness. Take our thanks to our elders in Coyaba. Tell them we are grateful to them for lending you to us. We send you back to them now. Travel well. Go in peace.'

The mourners trooped out of the cave to join the rest of the Taino outside. The final rites were for the priests and cacique alone to perform. Baba touched my shoulder, telling me to follow the others. I looked long at Caicihu. I felt as if powdered pepper had been sprinkled in my eyes, my nostrils, my throat. I longed for tears to wash away the sting, but the pool behind my eyes was empty. As empty as my heart.

My gaze travelled from his feet, his toes, resting on Daha's back, up his arched body decorated with the stars, sun and moon — images of Yucahu and our ancestors. It lingered on the small wound on his chest where the Kalinago arrow had pierced him. A fierce pride surfaced above the hurt. That wound was evidence. He had not been running away when he was killed but he had faced the enemy. If he had been fleeing, the arrow would have been in his back. The Taino boys who found him in the bush said he was clutching his axe even in death. My brother had died with honour.

He wore a parrot-feather headdress almost as magnificent as the one our father wore for special occasions. His necklace was one I had made for him, red beads, tiny white shells and beaten gold. His earrings were gold with small parrot feathers, and a ring of gold was strung through his nostrils. Everyone who saw him in Coyaba would know he was a cacique's son and would treat him with due respect.

I paused as I turned to leave. I unfastened the zemi of Atebeyra from around my neck and tied it to Caicihu's wrist.

'Earth Mother,' I whispered, 'look after my brother.' Then I turned and ran from the cave.

The other dead Taino were buried in the midden at the back of the village. I went with the rest of the village to hear the prayers said for them, but I heard none of the words the priests chanted. All I wanted to do was to curl up and follow Caicihu to Coyaba.

I longed for my mother. With her arms around me, her soft voice warming me, everything would be all right. I shook my head to free it of the thought. No one could make things right again. Without Caicihu and Bibi, my life would never be the same.

Back in the village, I went to our new caney and slung my hammock on the posts. I was suddenly weary and felt that I could sleep forever.

Nito's mother came in at the door but stopped when she saw me.

'Are you not well, Anani? The sun is still high but you are in your hammock.'

'My eyelids are heavy, Karaya. I did not sleep much last night.'

She frowned. 'Nor any night since the Kalinago raid? It is as if an evil spirit follows you.' Her eyes widened. 'Where did you sleep that night?'

'On the beach.' I knew what she was thinking. 'I kept a fire burning all night to keep away the evil spirits. I do not think one could have found me.' I did not add that I had fallen asleep before the day woke.

'You were alone? All night?'

I nodded. 'I did not know then that others had escaped.'

Karaya dashed over and gathered me, still wrapped in my hammock, into her arms. 'Oh, my brave, brave, Anani! All night alone with the spirits. And no one asked you how you managed. The whole of Iyanola will hear of your bravery.'

'What bravery is this?'

Neither of us had heard Baba entering the caney. The light visited his eyes for a quick moment as he listened

67

to Bibi tell of my night on the beach. But then he frowned.

'You have done well, Anani. But we must make sure no evil spirit has fastened itself to you. I will tell Bamako to perform the cleansing ceremony that will send the spirits back to Coyaba. Then we must change your name, so if any spirits return they will not find you.'

'I have already chosen a new name.'

Their eyebrows rose together.

'Well? Do not keep us guessing. What is it?' Baba had a small smile playing around his mouth. It was the first I had seen on anyone since the raid.

'Maruka,' I said. 'My name is Maruka.'

The smile vanished, chased away by the frown which folded Baba's forehead.

'Maruka? That is a strange name. What does it mean?'

I felt the blood loud in my head as I thought of Caicihu alone in the burial cave, of my mother . . . A roar of voices shouting for revenge almost deafened me. I felt the wrath of Huracan, god of thunder himself, and I knew what the name meant to me.

From now on I was no longer Anani – Water Flower – but Maruka – the one who avenges.

Kiskeya

9

Strangers

'Nito! Now!' I yelled again. Her gaze travelled past me out to sea and her mouth opened in a silent shout. I grabbed her hand and together we shot through the trees towards the compound. Neither of us spoke. We could not waste time or breath in words. We had to warn everyone as soon as we could. I had to slow down for Nito and it almost killed me. How could this be happening again?

We burst into the compound almost too out-of-breath to speak. I could not believe that the women were still sitting around the fire chatting, the men still lying in their hammocks, the children still running in and out of the *bohios* when our world was about to end. 'Kalinago!' I said, too softly for anyone except Nito to hear.

She looked at me and her eyes widened with shock and fear. Then she screamed, 'Kalinago! Kalinago! The Kalinago are coming!'

Chaos awoke. The women ran like scattered hens, scooping up children and heading for their *bohios*. They bumped into the men, who were running for their axes, clubs and bone-tipped spears. And all the time Nito kept screaming, 'Kalinago! Kalinago!'

Then my father was there, his hand on both our shoulders.

'Very well, Nito,' he said. 'You have told us.' He raised his eyes to mine and they were troubled, remembering . . . 'Where are they?'

'On the sea, Baba. Coming from the way to Boriken.' I was relieved to find that my voice was working again.

'How many canoes?'

'Three.'

My father frowned.

'Are you certain, only three? It is not the Kalinago way to go hunting with so few.'

'These are not ordinary canoes, Baba. They are like – like giant birds moving on the water. They are many times bigger than the ones which came to Iyanola. They have wings.'

'Winged canoes.' My father frowned. 'Go, find your mothers.'

He pushed us in the direction of the *caney* and

hurried away. The *guamo* wailed above the shouts and screams, summoning the Taino to war.

When I looked back, my father was surrounded by the elders. He said something, and two men armed with axes sped away towards the sea, melting silently into the darkness. Another two dashed off to the right of them and another two to the left.

I turned. Nito had already disappeared into the *caney*. My father's four wives were hurriedly gathering the young ones.

In the flickering light of the torch which one of my mothers held, the faces of the women and children were distorted into twisted masks of fear.

I swallowed. My mouth was dry.

No one knew what anyone should be doing. People rushed about, bumping into each other like a colony of ants disturbed by a digging stick.

I ran for the doorway. Then I stopped. The wail of the conch shell had changed. It was no longer a frantic bellow but was now a solemn wail. Not a war cry, but an assembly call.

The mad rush slowed and everyone headed for the ball court in front of the *caney*.

Father was already there, surrounded by the elders whom he had sent to the sea. It had been a long time since the Taino had assembled like this at night.

A hand crept into mine. I looked down into Nito's frightened eyes and squeezed her hand. I needed

71

someone to comfort me as well. Someone to tell me that my nightmare was not coming true. That the Kalinago had not followed us all the way to Kiskeya, to finish what they had started three dry seasons before.

10

Consulting the *Zemis*

Father looked around and his eyes rested on Guabonito and me. He beckoned to us and I walked on stiff legs towards him, pulling Nito along with me.

'Taino,' he said. 'We have visitors.'

A murmur went up from the crowd and he raised his hands for silence. 'Tonight my daughters Maruka and Guabonito, while they bathed, saw canoes heading for Kiskeya. They came to warn us that the Kalinago were coming.'

There were cries of fear and panic. I shivered, though the dark was warm and scented with blossoms of rose apples and nutmeg. My father shook his head and the Taino fell quiet.

'I sent men to see how many canoes the Kalinago

brought, but my men tell me our visitors are not Kalinago.'

A sigh of relief rose from the Taino. Shame coloured my relief. I had been wrong.

'Who are they?' one of the behiques asked. 'Are they friends?'

'We do not know,' my father said. 'But I will let the men tell you themselves what they saw.'

One of the men stepped forward. It was Bamako, the chief behique.

'We saw the giant birds on the sea. They moved without oars. We rowed out towards them, but we were careful not to get too close.'

A gasp of fear and admiration came from the Taino.

'We saw things moving in these birds, but as it was dark we could not be certain what they were, though they moved like men.'

'How can canoes move without oars?' an old man asked.

'They move with the wind,' Bamako said. 'Now that the wind has fallen, they are still.'

My father spoke. 'We do not know who they are, or if they come in peace. We will ask the *zemis*.'

We waited in silence outside the house of the *zemis* while Father and the behiques consulted the messengers of the Supreme Being.

I wiped my palms on my thighs, but they remained damp. I looked around at the Taino waiting beside me. Their faces said they were as nervous as I was.

The smell of the tobacco crept out of the house and we knew that the men inside were entering the trance, that they now spoke to the spirits. Not long before, we had heard the noises as they vomited, using sticks in their throats to make sure their stomachs were empty. It was important, before they spoke to the *zemis*, that they cleansed themselves of anything that was impure. The *zemis* might not answer or, worse, might punish them if the priests and cacique were unclean before them.

It was strange, sitting in front of the house of the *zemis* like this at night. We had only ever consulted the *zemis* in the daytime. The night belonged to the dead.

In the light of the torches, many of the Taino looked as if they had come from Coyaba. The light flickered on our painted bodies, making pictures that danced on our skins.

I bit my lip until I could taste the salty blood on my tongue. What would the *zemis* say? We all rose when the men appeared in the doorway. My gaze sped at once to my father's face, but I could read nothing there. We did not know what to think. Never before had we been unable to read the *zemis'* words in the cacique's face.

He stumbled against the doorway and my breath lodged in my throat.

'Let us to go bed. In the morning we will welcome our visitors,' he said.

But he did not smile.

11

Making Ready

That night we did not sleep. We felt the presence of the monster canoes sitting on the sea, their wings folded – waiting.

The *guamo* sounded before the sun woke, but everyone was already washed and painted. I had painted red stripes all over my body, and black and white circles of clay and soot around my eyes. I had taken great care to thread the string of beads through my hair – and I had fastened the gold rings in my ears and nose.

The table where we kept Caicihu's skull and the other *zemis* was empty, as if my mothers were still not sure about the strangers, in spite of my father's words. I could not blame them. What kind of people visited at night? I would have liked to talk with the *zemi* of Caicihu too, but I dared not ask where it was hidden.

The fire-coloured *zemi* of Atebeyra which I found by the river I tied around my neck. I knew there must be a reason I had found it just before the visitors arrived.

My father looked up when I came out of the *caney*. He was on his seat and four men were getting ready to lift him on to their shoulders, but he motioned them to wait as I approached him. He wore his ceremonial dress and I realized how important our visitors were. Father did not often stand on ceremony, though he was chief cacique in this part of Kiskeya.

He looked at me and shook his head. I stopped, puzzled.

'Father?'

'Have you not heard, Maruka? Only the men will go to meet the strangers.'

I stared at him, disbelieving. 'But, Father, you said we would welcome them.'

'And so we will. But first we must know who they are. Until we do, I have decided that the women will remain here.'

A feeling of deep despair washed over me. I knew then that I had to meet the strangers. I did not know why, but I felt that was what Atebeyra was telling me when she sent me her image that morning.

'Baba, please. Let me come with you.'

'Maruka, I have spoken.'

I turned, my throat tight and stinging with unshed tears. I could not argue with the cacique in public, even though he was my father. I did not want to cry in the presence of the men either, but I knew I would give way to tears if I stayed to watch them go.

'You should remember you are not your brother, Maruka. Stop trying to take his place.'

I had not even noticed Azzacca there beside my father. Azzacca had been born in an old man's skin. His pompous words did not sit well on his young shoulders. When he spoke I felt fierce anger rise up like live coals inside me. It melted the lump in my throat and lit a fire in my head. Why had he escaped the attack on Iyanola? Why couldn't Caicihu have survived instead of him? I turned on my cousin like a cornered iguana. But before I could say anything, my father spoke.

'If you come with us, you must promise to stay by my side.'

Relief like a flood swept over me. Azzacca should have known better than to mention my brother. My father often saw Caicihu living in me, and at a time like this the cacique would want his firstborn son with him, if only in spirit.

'I will go and get some cassava bread, Father,' I said. 'A gift for our guests.'

'That is a good idea.' My father smiled. 'We will wait here for you.'

When I returned I saw that the *nitainos*, the nobles of the tribe, all had gifts for our visitors. Some had balls of cotton, some parrots, some fruit. My father carried a mask made from gold and green stone, our two most precious materials. Had the *zemis* told him more about the visitors than he had told us? Only the greatest lords would be worthy of such a present.

I looked at him, a question in my eyes, but he was busy directing the procession.

I fell into step beside the men as they hoisted my father's seat on to their shoulders. At that moment, all that mattered was that I was going to meet the visitors as Atebeyra wished. It did not matter what the *zemis* had said.

I would have thought differently if I had known then what my father knew.

12

First Contact

The shells and coral on our arms and legs rattled as we walked and the gold in our ears and noses shone in the rising sun.

We came through the trees and the breath hid in my throat, too terrified to join the air outside. The strange canoes were much closer to land than they had been the night before. They blotted out a vast stretch of the horizon and loomed like mountains towards the sky. My mouth gaped and I knew my eyes all but filled my face. They were more enormous than I ever imagined any canoe could be.

The sea rushed towards the land, hurrying across the sand as if anxious to escape the creatures on its back. A wind dashed across the waves, clutched us in its cold hands for a little while and then hurried off into the forest behind us. The waking sun peered over the edge of a cloud, then slunk back to hide, trailing a red finger across the face of the ocean, turning it to blood.

We watched in silence as the white-winged vessels gave birth to baby canoes. These were moved backwards by strange creatures. As they came closer we could see they were men, but not like any men the Taino had ever seen before. With all my being I longed to run away, but I could not shame my father by being a coward.

Someone behind me gave a loud gasp. 'Covered men!' His voice was full of the disbelief we all felt.

'Hold your tongue!' I could hear the tightness in my father's voice. His bearers lowered him from his seat and he stood erect, looking assured as the cacique should; but standing close beside him, I could hear how the breath hurried from his body, and I felt the tremor as his hand brushed against mine.

They stumbled on to the beach like people unused to walking on land. Their feet hit the sand as if surprised to find it there and their bodies swayed like a young tree in a strong wind. I knew my mouth was hanging open, but I could not help it.

They were completely covered in cloths of different colours. Each head was covered with what looked like an upturned fruit bowl. All we could see of their bodies were their hands and faces. And what ugly faces they were; their foreheads unflattened, their chins, cheeks and upper lips covered with hair. I looked away quickly, ashamed for them. How could they let others see them with their hair unplucked? It was bad manners to gaze at another's indignity, but I felt my eyes drawn to them once more, almost against my will.

Their skins were as pale as the belly of the tree frog, as if they had never been stroked by the sun, and when I met the eyes of the one who led them, I felt alarm flutter inside me like a trapped bird. I had never seen eyes like those before; eyes which had captured the sea and the sky.

I guessed he was their cacique by the way the others stood aside to let him through. Besides, he wore red, the symbol of high position. His hair under its covering flashed fire too, and red hair spread across his chin like flames over the bottom of a cooking pot. Even his skin glowed red as if there was a fire burning underneath.

He beckoned to three of his followers who each carried a square of cloth attached to a pole. Two red tree branches crossed each other on the bright white cloth. He pointed to the squares and said something in a language none of us had heard before and they planted the poles into the sand.

The cacique fell to his knees and, clasping his hands beneath the hair on his chin, closed his eyes and started a rapid incantation.

A murmur of fear went through the Taino. I trembled like a leaf in a storm and cast a quick glance at Baba. His face was rigid, like a stone *zemi*'s.

We waited in dread for the spell of the covered men to start working. I fingered the *zemi* around my neck, praying for protection from the magic. Every one of the Taino was doing the same.

The cacique got up and dusted the sand from his knees. His sky-coloured eyes scanned the assembled Taino and came to rest on my father.

They took in my father's ceremonial dress: the band of parrot feathers around his head, the matching cape around his shoulders, the belt of shells, the necklace of beads and gold, the bands of gold around his arms and legs. A light entered his eyes as he stared at the gold. It seemed to hold him under a spell and it was a while before he spoke again.

More of the strange words tumbled from his mouth, falling over each other so that they made no sense to our ears.

'Greetings,' my father said. 'You are welcome to Kiskeya.'

Baba spread his fingers in greeting, showing that he carried no weapons. The pale stranger did not return the greeting, but thrust his hand in front of him towards Baba. Baba was puzzled, as we all were.

He seemed to be asking to look at Baba's hand.

I frowned. How rude! Could he not see that my father's hand was empty? Did he think there could be a weapon under the skin? How could he insult the cacique by doubting him like this?

Baba stared at the pale hand for a few breaths, and then slowly raised his own to touch it. The stranger closed his hand, and Baba's disappeared. He shook Baba's arm. If there were any weapons hidden in it they would have fallen out. Satisfied now, he let go.

Baba looked fearfully at his hand but it was exactly as it had been before it was captured. I let out the breath I had been holding and my shoulders relaxed. He had not harmed my father.

More meaningless words hurried from the stranger's mouth. He could see we did not understand, so he drew his words with his hands. He pointed to the sea and then to the sky. Then he seemed to remember something.

He turned and spoke to the others and they parted. Then we saw them. Ordinary men. We had been so overcome at the sight of the strangers, we had not noticed them coming out of the last boat.

'Greetings,' one of them said. 'We are Lucayan from Guanahani.'

'You are welcome here,' my father said. I could see he was bursting with questions for the Lucayans, but even at this unusual time he remembered his manners.

'You must be hungry,' he said, motioning to the fruit and cassava bread we carried. 'Will you eat?'

The Lucayan who had spoken before shook his head. 'We cannot eat before our guests,' he said. 'We must first feed the ones from the land of the dead.'

13

Spirits

'How do you know they are from Coyaba?' Baba asked after the silence had stretched to breaking point.

'They told us.'

Baba's eyebrows rose to kiss his fringe. 'Do you understand their language?'

'They told us with signs, as they told you now.' The Lucayan pointed to the sea and then to the sky as the pale-skinned cacique had done.

The cacique stepped forward and held out shells that shone in the light. He shook them and they cried loud, 'Peleng! Peleng! Peleng!' The Taino fell back in wonder.

He held the shells out to my father and I could see that Baba was as confused as I was. The strange man did not take food before exchanging gifts. The custom must be different in Coyaba.

Baba reached out for the shells, the shells which spoke like the maracas the behiques used when they talked to the *zemis*. He beckoned to one of his gift-bearers and the man crept forward with the balls of cotton. The strange cacique took them and handed them to one of his men. He smiled his thanks, beckoned to another of his people and took from him some cloth. It was as red as the *roucou* with which we painted our bodies. Red as the face of the sacred rainbow serpent we learned about in our *areitos*, the dancing and story-telling sessions where we remembered our history. If we had any doubts, they were now blown away in the wind. These gifts told us our visitors had been sent from Coyaba. But why had they come?

My father beckoned for the parrots, gifts of the nobles. He offered much cotton thread to show that we were tied together in friendship, spears, arrows and digging sticks so that they might hunt and fish; and gold, to ward off evil and keep them from disease.

The cacique took the gifts and gave them to his servants, but when he saw the gold, a strange light crept into his eyes. It was the look a traveller gets when he has not eaten for many days and he sees the welcome feast. His fingers closed around it as if he would never let it go and he stepped closer to Baba.

He held out the gold and gabbled his strange noises again. My father was bewildered.

'What does he say?' he asked the Lucayan.

The pale stranger was pointing to the gold and spreading his hands wide as if he had lost something. The Lucayan watched for a moment, and then nodded.

'I think he wants to know where to get more gold,' he said.

I felt a deep sorrow for these men. Now I understood why they were so pale, why the blood showed through the skin on their hands, and why they did not pluck the hair on their faces. They had no gold to keep them from sickness. I peered into each face in turn. Perhaps one of these spirits might be Caicihu. It frightened me to think that he might be so changed by living in Coyaba that we would not recognize or understand each other.

Father was talking again. 'There is a little gold here on Kiskeya,' Baba said. 'But much gold is on the island of Caonao, near Matimino.'

The stranger tried to repeat what Father had said, like a baby learning to speak.

'Civao,' he said. And then, 'Cipango?' He spread his hands questioningly and we understood that he wanted to go there. We did not understand why he called Caonao, Cipango. Perhaps that was the name they used in Coyaba.

Father pointed to the sea.

'That way,' he said.

The pale cacique nodded vigorously, looking like a dog which had just discovered a pot of unwatched coney stew.

The basket of cassava bread was gaining weight in my arms. I could see that the other bearers wished we had followed the custom and eaten first. They were fidgeting, trying to get their baskets into a more comfortable position.

'Baba, when do they eat?' I whispered, almost afraid to open my mouth in the presence of these beings.

Baba turned to the pale cacique again. He pointed to the *casabi* I held and mimed eating. Then he raised his brows. The cacique looked at me and nodded, smiling, but he did not look at the bread. His eyes stayed fastened to the gold in my ears.

They ate the *casabi* as if they were not used to eating, carrying the bread slowly to their mouths, touching it with the tips of their tongues before nibbling a baby's bite. They ate the fruit with more spirit, but they let the juice of the mangoes escape down their hands and chin.

I noticed the long sticks they all carried at their side.

'Those are strange digging sticks, Baba,' I whispered to my father.

'Yes,' my father said softly. 'Shiny.'

The man behind the pale cacique saw us looking at his stick and he laughed. He held it out to me. My eyes grew to the size of the cassava basket. I could not accept such a gift. I had nothing so good to give in return. Father saw me hesitate and gave me a gentle nudge.

'Take it,' he said. 'I will give them a mask.'

I stared at Baba. The shiny stick winked at me as the sun kissed it and I stretched out my hand, eager to feel it.

I felt a bite on my palm, sharp as the bite of an angry dog's teeth, and I drew my hand back in fright. It bled where I had held the stick. I looked at my palm and then at the man. He shook his head, laughing, then he stuck the stick back at his side. He had not meant it as a gift. And he did not even bother to cover his mouth as he laughed.

'Baba?'

He looked down at me from his chair. 'Mmm?'

'Our visitors.' I scrabbled about in my mind for a way to form the words in my head. Baba waited, silent, giving me the time I needed to hunt my meaning.

'If they are Taino returned from the land of the dead,' I said at last, 'why do they not look like Taino?'

My father thought for a while, then motioned

to his bearers to lower his chair. He searched about the ground then picked up a rotting mamey apple. I frowned. He was not going to eat that, surely. The flies he had disturbed were already buzzing round his head, demanding he give them back their meal.

Baba swatted them away and held the fruit out to me.

'You see this fruit,' he said. 'It has died and is now rotting. What will happen when it has rotted and is under the earth?'

I wrinkled my forehead, confused. What did a rotten mamey apple have to do with my question? Sometimes I wished Baba would answer a question directly rather than telling a story for every answer. I shrugged.

'It grows into a mamey apple tree.'

Baba nodded. 'Does the tree look like the apple?'

Understanding was born in my mind. 'So when the Taino die, they become new, different beings.'

Baba smiled. 'And as the tree does not remember being an apple, so the spirits do not remember being Taino. But when they have grown into spirits, just as the tree bears new apples, so they bear new Tainos, whom they send to us from Coyaba as babies.'

I looked up into the sky. At night we could see tens and tens and tens of fires in the skies where other spirits in Coyaba were cooking their evening meals, and although I could not see them now, I felt closer to them than I ever had before. One of the spirits in the giant canoes could be Caicihu, but we would not know for sure, and he would not remember. Just as I did not remember my home in Coyaba before I was sent to Baba and Bibi.

14

No Iguanas

'What terrible thing do you think they hide beneath their clothes?'

I grated another piece of cassava, holding it between my thumb and forefinger. Guabonito waited until I had finished and had reached for another piece of cassava.

'Well? What do you think?'

'You should not speak like that about our guests.'

'Do you think they have tails?'

'Nito!' But I had to hide my smile behind my hand.

'Perhaps they have large lumps underneath the baskets they wear on their heads.'

'I think they go covered to protect themselves from

the sun and the wind,' I said. 'I do not think the sun shines in Coyaba.'

'I know!' Guabonito carried on as if I had not spoken. She often ignored what she did not want to hear. 'They must be *caracaracol*! They must have scaly skin like the man in the stories Father tells at the *areitos*.' Her eyes were shining with pride at her cleverness.

'There are no sores or signs of disease on the skin of their hands and faces, Nito. They cannot be *caracaracol*.'

Her mouth turned down in disappointment, but only for a breath.

'Perhaps the sores are only on the parts they keep covered,' she said. 'Why else would they hide their skins like that?'

I shook my head and got up, lifting the bowl of grated cassava on to my hip. 'Come and help me squeeze this,' I told her. 'You think too much.'

Just then my father and Azzacca came striding from the forest. Azzacca carried a coney and Father a string of parrot fish and crabs, but they were both unsmiling. Baba looked as glum as a caterpillar in a hen's beak.

'Baba, you have caught so much fish!' Nito scampered to run her hands over the bright pink scales and I followed close behind.

'But it is not enough, little one.' My father sighed.

95

'All morning we have hunted, but no one has seen an iguana. How can we honour our guests without iguana meat? It will be a sad feast tonight.'

'Maruka knows where to find iguanas.'

My silencing nudge in Nito's side came too late, and only then did I remember I had not told her to keep that information secret.

My father's face wore a look of hope mixed with surprise. 'Is this true? You know where we might get an iguana?'

I scratched at my ankle with my big toe and shifted the bowl of cassava from my left hip to the right. I could not tell Father where I had seen the iguanas without getting into trouble. My father was not easily angered, but when he was it was best to keep out of his way. He would be outraged that I had been to the sacred caves.

'I saw some iguanas once, Baba. But it was a long time ago. They might not be there now.'

The hope slunk from his eyes. His broad forehead wore three lines of worry. I could not bear to see him like this. I could not stand by and see him dishonoured at the welcome feast for the visitors.

'I will go to see if the lizards are still there, Baba,' I said.

He smiled and the light crept back into his eyes.

'Take Azzacca with you.' And he turned and walked off towards the cooking fires before I could protest. I closed my eyes to hide my dismay, but Azzacca knew well enough he was the last person I wanted to go hunting with. He could not hide the pleasure it gave him to see me so uncomfortable. His lips parted in a smile which did not visit his eyes.

'Wait here while I give the women this coney,' he ordered. 'It will not take me long.'

'May I come with you, Maruka?' Nito begged.

'Your place is here with the women, Guabonito,' Azzacca said. 'Do not let Maruka put ideas in your head. Women do not go hunting. It is not the Taino way. Go and help with the cooking.'

Nito's face crumpled. Her bottom lip trembled as she tried to keep back the tears. I could have hit Azzacca. I bent towards Nito and put my arm around her.

'Do not be sad. I will bring back a baby iguana for you to keep in the compound. And later, perhaps next dry season, I will teach you to hunt as Caicihu taught me.'

Her smile was as bright as the plume of the rainbow serpent.

'This is the way to the sacred caves!' Azzacca stared at me as if I had suddenly sprouted a tail on my nose.

'You do not have to come.' I turned and continued up the path that wound up the mountain. It was so rarely used it was barely passable. Azzacca scrambled up behind me and grabbed my arm, yanking it off the guava sapling I was holding on to, to pull myself up.

My feet slid from beneath me and I fell back hard against him. He was unprepared and his look of surprise and alarm would have been funny at any other time. And then we were tumbling down the hill.

We lay, limp, on the damp earth at the foot of the path, all the air knocked from our bodies. I was first to find my breath again. Slowly, I pushed myself on to my hands and raised my shoulders from the ground.

Damp leaves clung to my skin, and my knees and elbows stung where they had connected with the rocks on the path. The cut in my palm from the pale stranger's stick was aching. I touched my fingers to it and they came away moist.

The anger started as a small seed inside, but soon it was a towering tree. Azzacca cowered in its shadow. He stared at the fire in my eyes and his hand got up to cover his head before he thought better of it and left it hanging halfway between his chest and his shoulder.

My chest was rising and falling as if I had run a long, long way.

'You hen-brained son of a sea turtle! You could have killed me!'

'Do not be stupid. We only fell a little way.' But he did not say it with his usual confidence.

My breath rushed from my lips in short, sharp bursts. I could hardly speak for the anger inside.

'If you value your safety you will stay far from me,'
I said slowly, quietly.

'Do you threaten me?'

'Keep away from me, Azzacca. I will not tell you again.'

His eyebrows shot up. As my father's heir, he was not used to being spoken to like that. I spun around and started back up the mountain. Halfway up, I found my spear and axe which had fallen when we slipped. As I picked them up I glanced back at him. He was still lying on the ground, staring at me, his mouth half open like a lizard hunting flies.

15

The Hunt

I heard the flies before I saw the animals. The insects followed them everywhere, feeding on the liquid which seeped from their eyes. The two great lizards were lying on a boulder and it would have been easy to mistake them for a part of the moss-covered stone, except that now and then they tossed their heads to dislodge the flies.

They were almost as big as the one I had hunted on Iyanola, on that terrible day three dry seasons before. I stood for a while, my mind working fast. I knew I could not hunt them both, so I needed to separate them.

I backed away, slowly, so that I would not attract their attention. Out of sight of them I picked up a handful of pebbles.

They had not moved. I hid behind a palm tree and

took careful aim. The first pebble landed on the snout of the female. I knew she was female because she was the smaller of the two. Besides, two males could not be together without fighting. She threw her head up in protest, looked around, then settled back to her basking.

The second pebble landed harmlessly on the male's scaly back. He did not even notice. The next was more accurate and I grinned as he growled, shook his head and slithered off the rock.

As soon as the retreating iguana was out of sight I took an arrow from my pouch and fitted it to my bow, keeping my eyes on the female all the time. I did not want to make the same mistake I had made on Iyanola. My aim had to be perfect.

The arrow flew straight to the soft place between the eyes. The iguana reared on her back legs with a bellow and tossed her head from side to side, trying to dislodge the weapon. I had another arrow ready and as she raised her head again I let fly. The arrow found the throat and pierced the skin. The lizard lurched to one side, then half stepped, half tumbled off the boulder. She tried to raise herself but her frantic movement had helped the poison on the tip of the arrow to work faster. She sank to the ground with a last roar of anger.

I stood for a while staring at the iguana, expecting her to get up and chase me. I could not believe it had been so easy.

I moved warily towards her, stepping noiselessly, in case she was still alive. She did not move. I carefully prodded her with my bow. Nothing. The flies which had been startled away by her death dance had found the drops of blood around the arrow in her forehead.

I bent and pulled out the arrow. A twig snapped behind me. I spun around, my heart pounding. What if the iguana's mate had returned?

Azzacca was staring from me to the iguana. 'Did you kill it?'

I had almost forgotten him. I glanced around the clearing. 'I cannot see anyone else here, can you?'

'Well, we had better get back if the women are to cook it for the feast. We have not got time to stand around admiring your kill.'

No word of praise. No acknowledgement that I had done well. I smiled inside. It did not matter. There would be praise enough when I returned to the village. It was easy to see that Azzacca was jealous and angry that I had been the one to get the lizard. His gaze moved from me to the mouths of the sacred caves behind us, a little way from the clearing, and a satisfied look clothed his face.

'I was right. You have been to the sacred caves.'

'I did not kill the iguana inside the caves. It was sitting on this boulder when I shot it.'

'But have you been inside? You know it is forbidden

for anyone but the cacique and the behiques to touch the floor of the caves.'

I turned away from Azzacca. 'Will you tell Baba?' He thought for a while. 'You might have brought bad luck to the Taino, but I will say nothing. You have saved my uncle's honour.' He picked up the iguana. 'Come, I will help you to carry it part of the way.'

'I have to do something else first,' I said. He frowned, a look of suspicion stealing across his face.

'What do you have to do that is so important you would keep the village waiting?'

'I have promised Nito a baby iguana. I am going to find one.'

'Do not be silly. Guabonito will understand that you had no time to get her iguana, but my uncle will not be pleased if there is no lizard for the feast. These visitors are spirits, remember. We should not anger them.'

My mind fought with itself. I thought of entering the village with the iguana on my shoulder and the look of surprise and pleasure on my father's face, and a warm glow started inside and spread through my whole body. Then another picture forced itself into my mind: Nito's face, dark with disappointment. I shook my head.

'The visitors will have to wait. I cannot disappoint Nito. Better a hungry spirit who knows he will be fed than a sister choking on a broken promise.'

Azzacca lowered the iguana, but he was not pleased.

I hesitated. There was a way to solve both problems. I could send Azzacca with my kill while I caught Nito's lizard. I had pictured myself striding into the compound with the huge lizard on my back. I could almost hear the praise songs sung for me at the *areito* that night. Even those who disapproved of my hunting would be filled with admiration.

If Azzacca brought the iguana home I would still have my praise songs, but it would not be the same. Yet I could not see any other way.

'Perhaps you could take the iguana back for me.'

He stared at me as if I had said goodbye to my senses.

'It is not my kill. A hunter should carry his own game.'

'I know. But do you have another solution? This way the spirits will be fed and Nito will get her iguana.'

He was still undecided. 'Are you sure?'

Reluctantly I nodded.

'Then I will see you back at the village,' he said.

I noticed that my second arrow was still lodged in the iguana's throat. I yanked it out as Azzacca turned away. The rubbery skin had closed around the head and was unwilling to let go.

There was a crack and the arrow was in my hand, but without the head.

I should have kept the broken arrow, but I didn't. I flung it to the ground in annoyance and strode into the trees.

16
Treachery

The smell of roasting meat greeted me long before I got to the compound. As I stepped from the trees Karaya saw me and hurried from her place among the women round the fire.

'Maruka! Where have you been? You missed all the excitement.'

I blinked, a terrible feeling springing to life inside me. 'What excitement?'

'Azzacca caught a huge iguana. We are roasting it now. He has saved your father's honour.'

'He has?' My voice sounded like the croak of the dying iguanas. Karaya peered at me.

'Are you not well, Maruka? You sound – strange.' She noticed the animal in my hand. 'Oh, you have caught an iguana as well!' She frowned. 'It is quite small. Perhaps we should fatten it up a bit before we cook it.'

I held the baby lizard closer to my chest and it wriggled in protest. 'This one belongs to Nito,' I said fiercely. 'No one else can have it.' I was still trying to work out what had happened.

She smiled warmly. 'That is very considerate. Guabonito is over by the stream, trying to catch crabs.' She shook her head. 'I hope she is not going to hunt as well. One female hunter in the family is sufficient.' She ruffled my hair to show she did not mean it unkindly and turned back to help the other women with the cooking. 'When you have given Guabonito her present, come and help us with the feast. You can watch the roast while we make the *casabi* and stew.'

I wanted to tell her the truth, but my throat was so tight that no words could find a way out, and anger and disbelief clouded my brain. How could Azzacca have been so dishonourable? Surely he knew that I would not just stand quietly by while he stole my prize?

I would find him and confront him with his dishonesty. Then I would force him to admit to everyone that the iguana was mine; that the words of praise belonged to me. But first I had to give Nito her lizard.

Azzacca came up to me as I was walking towards the stream at the back of the village.

'What did you say to Karaya?' He must have been watching us.

'What do you think I said? Azzacca is a liar and a thief?'

'You did not?' He stared at me, then repeated more confidently, 'You did not. I did not steal your iguana. They just – assumed I had killed it.'

'And you did not tell them they were wrong?'

'It was difficult. They were so pleased that their future cacique was a good hunter, finding an iguana when all the others had failed. I did not want to disappoint them.'

'Future cacique!' I made a noise of disgust in my throat. 'You are not fit to sit on my father's *duho*. You are not cacique yet, Azzacca. Just because you are the oldest nephew, do not think you are the chosen one. When my father finds out how dishonest you are . . .'

'You will not tell him.' It was not a question or a plea, but a statement. I raised my brows and my lips curled. I did not try to hide my contempt.

'And who will stop me?'

'It will be your word against mine.'

'I am the cacique's daughter.'

'And I am his heir. I will be believed.'

'*I* am Taino. Our people do not lie.' Azzacca flinched. He was only half Taino. His mother, my father's sister, had married a Macorix cacique and he had grown up among them until his tenth dry season. Their ways were different from ours.

Azzacca's eyes narrowed. 'If you tell them you

killed the iguana, I will have to tell them *where* you killed it.'

'You may do what you like.' My voice sounded weak even to my ears. I cleared my throat and tried again. 'I am not afraid.'

'Perhaps, but how about my uncle and his wives, and all his other children? Will they feel as you do? I cannot wait to hear what my uncle has to say about it.'

I swallowed. I had been stupid to think my actions would affect only me. I had not thought about the disgrace I would bring on my family by entering the sacred cave. I hung my head in shame. I tried to walk away but Azzacca stepped in my path.

'Well?'

Although the words found the way to my mouth reluctantly, I had to ask. 'I have your word you will not say anything?'

'You have my word.'

I sighed. 'Then I will not tell anyone you *stole* my iguana.'

Azzacca scowled but did not protest. Instead, he examined my face as I had examined his. 'I have your word?'

I poured as much scorn as I could into my look. 'I have told you before. *I* am Taino.' This time when I moved he stepped hastily out of my way. I felt him watching me as I marched off, but I did not look back.

'Why do you not tell them?'

I stopped jabbing at the sweet potato and turned to stare at Bijirita.

'What did you say?'

She lowered her head and stared at the ground. She raised her gaze to my face then looked hastily away.

'What is it, Biji?'

'I am sorry. Forgive me. I did not mean to listen but I was digging the groundnuts for the feast when you stopped by the fence and before I could tell you I was there Azzacca had come and was talking to you and it was too late to say anything after I heard . . .'

My heart leaped in alarm. 'What are you talking about, Biji?'

She looked around quickly. 'Forgive me, Maruka, but I heard what he has done. It is a terrible thing and I think you should tell your parents.'

I tried to calm my thoughts. If Biji had heard our whole conversation, she would know that I had a secret too.

I shook my head and bent towards her. My words were urgent, but I tried to look as if we were having a normal conversation.

'Biji, I do not want my parents or anyone else

to know what Azzacca has done. You must not say anything. Promise?'

She frowned. 'But why, Maruka? I do not understand why you let him escape with such behaviour.'

I smiled grimly. 'One day, perhaps, I will tell you. But for now it has to be our secret. Do you promise?'

She nodded reluctantly. 'It pains me that Azzacca will be accepting praise he does not deserve, while you . . .'

'Shh! My mother comes. I will speak with you later.'

I turned to face Karaya and helped her to lower the basket of sweet potatoes to the earth.

'More for you to roast, Maruka. There will be many mouths to feed tonight.'

I started laying the potatoes on the glowing coals and I speared the cooked ones into the empty basket.

'These are ready,' I said. I smiled at her as if there was no other thought in my head except roasting potatoes. But my gaze followed Biji as she went back to her task of squeezing the poisonous juice from the cassava.

17

Feast

The ball court in front of our house had been swept clean. The communal fires in the centre still smouldered, keeping the food warm. And what food there was!

The spicy smell of pepperpot teased my nostrils, but it had to compete with the aroma of the barbecued iguana, roasted maize and sweet potatoes. Piles of *casabi* were stacked on plates, the white of the breads bright beside the brilliant reds, greens, yellows and purples of the bowls of mangoes, pineapples, sweetsops, guavas, star-apples, mamey apples and pawpaws.

The Taino had spent as much time on themselves as on the food. The first to arrive in the ball court were the sub-caciques from the neighbouring villages. They reminded me of the beautiful parrots of the forest with their feather headdresses and bodies painted white, black and red. My father went to greet them and I felt pride swell like a ripening fruit inside me.

He strode towards his guests like the lord of all Kiskeya, the shells around his neck, arms and ankles swinging in time to his movements.

The feathers in his headdress were the longest there, the blues, greens and reds brighter than any other. As he turned from one cacique to another the sunlight kissed the gold in his ears and nose and the green stones and gold of his belt so that they sparkled.

I touched the gold in my ears and the shell and bone necklace around my neck. They were the best I had, the shells the brightest pinks and the purest whites, and the bones bleached almost transparent by the sun.

The red beads around my ankles were interspersed with white and the bright yellow of more gold. Karaya had taken great care with my body paints and I hoped I looked as wonderful as I felt.

She led my father's other wives from the house and I wished that I had had my age-ceremony at the last dry season. The women's ceremonial skirts were the colour of hummingbirds' wings. The cotton had been dyed dark blue and the threads woven with red, white and black beads which shimmered as they moved. After my age-ceremony I would be a woman and able to wear such things on days like this.

Except there were not many days like this. Never

before had the Taino held a feast where the guests of honour were the spirits. Spirits who were now following the Taino men who had been sent to escort them into the ball court.

Many of the Taino had not seen the spirits before, and though some had stolen away to gape at their enormous canoes and had glimpsed one or two of them on the beach, the sight of the visitors all together was still overwhelming.

I heard the gasp from the visiting caciques and their wives, and smiled behind my hands. We had done the same when we had seen the spirits for the first time.

The pale visitors sat in the *duhos* my father had made ready for them and, although the ceremonial stools looked big to me, they disappeared under the bulky coverings the spirits wore. So much cloth on one body seemed strange.

But I did not have time to wonder. Now that they had arrived, the feasting could begin, and I was needed to help serve the food.

I took the bowl of pepperpot from Karaya and handed it to Baba. He passed it reverently to the pale cacique.

The visitors sat together, and though we tried to conceal our curiosity, they did not bother with that courtesy. They stared openly at us, and it seemed they could not take their eyes off the gold we wore. They were especially fascinated with the large flattened pieces which hung from my father's ears.

They took the food and examined it for a while before dipping the calabash spoons into the bowls. They raised the spoonfuls slowly to their lips, as if they thought it might contain the poisonous juice of the bitter cassava. They did not seem to recognize any of the food.

The pepperpot was not as popular with the visitors as I had expected it to be. The spicy dish of meat, fish, callaloo and hot peppers was my favourite and as I stuffed my mouth I could not understand how anyone could not like it. My tongue tingled deliciously with the heat from the peppers. Most of the strangers, though, put it to one side, and all had a red paint under their skin after the first mouthful.

Then Karaya was handing round the roast iguana and I lost my appetite. The covered men seemed to like that as much as the Taino did. They smiled and nodded approvingly as they ate it, and my father's smile seemed to link his ears.

'Well done, Azzacca,' he said. 'It would have been a poor feast without your iguana.' He looked from Azzacca's satisfied face to mine and his smile wavered. He got up and came towards me.

'Do not look so sad, Flower. You also did well. If you had not found the iguanas, Azzacca would not have been able to catch this one.'

I opened my mouth, but no words could get past the lump in my throat. Baba smiled.

'You are upset because Azzacca's lizard was so much bigger than yours.'

I shook my head.

He sighed again. 'I have said many times, Maruka. You do not need to try and replace Caicihu. I know his spirit lives in you, but you are still a girl. There are some things a male will always do better. There is no disgrace in that.'

I remained silent. What could I say?

Baba went back to his seat, between the pale cacique and Azzacca.

Karaya walked over to him and handed him something. They both turned to stare at me and talked together for a little while but I could not hear the words. Karaya returned to the pots and Baba continued to watch me, surprise in his eyes, but he said nothing. I frowned, but had no time to ask him what was wrong.

One of the visitors came over to Karaya and gestured that the meat was good. Karaya smiled and gave him some more. He thanked her and made signs that he wanted to know what the meat was. She tried to tell him, but he looked puzzled. I beckoned to Nito.

'Go and get your iguana,' I said. 'The spirit wants to know what he is eating.'

Nito sped away and returned with the lizard clinging to her shoulder.

Karaya took the lizard from Nito and, beaming, thrust it towards the stranger's face. He stepped back, slightly alarmed.

'This is it,' she said. He did not understand. He thought she was giving him a present. He reached out tentatively for it but she pulled it back, shaking her head. She pointed to the big bowl with the rest of the meat, pointed to the lizard, towards the bowl again and then to her mouth.

He understood then. Karaya waited for the look of pleasure but it did not come. Instead, the face of the stranger went paler, so that he almost seemed transparent. He stopped chewing and made a strangled sound in his throat. Then he turned and ran towards the nearest house. As he went he yelled to his companions. They all stared at the lizard in Karaya's hands. Then two others followed him and we heard them emptying their stomachs. I looked at Karaya with a question on my face. She raised her eyebrows and shrugged. The ways of the strangers were a mystery to her too.

The others put their bowls on the ground as if the vessels had suddenly grown fangs. One of the strangers spat out the food in his mouth, right there in front of everyone. We turned our heads, pretending not to notice. For the rest of the feast, the strangers ate only the fruits.

18

Areito

By the time we had finished eating, dusk had fallen and the lanterns were lit. Guabonito and I had prepared a special dance for our visitors, and while Father told the story of the first Taino, I fidgeted and squirmed. My palms were wet and my body felt clammy. What if I forgot the steps? Would the spirits be angry? It was fine, dancing for the spirits when we could not see them, but harder when their colourless eyes were fastened on us.

I glanced at Nito, thinking she must be even more nervous than I was, but she gazed at Baba, her eyes wide with expectation. I shook my head. However many times she heard the story Nito always looked as if it was the first.

Baba had finished welcoming our visitors to the

areito and was about to begin. His voice deepened and his eyes looked past us and far into the distance of time, before any of us were born. He told the story as if he was seeing it unravelling in front of his eyes, and I allowed myself to be lost in the music of his voice. As he spoke he mimed the parts. His flying fingers sketched pictures in the air. His body doubled and twisted as he made the journeys with the Taino of old.

'*Long ago, when time was still in the cradle, all people lived in two caves in Caonao. In those days it was forbidden for men to see the sun. In the large cave lived the Taino. All the other peoples lived in the smaller cave. The guardian of the caves was Macocael.*

'*One day Macocael was late returning to the cave. He stayed until the sun awoke and was turned into stone. Guahayona, one of the men inside the cave, when he saw it was unguarded, persuaded all the women to go with him, to search for other lands. They arrived on the island of Matimino, where he left them. To this day there are only women on Matimino.*

'*Guahayona came to the island of Guanin, where he met a medicine woman called Guabonito.*' Baba paused and took a sip from his cup of cassava wine.

I felt Nito squirming beside me and I smiled. I squeezed her hand and she grinned at me, her eyes shining. This was her favourite part of the story. Baba went on.

'*Guabonito saw that Guahayona was* caracaracol. *There were scabs on his face and his skin was flaking on his hands, elbows and knees. The rest of his body was red and itchy.*

'*Guabonito washed him with digo plants and put him in a place called Geranara until he recovered from his sores.*

'*When Guahayona was well again he asked Guabonito's permission to leave. She agreed. But before he left she gave him the gold and cibas to protect him from illness. The Taino had never seen gold or the ciba stones until then. She showed him how to wear them in his nose, his ears and around his arms and ankles. That is why the Taino wear them to this day.*'

I fingered the necklace around my neck. In between the shells and beads which were threaded on the cotton string were tiny pieces of gold which flashed when the sun kissed them and bright ciba stones which sparkled with green fire. Beside me Nito was stroking her own necklace. So were many of the Taino. We all took comfort from knowing that as long as we wore them we would be free from sickness.

The pale visitors were trying to look interested, but I could see they did not understand what Baba was saying. A few were listening, but with a puzzled look. The others were gazing around the square, peering into the *bohios* as if they had lost something which they thought might be hidden in the houses. And all the time their gazes kept returning to the gold we wore.

'Tonight,' Baba continued, 'we have been honoured. The spirits have left their homes in Coyaba, have come down from the skies to visit us.'

There was a murmur among the Taino and the elders nodded and smiled at our visitors. They smiled back uncertainly.

'Welcome, spirits. Our homes are your homes. Whatever we have is yours.'

His glance swept the crowd and a smile softened the lines on his face.

'Now we have others to honour.'

He beckoned to Azzacca and I felt a dark pit open in the bottom of my stomach. This was the part of the evening I had been dreading. Each word was like an arrow tip in my heart.

'Most of us have enjoyed the delicious iguana meat.' He looked at the visitors and one or two Taino smiled behind their hands. 'We have Azzacca to thank for that. Azzacca!'

The Taino punched the air with their fists. 'Azzacca! Azzacca! Azzacca!'

I did not join in. I felt my father's eyes on me and knew he was disappointed. He thought I was still sulking because Azzacca had been more successful in the hunt.

Bamako got up after the cheering had stopped and sang a song of praise to Azzacca, the brave hunter who had succeeded where all the other hunters had failed.

I squeezed my eyes tight to shut in the tears.

When Bamako finished, there was more stamping of approval and shouts of 'Azzacca!' I stared at the red earth and prayed for it to stop. I did not hear Baba announcing our dance; did not know it was time until Nito was pulling me from my seat.

'Come on, Maruka.'

Panic clutched me to its chest. I could not dance when my heart was a heavy stone in my chest.

My feet felt as if they were wading through a swamp. My body was heavy and strange, as if someone else moved inside my skin.

Nito's feet flew like wind across the ground. I felt her anxious glances as I stumbled and shambled after her, but I could do nothing right.

Afterwards there was a polite stamping of feet. I knew it was only for Nito. The pale visitors banged their palms together and shouted, 'Ole! Ole!'

I could not look at Nito. She had been looking forward to this so much and I had spoiled it for her.

I ran into the *caney* and climbed into my hammock. I buried my face into the cotton and waited for the tears to come. But even the tears were ashamed and wanted nothing to do with me. When Nito called my name from the doorway, I could not answer. I held my breath until she went away. Then I rolled over and stared through the smoke hole into the sky. I gazed at the fires of the people in Coyaba.

'Why, Atebeyra? Why?'

But there was no answer.

I could remember only one other time when I felt as miserable as I did now. My mind travelled the tracks of time back to Iyanola, to the days following Caicihu's burial.

Iyanola

19
Right or Wrong?

I sat cross-legged on the warm earth, my new spear in my hand. I stopped sharpening the point to watch the men rebuilding the last of the bohios. *The smell of fresh-cut coconut boughs tickled my nostrils and mingled with the aroma of the pepperpot which would be part of the second meal. The stew was a new one as the old pepperpot which had been cooking for weeks had been destroyed in the Kalinago raid.*

I went back to sharpening my spear but looked up as a shadow fell across my lap. A half-smile flitted across his lips, though it was not strong enough to chase the sadness from my father's eyes.

'I am glad to see you are going hunting again. What will it be? Birds or coney?'

I shook my head. 'Neither, Baba. This is a special spear. It is for hunting Kalinago.'

Baba's eyes widened in shock. He squatted in front of me and laid his hand on mine where I clutched the spear.

'Anani – Maruka . . .' He was not yet used to my new name. 'We do not hunt people. That is not the Taino way.'

Doubt and confusion puckered my forehead. 'But, Baba, they hunted us. They captured my mother and . . . and . . .' The words would not come. I could not tell him. Instead I asked, 'What about all the Taino women and girls they have taken? Are we not going to rescue them?'

My father placed his hands on either side of my face so that our eyes talked with each other.

'Maruka, Flower, the Kalinago are trained killers. The Taino are peaceful people. Many more Taino would be killed if we went to war. Is that what you want?' I shook my head and his hands left my face. 'Besides, a Taino should not take the life of another human, you remember that, don't you?'

I thought of the Kalinago boy lying on the stones by the growling waters. I had not told anyone about him and now I was ashamed and terrified to admit I had taken a life.

'I know that, Father, but it is right for a Taino to take revenge.'

'Other means of revenge are always preferable to taking a life. A life is precious. A gift from the gods. We cannot throw it away lightly.'

We were both silent for a while.

'What happens if a Taino takes another life, Baba?'

Baba shook his head as if it was too terrible to consider.

'He would have to pay for it when he reaches Coyaba. He might even be kept out of Coyaba forever, like the lost spirits which have drowned at sea and not had the travelling prayers said over them.'

I bit my lip. A dark feeling of guilt and fear made a nest in my heart, and started feeding on Baba's words.

'And are all spirits kept out of Coyaba if they have not had the prayers said over them?'

'All Taino, yes.'

'What about Kalinago?'

Baba looked closely at me. 'We are not going after the Kalinago, Maruka. I have said.'

'I know, but what happens if a dead Kalinago has not had the prayers said over him? Would his spirit remain on Kiskeya forever?'

Baba's eyes narrowed. 'On Kiskeya?'

I had said too much. Baba held my chin and peered into my face. His voice was soft but firm.

'What is it, Flower?'

I could not keep this secret any longer. I cringed as his face darkened and his lips narrowed into a thin line.

'This is not good. The Kalinago never leave their dead on the battleground. They will be back for him.' He rose swiftly and my gaze followed his to the sea.

'There is no time to lose,' he said. 'I must talk with the elders.' He strode away to the house of the zemis and a

126

short time later the sound of the guamo *called the council to assemble.*

I raced to our caney. *My bow and arrows had to be checked, my axe prepared. Although I remembered what Baba had said, I knew a Taino was allowed to defend himself if attacked. I had to make sure I was ready.*

My father called the caciques from the other tribes on the island. They were in council until the sun started its homeward journey. Then the other caciques left. My father spoke to his elders and later talked for an age in the caney *with my other mothers.*

Just before dusk the men went to the canoe house to check on the boats. My spirits soared. It seemed we were not going to wait for the Kalinago after all but we were going to find them before they found us again. My weapons were all ready and waiting, and I was anxious to get started. I wanted to avenge my brother and my mother, and I wanted to avenge my brother and my mother, all the Taino we had buried in the midden. I was so happy that my father had changed his mind. The other caciques had obviously persuaded him it was the right thing to do.

We went to sleep with a feeling of excitement and anticipation. I was up and washed while the sun was still shaking itself awake. I sprinted up the track from the river but stopped when I entered the compound.

The women were packing travelling baskets. The pots,

the griddles, the wringers we used to squeeze the juice from the cassava were being stuffed hurriedly into containers. Karaya saw me and beckoned.

'Come and help, Anan – Maruka. There is much to do, and little time to do it in.'

'What is happening? Why are we packing all our things?' I did not think we would take all our belongings to war.

'We are leaving,' she said. 'Iyanola is no longer a safe place to live. That is what your father and the council have decided.'

He could not do this. I turned from Karaya and ran towards the ball court. I had to let Baba know how important it was for us to stay. If we left Iyanola, we would be going further away from Bibi. She would never be saved.

He was with the priest in the house of the zemis. It was the only building which had not been damaged in the raid, because it was away from the other houses. Baba and the priest were taking the zemis from their duhos and stacking them carefully into baskets. I cleared my throat to get his attention.

He hurried over to me. 'What is it, Flower? Is something wrong?'

'Karaya says we are leaving Iyanola.'

'Yes.'

'Is it true?'

'We cannot stay here, Maruka. The Kalinago will be back.'

'So we are running away?'

He frowned. 'Would you rather we stay and be killed?'

'But what about the Taino who have been taken? They will be waiting for us to rescue them. Besides, Bibi—'

'Will understand.' He stopped my words before they could leave my lips. 'Listen, Maruka, the Kalinago have attacked us before. You were only a baby the last time, so you will not remember. We lived on Oualie then. Once the attacks start, they never cease. We would have to fight all our lives. The only thing to do is move on.'

'But we have to help Bibi.'

'Maruka, I understand you miss your mother. Do you think the pain of loss is yours alone? I have said all that is to be said. Go now and help your other mothers to pack.'

'But, Baba, you do not understand. Bibi needs us—'

'Enough! I do not want you to speak of your mother any more. You must accept that she is gone. Thinking of saving her will only prolong the pain.'

'Baba, will you listen to me?'

'No, Maruka, you listen. There is to be no more talk of rescuing your mother or anyone else. I have spoken.'

He turned and re-entered the house of the zemis and I stormed back to the caney. Anger, like a volcano, erupted inside me, blinding me so that I charged into Guabonito who was coming out of the caney as I entered. She swayed for a breath and then fell down on the packed earth.

129

Nito stared at me. Fear fluttered across her face and it crumpled like a sodden cotton petal. Her wail filled the caney *and pulled her mother to her side.*

I stood looking down at my sister, but my brain was slow to surface from the angry fog into which it had fallen. Karaya's voice pierced the daze.

'Maruka! Have you said goodbye to your senses? Why are you attacking your sister?'

'Oh. I am sorry. Forgive me, Nito. I did not see . . .' I shook my head and reached for Nito, anxious to make amends, but she buried her face in her mother's neck and Karaya turned from me and went back to her packing, with Nito sticking to her side. I went outside and found a quiet spot at the back of the compound. I sat on the hard earth and felt the thorns of macka grass digging into my bare skin with a twisted sense of satisfaction. I deserved to be punished. I should not have let anger take control of me so that I was a danger to others. Why was I cursed with such an awful temper? None of the other Taino ever showed such violent emotions. Why was I so different?

I buried my head in my hands, feeling that my whole world was folding in on itself. Why would Baba not listen to me when I tried to tell him about Bibi? Did he not care about her? Why did he shut me from his thoughts?

An idea leaped into my mind. I could not force my father to do what I wanted; could not force him to listen to what I had to say. If Bibi was to be saved, I would have to do it myself.

Kiskeya

20
Storm

The day after the *areito* I was carving a *zemi* from the shell of a calabash. I had not finished work on my canoe, and I was afraid I was running out of time. Soon the great storms would come and I could not go on my journey then. I would have to wait until another dry season, and my mother would spend another cycle waiting to be rescued.

I turned to my carving and drew the sharp stone over the thick shell of the calabash, as I tried to work out how long it would take me to finish the canoe. I had almost finished the *zemi* I was carving when thunder grumbled over the tops of the trees and I glanced at the sky. It glared back at me with bloodshot eyes. The wind growled and lashed the trees, pushing their heads towards the ground, and I saw the birds speeding inland from the sea.

Like chickens chased by dogs, the Taino were dashing here and there, snatching pots, bowls, griddles and jugs from the communal fireside and calling children into the *bohios*. I dived into the *caney* just as the first drops of rain hit the ground like silver arrows from the sky.

Huracan, god of thunder, was fuming. Branches tore themselves from trees and fled from his fury. The roofs of the *bohios* scattered to hide from his anger.

The *caney* shook, leaning first one way and then the other, as if a giant hand was rocking it, trying to tear it from the ground. I felt sure the *caney* could not hold out much longer and I shuffled closer to Baba. Soon we would be exposed to Huracan's wrath.

Cico was huddled at my feet, making small wuffs of terror, and I reached down to pat his head. Huracan cracked his whip again. The thunder seemed to split the earth. Nito screamed and I had to bite my lip hard to keep from screaming too. My head ached from the noise and tension, the sudden darkness and the driving rain. It seemed to go on forever.

Then, as suddenly as it had started, the storm stopped. The silence was even more terrifying than the noise. It felt as if Huracan was waiting for us to come out of the *caney* so that he could strike us. The others must have felt it too, because no one moved.

The first high-pitched wail cracked the silence and

shocked us into action. Baba was the first to reach the opening, and by the time he got there the air was full of shrieks, wails and screams. I followed Baba and the women to see the devastation Huracan had caused. But Nito and the little ones continued to huddle in the corner, some of them sobbing in fright.

I gasped at the sight before me. The village looked as if every one of Huracan's bolts had found its mark there.

Trees which had stood tall and strong for many dry seasons lay on the ground, roots pointing to the sky, branches stripped clean of leaves. *Bohios* had been torn apart. All that remained of some were the central poles pointing accusingly at the sky. Others had been ripped out, pole and all.

The square itself wore a garland of leaves, fruit, pots and gourds, washed into piles around its edges. The stream behind the compound had mounted its banks and was rushing in brown torrents through the maize field. Except there was no maize in the field any more.

The Taino were walking amongst the rubble which remained of their *bohios*. Some were crying aloud, some moaning softly and others seemed too dazed to make any sound.

Baba went over to where a man sat on the fallen centre pole which was all that was left of his *bohio*. He straddled it, as if he was about to paddle it down the river. That thought brought another to my head. My hands flew to my mouth. My canoe.

Nito and I had not covered it when we saw the pale men's canoes arriving, and I had not been back to hide it. It had been left out in the storm.

Before I had time to think, I was running towards my secret place. It was hard to run when the path had been washed away. By the time I reached the place where the canoe should have been, the sky was scowling again and the wind was muttering. I did not have much time. Huracan was just resting, the storm was not over.

I slipped and slithered down the slope.

I scrabbled through the mounds of leaves and branches strewn on the ground, though I knew the canoe would not have been hiding under them. I scrambled towards the river and peered into the swirling brown waters. What if it had been washed out to sea? The thought was a knife in my brain.

Then I saw it. Wedged between the trunks of two giant kapok trees. I stood still for a few breaths, grinning at the boat and feeling weak with relief.

I slid towards it and ran my hand over the wood. There were no cracks or splits in it and the tension slunk from my body. I patted the trunks of the kapok trees, thanking the spirits inside for looking after my boat.

The brown cascade gurgled round my feet and

climbed from my ankles to my calves. It was rising. I had to get out before the whole valley was flooded. I glanced at my boat. Should I try to move it? It was probably safe between the trees and a quick inspection of the sky's glowering face told me that I was running out of time.

I scooted towards the slope, fighting to get footholds in the slippery clay. The shrubs and grasses which had served as handholds before were now on their way to the ocean. I found myself slipping back towards the river and sank my fingers into the earth. They came away with a lump of mud. I fell back into the water with a splash.

Something hard was digging into my palm; probably a stone or shell embedded in the soil I was still clutching. I raised my hand to throw it away, then paused. It might be suitable as an arrowhead. It felt hard enough.

I gaped at the thing in my hand. Unable to believe what my eyes were telling me, I lowered my hand into the water and washed the dirt away. The piece of gold winked at me in the unnatural light left by the storm. It was the biggest piece of gold I had ever seen. Even Baba's armbands had had to be made from several pieces melted together. But this was almost big enough to make an armband by itself.

I whooped with joy. I could not wait to show it to the others. A thought spoke to me and immediately I sobered. I could not show it to anyone. They would want to know where I had found it. They would ask what I had been doing here. I would have to keep it hidden. The basket which held the ornaments for my age-ceremony would be a good place to put it. No one else would look in there.

21

In the Eye of the Storm

I glanced anxiously at the sky. Its face was drawn, dark with displeasure. Clouds scuttled away in fear, and an angry wind shook the trees. I scrambled up the slope, careful now to dig my fingers and toes deep into the clay. It was difficult because I clutched the gold in my left hand and could only hold on with my right. I let out my breath in relief when I reached the top, but I would not be able to get back before the storm broke again. Something heavy lodged in the bottom of my stomach.

A finger of lightning zigzagged across the tops of the trees. It was a while before the deafening clap of thunder followed and by then I was almost fainting from holding my breath. I unclenched my fists and there were little half-moons where my nails had dug into my hands.

My eyes darted around the forest. There was nothing but trees. I could not stay there. Not with Huracan shooting arrows at the earth. There was only one place I could hide. My mind closed up against the thought but I forced it open again. It was forbidden, but where else could I go? By the time I got to the village I would be drenched or worse.

My heart was pounding and I touched the *zemi* around my neck. With a silent plea to Atebeyra, I turned and ran away from the village.

I stood for a long time looking at the opening. The raindrops were pointed arrows against my bare skin, but still I held back. I blinked the water from my eyelids and licked my lips. The water was cool and tasted of rose apple blossoms. Steam rose from the earth in a white sheet that quickly covered the tops of the trees below me.

I should not have come here. I turned to retrace my steps and a demon's tongue of lightning sizzled through the sky. The air crackled as if it had been set on fire. I spun round and dived into the sacred cave.

When the thunder came I had my eyes shut tight and my teeth were trying to pierce my lips. The shock of the bolt seemed to split the earth and caused the floor of the cave to rock beneath my feet.

My scream bounced against the walls of the cave before skidding off into the blackness deep inside.

It went echoing on to join the last of the thunder rumbling into the bowels of the earth.

I was instantly ashamed and slowly opened my eyes. In this of all places I should not have shown such a lack of courage. I was glad there was no one there.

My glance explored the cave. It was much larger than the one into which I had chased the coney. At first I could see very little, a shape here and there, and vague outlines on the walls, but as my eyes became accustomed to the gloom I saw that the shapes were *zemis*. There was Opiyelguaobiran with his dog's head and Atebeyra with her swollen belly. Beside her, her son Huracan stood with his mouth wide.

I looked hurriedly away. The lightning and thunder and the furious wind and rain outside told of Huracan's wrath. Perhaps my presence in the sacred cave would make him even angrier.

I dropped to my knees and clutched my amulet in both hands. The shell was cold against my fingers. I turned to face the *zemi* of Atebeyra but kept my eyes on the sandy floor of the cave. 'Atebeyra,' I pleaded, 'please do not be angry with me. I have not come to do wrong in your sacred place. I have come to shelter from the storm. Speak to your son and the other gods so that they do me no harm.'

I knelt like that for a long time, until the pain of the sand biting into my knees was too much to bear.

The storm was quieter and I guessed that Huracan's anger was passing. I rose to my feet, stretched my toes and moved my neck and shoulders to get rid of the stiffness.

Suddenly there was a sound at the back of the cave. I froze in terror. It was dark and I could not be sure, but it seemed to me that something, a shadow, moved.

'Be merciful, Atebeyra,' I gabbled, 'and I will bring you an offering every day. I will go now and will not defile your sacred place again. Spare me, *zemis*, and every day I will feed you.'

I was rising as I spoke, my eyes never leaving the spot from which the sound and movement had come. I crept backwards towards the mouth of the cave, gabbling all the while. I cannot remember now what else I promised the *zemis*. I wanted to turn and fly from the place, but I could only move slowly, careful not to disturb any of the offerings on the floor of the cave.

I had just reached the door when the shadow moved. There was someone there! I turned and fled. For once I was careless of the noise I was making through the forest. I was not the hunter now, but the hunted, and I ran as if all the inhabitants of Coyaba were after me. The wind tried to lift me from the ground and slammed me against a tree. Sparks fizzled in my brain as pain ripped through my body. I took a deep breath to calm myself. Then I was off again, dodging the rocks and branches being washed towards me, splashing like an enormous manatee through the rivers which had appeared.

By the time I reached the compound, Huracan had spent his anger, and the torrent had settled into a steady drizzle with the occasional rumble of thunder in the distance. The Taino were beginning to emerge again from the *bohios* and my father, coming out of our *caney*, spotted me straight away.

I had been so scared that I had not considered what the others would think. My father stopped in front of me, and I could guess from his expression what I looked like: my hair plastered to my head like a drowned blackbird's feathers to its carcass, my chest heaving and the breath rushing from my mouth in clouds of steam; my body bruised, scratched and muddied.

I felt my father's hand on my chin. Gently but firmly, he lifted my head so that our eyes said hello.

'What is the matter, child? Where have you been?'

'I was in the forest, Baba. I was caught in the storm.'

Baba frowned. 'I thought you were in the *caney* with us. Were my eyes making a fool of me?'

'I came out when the storm rested.'

Baba's frown deepened. 'But why? Did you not realize the storm had not finished?'

'Yes, but I wanted to see . . . to see what damage Huracan had done.' I could not tell him about the canoe and my plans to save my mother. I could not tell him that I had stepped inside a sacred cave for the second time. He brushed the rain from his lashes and turned to the square where the Taino were already clearing the debris.

'Well, you could have studied Huracan's work right here. There was no need to put yourself in danger.'

He stared at me for a while longer, then strode off to offer help and support to his people.

'You had better get yourself cleaned,' he said as he left. 'You look as if you have seen a spirit.'

22

The Gods Are Angry

The pale cacique had lines running across his forehead, joining his temple. His lips were stretched into a thin line and the eyes which had captured the sky were clouded with worry. He gestured helplessly to where the remains of his winged canoe and his belongings bobbed like fallen coconuts on the water.

Baba took charge. Soon an army of Taino were paddling out to rescue as much as they could of the wreckage. Baba was able to tell the pale cacique, with words and signs, that everything would be all right. But I was not sure it would be.

Why would Huracan destroy the spirits' canoe? Had the spirits angered him? The gods were not usually so destructive unless they were displeased. Everyone knew that. Perhaps Baba would have the answer.

I found him at the house of the *zemis*, where he was directing the storage of the visitors' belongings. He listened to my question with a frown folding his forehead. He was silent for a while before he answered.

'The ways of the gods are a forbidden country to us. We cannot travel there without an invitation.'

However, I thought of the mess the storm had made in the village, and a seed of worry took rest in my mind.

'Can the behiques not ask? Huracan has destroyed the spirits' canoe, and he almost destroyed our village. He must be angry with the spirits, and he might be angry with us for welcoming them. Will we not draw more of his anger to us if we help them now?'

Baba looked long at me. His lips opened, but closed again before any words could escape.

'We will talk later, Maruka,' he said.

I turned to go back to our *caney* and my glance slid through the opening of the *zemi* house. It collided with Atebeyra's fixed stare, and I remembered. I had promised to take food to the sacred caves every day. Any promise to the *zemis* had to be kept, or misfortune would be a lifelong companion.

I took a bowl from the *caney* and ladled pepperpot stew into it from the communal fire. I thanked the *zemis* that everyone was busy either helping to save the pale visitors' belongings or tidying up after the storm.

No one paid any attention to me. Next I hurried to the storehouse where the dried fish and meat were kept. I hoped with all my being that the food would be acceptable to the *zemis*.

I stood for a long while at the opening of the sacred cave. Then I straightened my shoulders and took a deep breath. I held the bowl with the food at arm's length in front of me, took one step into the cave and waited. There was no sound. I took another step, tensing my body as if against a blow. Another step took me all the way in. It was as silent as death, and cool inside, but I felt the moisture of sweat on the top of my lip.

Carefully, I lowered the bowl to the floor, keeping my gaze on the back of the cave where I had seen the shadow before. Nothing moved. I felt I should say something, but I was frightened of breaking the silence. If the *zemis* were asleep I did not want to wake them.

I took a step back. Then another. In two more steps I was out of the cave and running.

I was gasping for breath by the time I burst through the entrance of the *caney*. My heart threatened to leap from my chest and my legs wobbled as if the bones had been pulled from them.

I flopped on to one of the children's sleeping mats in the corner of the *caney*. Was this how it would be from now on? Would I have to endure this terror every day as I fed the *zemis* in the sacred cave? I could not live like that. No one could. Why had I made that promise? Why could I not have kept my mouth sealed? Perhaps Baba would know if there was a way out of my promise, but could I ask him without revealing what I had done?

The thoughts chased each other around my mind until my eyelids closed. But even in sleep I could not escape the *zemis*.

23
Dream

I had come to the sacred cave in search of something. It was very important for me to find it. I could feel the urgency welling up like a storm in my chest, but I did not know what I was supposed to find. I only knew that whatever I was searching for was in the cave, and finding it was a matter of life and death.

My spirit guide was with me, urging me on.

'Hurry, hurry, they are coming.'

I wanted to ask my guide who 'they' were, but the urgency in my chest pushed me forward, so I scrambled to the mouth of the cave.

It was dark inside. I could see nothing but blackness and I knew I would not be able to find what I had come for. Panic swelled inside me and I shouted through the mouth of the cave to my guide.

'I cannot find it. Come and help me.'

But my guide was hopping about frantically outside the cave. 'Come out, quickly. The mountain is falling!'

I scurried out and ran with my guide to stand a little distance away from the mountain. I did not understand what was happening. This was the sacred mountain of the Taino. How could it fall? And what had I been looking for in the cave?

We waited, but although it seemed to shudder and groan the mountain still stood. I turned to my guide.

'I am going back inside.'

'It is too late now,' my guide said sadly. 'They are here.'

I followed her gaze and my eyes tried to leave their sockets. My breath lodged in my throat and my knees huddled, shaking against each other.

There were men climbing up the rocks towards us. At least I thought they were men, but I could not be sure, because, except for their hands and faces, they were completely covered. They moved quickly, like land crabs in the rainy season, their covered feet gobbling up the distance between us. I could not move.

The sun kissed the shiny sticks they carried, so that blinding light bounced back to my eyes. I felt resigned, light in the head, as if my mind was making ready for my death. But the covered men went past us as if we were not there. At the bottom of the mountain they stopped and pointed the silver sticks at the rocks. The sticks growled and belched smoke, and suddenly the sacred mountain crumbled. I felt a terrible pain in my chest as the mountain fell and I cried out.

My guide grabbed me by the shoulders and shook me.

'Wake up, Maruka. It is only a bad dream. Wake up!'

Nito was shaking me and I woke with my screams in my ears and a dreadful pain sitting on my chest.

24
Advice

'Karaya, may I speak with you?'

She did not raise her eyes but continued to roll her spindle against her thigh, feeding the cotton carefully so that it was just the right thickness. She nodded at the ground beside her and I sat down.

'I was wondering when you would come. You have been wandering about like a lost spirit since you woke from your midday sleep. Anyone could see your mind was carrying a large load.'

I looked across the square to where the men were putting the last palm branches on the roof of a new *bohio*. Now that I had her permission to speak, I did not know where to begin. If only my mother was here. I had always gone to her when I had one of these waking dreams.

'The Taino have worked hard,' I said, changing the subject. 'No one would guess what the village was like only yesterday.'

'It looked worse than it was. Most *bohios* just needed a new roof.'

'We were lucky that Huracan spared our *caney* and the house of the *zemis*. Baba says not a single *zemi* was disturbed in the storm.'

'Is it the bad dream?'

'Karaya?'

'The thing that sits like a boulder on your mind. Is it the bad dream that frightened the whole village?'

I could not help smiling. That was the difference between Nito's mother and mine. My mother would have waited until I was ready to speak of my problem, however long it took.

'It was not an ordinary bad dream, Karaya. It is as real now as it was when Atebeyra showed it to me.'

Karaya glanced quickly at me and her eyes were smiling. I knew I sounded like my father.

'Maruka, in a few moons you will be ready for marriage, but you have not had your age-ceremony yet. You are still a child and the gods speak only to the behique and the cacique. They do not speak to children.'

'They have always spoken to me. And whatever they have said to me has happened just as they said.'

151

The spindle stopped in the middle of her thigh and the hand feeding the cotton stilled in mid-air.

'What are you saying?'

So I told her about the waking dreams I had on Iyanola. How I had seen my grandmother lying lifeless on the beach two days before she died by the sea. How I had watched the behique saying the funeral prayers over my grandfather the day before he went to Coyaba, how I had been chased by Kalinago ten days before they attacked Iyanola. Only I had thought they were demons . . .

Karaya was silent. She had been searching my face all the time I had been speaking, and her face had grown more alarmed as she had listened.

'Have you spoken of these . . . visions . . . to anyone else?'

She spoke in a whisper as if fearful she would be overheard.

'Only to Bibi.'

'And what did your mother tell you?'

'She did not think it was wise to let anyone else know. Especially not my father and the behiques.'

'That is good advice. They might think you are trying to take their place with the gods.' Karaya laughed, but there was no lightness in her laughter.

I was beginning to wish I had not said anything, but I had needed to tell someone. Bibi and Caicihu's absence was a spear in my chest now. I could have talked with them.

'The dream today; it was different from the others,' I whispered.

Karaya's brow climbed her forehead. 'How?'

'Before I was not asleep when I saw things. Today – I was asleep first, and then I saw what they did.'

'They?' Her voice was hesitant and alarm flitted across her face.

'The spirits from Coyaba. I saw the covered ones who came in their giant canoes.'

Karaya looked relieved. Her hands went back to their weaving.

'That is not surprising, Flower. After the excitement of yesterday it is not unusual you should dream about our new friends.'

'But in the dream they were not friends, Karaya. They had shiny sticks which spat lightning and destroyed the sacred caves with all the *zemis* inside.'

Karaya looked fearfully behind her. 'Do not repeat what you have told me to anyone,' she said. 'Everything will be fine.'

I wished I could believe her.

25

Friend of the *Zemis*

The next morning it was easier to enter the sacred cave. I had decided I could not live in fear. If the *zemis* were going to punish me there was nothing I could do about it. I could not stop them by worrying.

So I only paused for a breath before going through the opening. I almost dropped the bowl of pepperpot when I saw the one I had left the day before. It was empty.

We often took food to the house of the *zemis*. If the gods were not fed, they would be angry and would not send rain for the crops. They might stop the women from having children or give them too much pain during childbirth. The food was handed to the behiques who took it in to the *zemis*, but it was always left uneaten. The gods only ate the spirit of the food. But the food I had left was all gone, spirit and body. What did this mean?

I stood looking down at the empty bowl for a while and then my face stretched into a huge grin. It could only mean one thing. The *zemis* liked my food so much that they had eaten all of it. They had even cleaned the bowl. Not a crumb was left.

I felt like singing, jumping, dancing. I wanted to shout with the happiness inside. But I was in the sacred cave, so I whispered, 'Thank you,' then exchanged the bowls and left.

As soon as I was under the canopy of the trees, out of sight of the cave and certain I would not disturb the spirits, I whooped and yelled. A flock of parrots rose squawking from the leaves above me and I shouted to them.

'The *zemis* like my food.'

I grabbed hold of a sapling and spun round and round it, leaning away from the trunk. Holding the empty bowl up to the sky, I shouted at the sun that was just rubbing the sleep from its eyes.

'The *zemis* like my food.'

I was dizzy, and not just from spinning round the tree.

I sat on the ground to recover my breath and to let my head stop spinning. A ground lizard poked its head from underneath a pile of dried leaves and stared at me.

'The *zemis* like my food,' I told it. It raised its head in alarm and scuttled back under the leaves. It was no use. The joy was too much to keep inside. I started singing:

'The *zemis* like my food
The *zemis* like my food
They might be made from stone and wood
But they are alive and like my food
The *zemis* like my food.'

I got up and brushed away the damp leaves clinging to my skin. I was feeling so happy that I knew I would not be able to hide it and if I went back to the village someone was bound to ask what had happened. I would have to tell them – a Taino could not lie. But I could tell no one that I had been inside the cave.

I bit my lip. I had to calm down. But laughter bubbled up to my lips from deep inside.

I did not need to fear my trips to the sacred cave. The *zemis* were not going to kill me. They accepted me. I sang to the treetops.

'The *zemis* loved my food!
The *zemis* loved my food!
They ate the dried casabi
The *hutia* and manatee
They ate the fish

They cleared the dish
The *zemis* LOVED my food.'

I hoisted the bowl above my head, showing the ancestors in the sky how clean the bowl was.

I leaned against the trunk of the large cotton tree and sighed with contentment. I felt the axe in the pouch at my side. Perhaps I could go hunting to work off some of this new energy. But then I shook my head. I was in too good a mood to kill anything.

I could work on my canoe. Now that I knew the gods were pleased with me I would probably finish the canoe more quickly. I felt nothing could go wrong for me now. Nothing at all.

Soon I had a fire going in the bottom of the canoe. Scorching the wood would make it easier to carve. I hummed my new song as I worked and the river hummed along with me. I moved the coals around so that they could burn the wood evenly. Then I cut a large leaf from the eddo plants growing under the trees, and folded it into a bowl. I dipped it into the river and scooped up water, which I poured on the coals. I watched anxiously to see if the water left the bottom, and breathed easier when it formed a pool. My boat would not sink.

I emptied the water. It took all my strength to turn the canoe over and right it again, and I had to sit on the ground to rest before I could begin carving out the burned wood.

In the silence my stomach growled loudly and I realized that I had missed the morning meal. I looked around for something to silence my stomach until I got back to the village. There were guava trees a little distance away. They grew on the banks of the river and, from where I sat, I could see balls of yellow which meant the fruit was ripe.

I laid my carving stone carefully in the middle of the canoe, but took my axe with me.

I climbed the largest tree, sat on a sturdy branch and pulled a smaller branch towards me. It was awkward trying to pick guavas with my axe in my hand so I laid it carefully in the crook of the branch by my feet. Some of the fruit fell to the ground and splattered on the rocks as I disturbed the branch, but I was still able to get three good ripe ones.

I broke one open and the fragrance filled the air. I slurped the seeds and pulp. It was sweet and tangy at the same time; just the way I liked it. I bit into the empty shell and as I did, one of the other two fruits fell from my hand. I grabbed for it, missed and kicked my axe to the ground. It was the largest and least ripe one, which I was saving for last. I did not want to lose it, but I was more fearful that I might have damaged my axe. I scrambled from the tree, jumping from the lowest branch, and examined the axe closely. It was fine.

I hunted among the fallen fruit until I saw what looked like the guava I had dropped. I was about to bite into it when I saw that someone had got to it before me. Someone had taken a big bite out of it, and not long since.

I frowned at the fruit. My appetite had sneaked off. I looked around, knowing that whoever had started to eat this fruit might still be near by.

A lizard croaked to its mate on the trunk of the cocoa tree; a group of pitcheries squabbled in the tops of the large ceiba trees, chirping and fluttering as if they were the only inhabitants of the forest; a hummingbird hovered around the bright red flowers of a hibiscus plant, its wings whirring as it fed from the nectar. Nothing else moved.

My palms were suddenly damp and perspiration made a tiny river down my back. If someone had taken a bite out of that guava, they might have been watching me. They could have seen my boat.

I dashed back to my canoe, my heart pounding in fear, but it was still there. I let out my breath in a rush, but the next one caught in my throat. I moved closer, slowly.

My carving stone was lying in the bottom of the canoe, but not where I had left it. I remembered placing it in the middle of the boat, but now it was towards one end and resting against the side as if someone had dropped it in a hurry.

I scanned the trees for a sign of human movement. If someone was there he was a good hunter because I could see no sign of him. And yet I felt that someone was watching me.

I searched the riverbanks, but saw nothing unusual. I looked out to sea, but the calm blue was undisturbed. I raised my gaze to the top of the nearest tree. A large iguana stared back at me from a branch, then blinked and waddled away into the leaves.

I laughed nervously. 'Was it you I could feel watching me, old lizard?' My words sounded loud in my ears and did not lessen my unease.

I would have to move my canoe. Whoever had moved my carving stone would be back, either to find out who was making the canoe or to take it. I felt it deep inside.

But where could I hide it?

My eyes widened as a thought wriggled into my mind. I knew one place where my canoe would be safe. But did I dare take it there?

An unpleasant thought crawled into my head. What if a spirit had dropped the fruit and then moved my carving stone? What if it was watching me now; standing right next to me and I was unable to see it?

I rubbed my arms to get some warmth into my suddenly cold body. For the first time I realized how far from the village I was, and how lonely the forest felt.

I clutched the *zemi* around my neck. 'Please, Atebeyra,' I whispered, 'do not let anything or anyone harm me.'

I felt a strange calm as I said the words and I knew Atebeyra would protect me. I knew, too, that she would keep my canoe safe; that she would not mind if I stored it in her house.

I looked towards the sacred caves, then bent to pick up my carving stone. Dragging the canoe all the way was not going to be easy, but it was the only safe place I could think of. The spirits in the cave would not harm me. They had eaten my food. They were my friends.

26
Fort

I cocked my head to one side and examined the *caney* the pale visitors had made with the help of the Taino. It was different from ours. Square and wide instead of long and rectangular. It had three entrances instead of one, two in the back and one in the front. It also had smaller openings in the walls above the ground, so that the *caney* seemed alive, with eyes and a mouth.

'Do you think the houses in Coyaba look like that?' Nito asked.

'They must do.'

I smiled, my gaze accompanying Nito's to where two of the visitors sat under a guanabana tree, finishing a pot of turtle stew and cassava bread which would have fed ten Taino men.

'They are greedy,' Nito said.

'Hush!' I covered her mouth with my hand. 'You must not talk like that about the spirits.'

Nito was too young to know that some thoughts should live in the dark corners of the mind. But I silently wondered that her thoughts were such close relatives to mine.

27
Farewell

We watched the giant canoe glide across the face of the sea, without oars, carrying the pale cacique back to Coyaba, along with the Taino he had taken with him.

Biji's mother sobbed softly beside me. I put my arm around her and held her close. There were no words to comfort her. Bamako had told us it was an honour to be chosen by the spirits and we believed him with our heads, but our hearts rebelled against the thought. It was bad enough to journey to Coyaba when you had lived all your years in this world. It was too cruel to be taken there alive.

The pale cacique had loaded his winged canoe with hammocks, Taino canoes, and the parrots and ceremonial stools that he had asked for. He had cotton and masks, the best headdresses and bowls. He had taken bows and arrows, spears and food in abundance. He had taken the gold of the Taino, but he did not have the gold I had found by the river. That was hidden in my basket. And he did not have my canoe.

He had left most of his men in the small village they had made. Why could he not have left the Taino?

When the winged canoe was no more than a speck in the ocean we turned towards the village, our hearts laden with the emptiness that their absence had left. Would I ever see my friend Biji again?

28

Revelation

I was returning from my midday bath when I saw some of the Taino men leaving their *bohios* with their hunting weapons. Some had *coas*, the digging sticks which we sometimes used as weapons, some carried axes, others bows and arrows.

Baba and Azzacca were striding from the *caney*, their axes in their hands. I thought they might be going hunting and started towards the *caney* to get my bow and arrows. I expected Baba and Azzacca to head for the trees, but they were going towards the centre of the compound, past the ball court, towards the meeting house. I ran to catch them up.

'Where are you going, Baba?'

'The hunters are meeting to plan the hunt for the Maize Festival.' He had not stopped walking.

'May I come?'

He stopped then and his forehead creased into worried folds. 'Maruka, this is a hunter's meeting.'

'But I am a hunter, Baba. You have seen the meat I have caught. And I have been to the meetings of the hunt before.'

'This is different. The spirits from Coyaba will be celebrating with us this season. Nothing must go wrong.'

I struggled to hide the hurt his words caused me. After all this time I was still not good enough to be included with all the other hunters. I looked around the square. Some of the boys were younger than I was, and many of them could not catch half the number of animals *I* had caught. But they were not prevented from attending.

'Besides,' Baba continued, 'the meeting is in the house of the *zemis*. We need to ask for a special blessing on this hunt.'

My eyes widened. I gestured to one of the younger boys just going past us. 'Is Amanel to be allowed into the house of the *zemis*?'

Baba shook his head. 'The men and boys who are not on the council will sit outside the house. They will be able to contribute to the plans from there.'

My heart lifted. 'I could sit outside as well, Baba. I would not dream of entering the sacred house when the council sits.'

'You are not a man, Maruka. This is a meeting for men.'

I had been aware of Azzacca, quiet but disapproving beside me, and had been trying to block him from my thoughts. I whirled on him now, the angry words ready to tumble from my lips. I wanted to tell him something that would straighten the nasty curl of his lips, but I felt Baba's hand on my shoulder, calming me.

I turned my back on Azzacca and searched Baba's face for a sign that he had changed his mind. But although his eyes told me he understood, his lips were firm.

I fought to hold back the tears of frustration as I watched them walk away. It was not right that Azzacca should be respected as a hunter and I should be ignored. I was determined to make them admit that I was the equal of any of the boys. But how? I could go and get another iguana, but they would just think I was trying to compete with Azzacca.

Perhaps if I brought back a manatee to be dried for the maize harvest. Yes. I smiled to myself. Although the manatee was slow and docile, it was huge and took several men to catch. I could not catch it by using my strength. But I had learned to use my head as well as my hands.

I went to get my bow and arrows and set off for the beach.

I heard the noise from a long way away and stopped. There it was again. A giant splash, as if a boulder had landed in the water. It was as if someone was diving from a high place into the sea, but I knew of no one who would make such a commotion from diving.

I crouched low and crawled towards the group of boulders which hid the water from my view. Instinctively I placed my hands and feet on the damp, soft leaves where they would not make a sound.

I could see the water now, but not what was making the noise. There were ripples spreading in widening arcs on the blue-green surface, yet I could not tell if they were from something big or small. All was silent once more.

I was about to step around the nearest boulder when the surface of the water erupted. I gasped. The pale visitor shook his head and droplets of water showered from his long hair and beaded the surface with silver.

My mouth hanging open, I watched him swim up to the rocks opposite. His body did not divide the water like a Taino's, but seemed to battle through as if he was fighting strong currents. But that was not what surprised me.

The pale visitor was as naked as a Taino. His coverings were all crumpled on the sand and his body was even paler than his hands and face. Pale and hairy. I shuddered.

I suddenly realized that I was watching in secret and shame crawled through me. I should either leave or let the visitor know I was there. He clambered up the rock and I knew I should show myself before he dived again.

My right leg lifted to take a step forward. I left it hanging in the air for a breath then lowered it slowly. I could not believe what I was seeing.

The visitor was standing on top of the rock, poised for a dive. At that moment he was facing me and I could see his body from the front.

I let my eyes travel down to his toes then up to his face and back to the centre of his body. I blinked. Perhaps I had been deceived by the light. But no. There it was. The thing that separated men from the spirits. My mind was in confusion. How could this be?

His body hit the surface with a terrible commotion, and displaced water showered the surrounding vegetation. I wiped the splashes from my face. He was on his back now, floating, and there was no mistaking it.

Now I understood why the pale-skinned men had started to act as they did, stealing food from the Taino even though we fed them every day, and mistreating the men whom Baba sent to help them. Only the day before, one of the men had returned from the pale men's village without an ear. I had wondered what crime he had committed to anger the spirits so.

I turned and silently headed for the compound. I had to let Baba know at once. Our visitors were not spirits. I had seen the unmistakable evidence myself. His body clearly said he was a man.

29

Thwarted

The council of hunters seemed to be going on for days. I was hopping from one foot to the other with impatience. I was tempted to go over to the house of the *zemis* and blurt out what I had seen. But even in my impatience I was not foolish enough to disturb a council meeting. So I stood under the genip tree and watched anxiously for the first sign that the men were coming.

I was so intent on watching that I had not heard anyone approaching. I jumped when I felt a hand on my shoulder.

'I am sorry, Maruka, I did not mean to startle you.'

Karaya! I did not hear you coming.'

'No, your mind was far away on a journey. Will

you come and help with the evening meal? Now that we are feeding the visitors as well as ourselves, there is so much more to do.'

I was in two minds. I wanted to see my father straight away, but I could not refuse to help Karaya. I thought about telling her what I had seen, but I knew my father should be the one to find out first. Reluctantly I followed her to the communal fires.

I tried to speak to Baba at the evening meal, but he was deep in conversation with Bamako and I had no opportunity. They talked until it was time for the *areito* and afterwards we all went to bed. As I lay in my hammock I thought about what I had seen. I considered the dream I had been sent. It all began to make sense now. Spirits would not attack the sacred caves, but men might, especially men who behaved as our visitors did.

30

Search for the Pale Men's God

My sister tilted her head to one side and her gaze travelled from the golden earrings, over the necklace, and past my belt of red beads and green ciba stones, to my anklets of gold and white beads. Her eyes travelled back to the necklace and I could not mistake the admiration in her eyes.

'Ja, Maruka. You look beautiful. That is a lovely necklace.'

I frowned. 'You do not think this is too much gold?'

She shook her head. 'I hope I have a necklace like that when it is time for my age-ceremony. Where did you get it? Did Baba get it from the traders for you?'

I bent and pretended to straighten the anklet around my left foot. I hoped I could distract Nito and so escape having to provide an answer. I opened my mouth to ask her what she thought of the beads in my anklet, but Karaya spoke before I could.

'Yes, Maruka. You have not said where you got so much gold for your necklace. It was not your mother's, was it? I do not believe I have seen a piece so large before.'

I sighed inwardly. There was no way of avoiding such a direct question.

'No, it did not belong to Bibi. I found it. When I went to the river after the storm.'

'Oh. Why did you not show it to us before? It is magnificent. You will look lovely on your age-day.' She opened the basket and held out her hand. 'But that day is not for another dry season, so you can take off your finery now. I just wanted to see how well your ornaments would sit beside this nagua I am making for you.'

Silently I thanked Atebeyra that she had not asked any more questions. My gaze followed Karaya's to the stool where the nagua draped it like a cape. The cotton was threaded with beads of red and white which sparkled against the red and blue dyes of the cloth.

It was not as long as Karaya's skirt. She was the principal woman of the tribe, now my mother was gone, so her nagua was longer than any of the other women's, and reached almost to her knees. Mine would only come to the middle of my thighs, but to me it seemed like the most beautiful nagua I had ever seen. If only my mother was here to see me wear it.

A lump climbed from my stomach and nestled in my throat so that I found it hard to swallow. I must have made a sound because Karaya looked up from the floor where she was kneeling to undo my anklets. She peered into my eyes and read my misery there. Her face softened and she stood up.

'Why don't you go and show your father your necklace?' she said softly.

My spirit lifted. I knew my father would be proud of the way I had beaten the gold so that it was almost thin enough to see through. I had not seen him since waking and I still had not told him the truth about the pale men. Here was my chance. When I stepped through the opening of the *caney*, the rays of sun touched the gold and lent it its fire, so that it seemed that I was wearing the sun around my neck.

I found my father with Azzacca, two boys and one of the pale strangers. They were standing underneath the papaya tree by the side of the ball court.

The pale man was talking, and his hands chopped the air as he tried to make my father reap the meaning from his words. But Baba was shaking his head.

When he noticed me standing there, his eyes lit up.

'Come and join us, Maruka. Perhaps you can help us

understand the meaning of the spirit's words.' I wanted to tell Baba the pale man was not a spirit, but I could not blurt it out in front of Azzacca and the boys.

The pale man's eyes widened when he saw me and he almost jumped with excitement.

'Si! Si!' he yelled. His finger jabbed the air and he sprinted towards me. I turned to run, afraid he had lost his reason and was about to attack me.

'Wait, Maruka!' Baba's words halted me and I felt the pale man's hands clamped on my shoulders. I looked fearfully up into his face, but he was not looking at me. His hungry gaze was fixed on my necklace.

As if he was touching a newborn baby, his hand reached out and stroked the gold disc at the end of the bead chain.

'Si, si,' he said softly.

His gaze travelled reluctantly to my face. He pointed to the gold, then to his chest and spread his arms wide, and his words tumbled in a waterfall from his lips.

'Ah! My understanding awakes.'

I turned to Baba, relieved that he could find an explanation.

'The spirit wants us to show him where we got our gold,' he said.

'Most of the gold in Kiskeya is found in Cacique Caonabo's cacigazgo,' Azzacca said. 'We could take him there, but will he want to walk that far?'

177

I smiled. We had all noticed how the covered men slipped and slid in their foot coverings when they had to climb or walk on wet ground. He would have to go over a lot of slippery ground on his way to Cacique Caonabo's home. I thought about the place where I had found my piece of gold. There might be more there, but I did not intend to tell anyone about it.

Baba gestured that the way was long, but the stranger was nodding, his eyes bright with eagerness. He kept glancing towards the village and seemed in a hurry, as if he did not want the other pale men to know where he was. I suspected that any gold he found would not be shared among his friends.

'Who will take him?' Baba asked, looking from one to the other of us.

'I will go, Uncle.' Azzacca was always trying to get praise from my father. My lips curled scornfully but I quickly arranged my face into a pleasant mask. Azzacca was looking straight at me.

'Choose some others to go with you,' my father said. 'You will need help to carry anything Cacique Caonabo gives the visitor.'

I turned to go back to the *caney*. I did not want to have anything to do with the strange men. Now that I knew they were not spirits, I thought they should be treated as we would treat any other guest. As soon as the boys had left I would tell Baba what I knew.

My brows were furrowed and my thoughts were a nest of angry bees inside my head. Their buzzing blocked out the sounds around me so that I did not hear my father's voice until he touched me on the shoulder.

'Come back, Flower.' He was smiling but his smile was too weak to climb to his eyes. 'Will you go with Azzacca and the others to Cacique Caonabo's village?'

My eyes widened and the words flew from my lips before they could be seasoned with caution.

'I do not want to go, Baba.'

I found my senses again when I heard the gasp from two of the boys standing behind Azzacca and I tried to repair the damage.

'What I mean is that Azzacca will not want me to go with him. He will not want a girl slowing them down.'

'But I would like you to come with us, Maruka'.

I stared at Azzacca. What did he want? He could see I did not wish to go with them. I started to ask my father to let me stay but he had already turned away.

'Then that is settled. Get some food for the journey, Maruka, do not forget to take enough for our guest.'

'Baba, wait. There is something you should know.'

'Tell me when you get back, Flower. I must go and feed the *zemis*. The spirit has kept me long past their mealtime. I hope they will understand.'

179

And he was gone.

I was fuming. My anger was divided between my father, Azzacca and the pale man who was pretending to be a spirit.

Baba was always telling me, *Let the fires of your anger die down before you open the pot of action.*

I should have remembered that when I stormed out of the compound ahead of the others. If I had, I would have forced myself to calm down and then I would not have brought such trouble on myself.

31
Stepping Stones

We were silent, except for the clumping of the pale man's foot-covering on the hard mud track. He would not make a very good hunter, I thought. By now every animal on Kiskeya would be in hiding.

I was too angry to speak to anyone, and the other boys were too much in awe of the stranger and too conscious of Azzacca's rank to say anything.

Azzacca, after the first attempt to pass me and establish his position as head of the expedition, had settled behind me and kept silent.

The pale man was last. He was slashing at the bushes by the side of the track and at the branches overhead with his shiny digging stick. One slash was all he needed to have the branch come clattering down behind us, the bushes crumpled like an arrowed parrot on the ground. I did not understand why he needed to kill the plants. I could almost hear the spirits of the forest crying out in anger and pain.

The pace was too fast for the pale man. He shouted something and we turned to see that he had stopped. We had only been walking for a little while, but he was slumped against a star-apple tree. His breath came in short quick puffs, and the sweat poured from his face. He took off his head covering and fanned himself with it. It was not a good fan, and the plume kept poking him in his eye and nostril. I turned away so that no one could see my smile.

The other boys were covering their mouths too. Only Azzacca stood stony-faced, unable to see the joke.

Even my little dog Cico must have thought he looked strange, because he stood by me and wuffed at the man, his tail between his legs.

The visitor scowled at Cico and slid down to sit by the path. It was not yet time for the second meal. In fact I could still feel the load of the first meal in my stomach, but the man beckoned to me, pointing to the basket I carried.

I looked, questioning, at the others. Had I understood him correctly?

'Can you not see the spirit is hungry?' Azzacca asked impatiently. 'Give him some food.'

I set down the basket and took out the food I had

packed for our journey. I was carrying half the food in my basket and one of the other boys had the other half in his carrier.

I was about to separate a portion of the casabi and dried fish for him when his hand shot out and he tore the bundle from my grasp. Without thanking Yucahu for providing the casabi, he stuffed them into his mouth. One by one the cassava breads disappeared until there were only five left of the ten we had brought. The dried fish followed them down his throat and by the time he had belched and kicked the basket away, there was only enough food left for a couple of us.

I stared at him but his gaze skittered away from mine. I bent to pick up the basket and my necklace dangled in front of me. I cradled the gold pendant and straightened. I had forgotten I was still wearing it.

The pale stranger gestured to me and I turned to him, puzzled. He could not want more food, surely? He beckoned me to him, but I felt the footsteps of unease travelling up my back. The look in his eyes disturbed me. I did not move.

He lumbered to his feet and came towards me. I stepped back and looked at the boys for help. They stood in a bunch like trapped coneys and avoided my gaze. Instead, they looked at Azzacca, asking for guidance.

But Azzacca was staring at the stranger with the

same look of senseless hero-worship he had worn since he first saw the visitors. I would get no help from him.

I turned to run but I had waited too long. The pale man's hand closed around my arm and I was yanked against him. He grabbed my necklace. Then he yelled and I was free. He stumbled back and I saw Cico at his foot, teeth fastened to the man's leg.

I smiled with relief, but then the smile froze into a grimace of horror. The pale stranger had reached for his shiny digging stick.

Cico did not even have a chance to whimper.

We stared at the dog as if we had been turned to stone. I watched the earth drink Cico's blood until only a red stain remained of the pool which had spouted from the wound in his neck.

I lifted my head slowly and stared at the pale man. He stepped back, his right hand raised as if to defend himself, and the sun kissed the shiny stick in his hand. It shone fire, except for the part of the blade which had entered Cico's flesh. There, it was as red as the rainbow serpent.

Azzacca stepped hurriedly in front of me and I guessed he thought the pale man was about to use the stick on me. In a dark corner of my mind I felt surprised that he was protecting me.

The stranger gabbled his meaningless words again, then waited, expecting me to reply. I stared at him in silence. I wanted to ask him why he had killed my dog. Cico had only been trying to protect me. He had never attacked anyone in his life before. He had been so gentle. And now he was dead.

I wanted to rail at Cico's killer; beat his head to a pancake with my fists. The fury and grief were fires inside that threatened to burn me up. But I said nothing. Did nothing. I just stared.

'Come, Maruka.' The gentleness of Azzacca's voice surprised me but I shook his hand from my arm. I bent and picked up Cico; cradled him in my arms like a baby. His fur was warm against my skin, but his body was limp. I lifted his head and when I let go it flopped down again.

The tears came then. Slowly at first and then in a torrent. I nuzzled my face in his neck, uncaring that the blood stained my cheeks and chest. I heard the shuffle of the boys' feet as they shifted uncomfortably. I heard the heavy tramp of the pale man's boots as he walked away, but I did not move.

After a while I rubbed the back of my hand across my face and walked into the bushes with Cico. I laid him on the dry leaves under the cocoa trees and whispered a prayer to Yucahu for his safe journey to Coyaba. I had always thought Cico would accompany me to Coyaba as Daha had accompanied Caicihu. Now Cico had gone without me and, unless I could save my mother and redeem myself for killing the Kalinago on Iyanola, I might never reach Coyaba. I might never see Cico, Daha or Caicihu again.

I patted Cico's head one last time and turned back towards the path. The boys were waiting where I had left them, but the pale man was lounging against a blue mahoe tree as if nothing had happened. His gaze met mine and danced away.

Without saying anything, I took up the basket. I did not look at the others, but I felt their unease, their questioning glances. As members of the cacique's family, Azzacca and I were expected to lead. They would do whatever we did.

I turned towards the track and, once they could see the stranger peeling himself from the tree, the others followed.

The trees were thinning now, giving way to smaller shrubs, and the dirt track was replaced by gravel and small boulders. We had to be careful where we put our feet. Some of the small stones were pointed and quite sharp.

Then we were in a valley, cut out of the hills by a small river which twisted and circled the countryside as it travelled towards the sea. Usually it was wide enough and deep enough for a canoe to journey on, but it had been a long dry season and now it was hardly larger than a stream. It would be easy to cross. The water barely came up to my ankles.

The water was cool and soothing against my hot feet. Away in front of us the mountain rose tall and green, and I measured the distance, trying to judge how long it would take to climb. I was anxious to reach Chief Caonabo's cacigazgo and get away from the pale man. I could not bear to be in his company after what he had done to Cico.

It would have been good to sink my whole body into the water, wash away the stain of the last few segments of time, but instead I bent and splashed handfuls against my face and over my head, letting it trickle in cool streams down the back of my neck and down my chest.

The boys behind me were also splashing water over themselves. I straightened when I heard a shout from behind me. It was the pale man. He was beckoning to us to return to where he was standing on the bank.

At first we could not understand what he wanted, and when understanding visited me, I would not believe. I stared at him, my mouth open. Azzacca saw my expression.

'What does the spirit want?'

'I think he wants . . .' I shook my head. 'He . . . he . . . wants us to bend over, in a line, across the river.'

Azzacca's forehead creased in puzzlement.

'Why would he want us to do such a thing? You must be wrong.'

But from the way his words slowed as he looked

at the pale man miming his directions, I knew he had understood the same as I had. The pale man was now bright pink from his exertions and his gestures were getting wilder. He was talking more loudly, repeating the same word over and over, as if he thought we would catch his meaning through the repetition.

'Agachaos! Agachaos!'

Azzacca turned to one of the boys. 'Do as he says.'

I was horrified. 'Azzacca, you cannot mean that.'

'Do you have a better idea? Perhaps you would rather anger the spirit again and cause misfortune to fall on us too.'

'He is not a spirit!'

'What?' Azzacca sounded as if I had struck him. All the boys were staring at me as if I had committed a terrible crime.

I bit my lip. I had not meant to say anything; not before speaking to Baba. But now I had mentioned it, I could not swallow my words. 'He is just a man like you.'

Azzacca shook his head and turned to the boy he had spoken to before. 'Her mind has been affected by her dog's death. Now do as the spirit says.'

'Azzacca . . .'

'Do not say another word, Maruka.'

I opened my mouth to argue with him, but he had already turned his back to me.

He directed the boys to stand at intervals in the water so that the last one was just short of the far bank. The first boy was a man's length from the bank where we stood. Azzacca gestured towards the water.

'You go first.'

My eyes widened. 'Have you lost the use of your senses? I will not . . .'

'The sooner you go, the sooner . . .'

He did not finish. The pale man had grown impatient and grabbed hold of my arm. He shoved me towards the water and I stumbled to my knees. The basket flew from my hand as I grappled on the stony bottom to stop my face hitting a rock.

Before I could right myself, I felt the crunch of the pale man's foot-covering in the small of my back. I only just managed to keep from crying out. Then the foot was gone and I straightened, to see him walking to the other side on the backs of the Taino boys.

I retrieved my basket and followed the others as they left the river. No one spoke. The humiliation was too deep.

The angry tears begged to be released from their burning prison behind my eyes, but I refused. I would not add more disgrace to what I had already borne. A sudden thought occurred to me and I stopped abruptly. There were three other rivers to cross before we got to Cacique Caonabo. I could not be a part of the stranger's footbridge again. But how could I avoid it? There was

189

no other quick route and Azzacca was now in the lead. He was heading straight for the next river.

This time it did not take as long for the stranger to make his wishes understood. Like a coward, I headed for the opposite bank, hoping that there would be no need for me to bend over once all the boys had taken their position.

My luck had stayed in its hammock that day.

The water flowed more swiftly here and it was more difficult to keep our balance. I steadied myself on a large boulder, bent and waited.

I could measure the man's progress by the grunts of protest from the boys as the foot landed on each bare back. With every grunt my temper rose, and by the time I felt the hard, rough material on my skin, there was a red haze of anger before my eyes.

I had not planned to do it. The rebellion just happened. As the second foot joined the first on my back, I stood up, shrugging off the load. It was hard. He weighed as much as a manatee. With a surprised yell, arms flailing, he tumbled from my back. There was a crack as his head connected with the boulder, a splash and swish as his body hit the water, then silence. The silence was not altogether complete. The water still gurgled around our feet as the river continued its journey to the sea. The distant warble of a pitcherie had not stopped. Somewhere on the bank a cricket chirped and another answered.

We all stood, unmoving, in horror. I waited for the pale man to get up and punish me. I did not believe he was a spirit, but yet I feared him. I do not know how long we stood like that before I realized that he was not going to get up.

I flung the basket from me and grabbed hold of his head to lift it from the water. I turned to the nearest boy.

'Help me.'

They flew into action then. We lifted him and carried him to the bank. There was a purple bruise on the side of his head where he had hit the rock. There were also small purple lines under the thin skin of his closed eyelids. Apart from that there was no colour in his face.

I bent to put my hand by the side of his neck. The life did not leap there as it should. I looked up at Azzacca, who had come to stand beside me. He read it in my face.

'Maruka, what have you done?' His voice was a shocked whisper. 'You have killed the spirit.'

32

In the Council

'Tell us again how it happened.'

'It was an accident.'

Bamako's look was an arrow in my heart.

'Nothing happens by accident. Our thoughts are parents of our actions. Were you not angry when the spirit stepped on your back?'

I hung my head. I could not deny that I had been angry. I glanced at Baba, but his face was towards the ground, and I realized with shock how my actions had hurt him. His shoulders slumped. His hands hung loose between his legs. For the first time in all my years, I saw my father looking uncomfortable on his *duho*, as if the wood for his seat was too hard. I had to let the council see that, although what I had done was terrible, it was not as dreadful as they feared.

I licked my lips. It was hard enough to be in the house of the *zemis* with their all-seeing eyes focused on me. To be there on trial was dreadful. I wiped my palms across my thighs to dry them and took a deep breath.

'May I speak to the council?'

Baba's head jerked upwards. I turned my gaze from his awful stare and focused on Bamako, who was looking at me as if I had said farewell to my senses. I swallowed, but I could not go back now. I was not the only one who was unhappy with the ways of the strangers. Only the day before I had heard Karaya complaining that one of them had relieved himself in one of our cassava grounds. That was a whole season's crops wasted. We would not reap food from that polluted ground. Would a spirit have done that? Surely all Taino, dead or alive, would know not to do such a thing? Even worse, they had taken the women of the Taino for themselves, and like a cacique, they each took more than one. They did not care if the women were already married. The council would be happy to know they were not spirits.

'Forgive me, elders.' I turned to Baba, bracing myself against the sadness in his eyes. 'Noble Lord, there is something about the . . . strangers I think you should know.'

I waited, heart pounding, head bowed. I should have spoken to Baba before saying anything. But I had tried. He could not say I had not tried.

'Speak.'

My head shot up and my mouth hung open. Baba was looking at me expectantly, as were the rest of the council. I cleared my throat.

'I thank the noble lord. I thank—'

'Never mind the thanks,' Bamako commanded. 'What have you to say that could begin to excuse your actions?'

I took a deep breath and began.

'I was going to watch a manatee to see how best to catch one.' I stopped at the looks of disapproval on most of the men's faces. Perhaps this was not the best time to remind them I was a hunter.

I started again. 'I saw one of the visitors bathing in the place where the river greets the sea. He was without his covering.'

There was a sharp intake of breath from my right.

'You spied on the spirit?'

I whirled on Azzacca. 'I did not . . .'

'Never mind.' Baba waved away our dispute. 'What about the spirit?'

'He came up out of the water and I could see he was not a spirit, but a man like any Taino. Well, not like a Taino because it was shrunken and very small, but it was there. I could see it.'

Bamako raised his hand to stop me. 'Your words outrun your meaning. What could you see?'

I stared at them. Had I not said?

'His navel. I saw his navel. It was a small one, but it was there and everyone knows spirits do not have navels. So the visitors must be men!'

I stopped, a triumphant smile curving my lips. They were all staring at me incredulously and I felt light-headed with the effect my words had had on them. I could see none of them had guessed the pale visitors were men.

'That is it?'

I stared at Baba. What did he mean?

'You killed him because he had a navel?' Bamako turned to the council. 'Then we are all in danger.'

Azzacca snorted, but no one else laughed. I shook my head. 'But spirits do not have navels.'

'And that is all?' This was Baba again. I stared at him. He looked back, his eyes pleading with me to give them a better reason for my actions.

'There is more,' I said quietly. 'There is something else.'

The murmur of voices hushed and I had everyone's attention again.

'I had a dream.' A few jaws dropped, but no one said a word.

'I saw the pale strangers with shiny sticks attack the sacred cave. They destroyed the *zemis*.'

Silence. I could not stand this waiting silence and I rushed on when I should have stopped talking.

'The dream was sent to me by Atebeyra. I know that. She has sent me dreams before and things have happened as she showed me they would. And now she has shown me that the visitors are not our friends, they—'

'Quiet!'

My father's voice was like the crack of an axe on stone.

'Do you speak like this in the presence of the *zemis*, child? Have you not been taught in the ways of the Taino?' Bamako asked.

I tried not to look at Baba, but my gaze was drawn to him, his head bowed in shame.

'You darken this council by words without knowledge. Do you, a child who has seen little more than ten and two dry seasons, have the ear of the *zemis*? And does Atebeyra ignore her trusted servants, her priests, the behiques and even our noble lord the cacique to talk with an infant?' Bamako turned his face from me. 'Go now. We must find out from the *zemis* what is to be done with you.'

As I rushed from the house of the *zemis*, I heard Bamako's voice behind me.

'Remember, no one is to tell the pale men about this. We must first hear what the *zemis* have to say.'

33

Isolation

'Come, Maruka. You must eat. You cannot stay here all day. The sun will be going home soon.' I peered out of the little cave at Karaya's concerned face. How had she found me? I had thought no one knew about this place where I went to be alone.

It was a little cavern made from the river eating away at the earth. The river had drawn itself away over the seasons so that now the cavern had a wide stony beach in front of it. This was the place I liked to bathe and when I was not hunting, working on my canoe or working in the fields, I would lie in there and look out to sea. I knew it was impossible, but I would dream of a large canoe coming to the mouth of the river, bringing my mother back to me.

A tearing emptiness took hold of my heart. I

wanted her so badly now. Nito's mother could not take her place, even though she tried. I crawled slowly from my hiding place.

'How did you find me?'

'We have been searching all day. Nito told me that you like to bathe here.'

She waited, but when I did not respond she carried on, speaking quickly to drive away the uncomfortable silence.

'I nearly missed you. Luckily I saw your foot sticking out. It is a good hiding place.' She stopped and cleared her throat and I knew she was trying to find the courage to say something I did not want to hear.

'I am not ready to go back,' I said quickly. 'Go on. Have the evening meal without me.'

She looked at the sky.

'The spirits will be walking soon.'

I shivered, but stuck out my chin, 'I am not afraid of spirits.'

She turned towards the village. 'Oh yes. I forgot. You are the girl who sleeps with spirits.' She stopped and turned again to face me, her face serious. 'And now everyone knows you are also the girl who talks to *zemis*.'

I hung my head. She had told me to say nothing. I should have listened to her. I waited for her to ask me why I had ignored her advice, but instead she said:

'The council has returned. They will want to talk to you.'

My head shot up. 'Returned? From where?'

'From the sacred caves. They wanted to make sacrifices for . . . for you and to ask advice of the gods.'

The village was having the evening meal when we entered the compound. Nito got up from her place and ran to hug me. I returned the hug awkwardly. Her face was decorated with the dry riverbeds of her tears. Guilt flooded my heart. I knew I was the reason for her sadness.

Karaya led me to the communal fire and scooped a bowl of pepperpot from the bubbling pot.

No one said anything, but their silence spoke enough. I pushed the bowl away and got up. Nito looked anxiously at me and made to stand, but I shook my head and walked towards the *caney*. No one stopped me.

Inside I sat before the altar and tried to talk to the *zemis*. I needed their help. But no words came.

I sat like that until I heard the Taino leaving the fire. That is where Azzacca found me.

'The council wishes to speak to you,' he said.

34

Judgement from the Caves

Bamako was speaking but he stopped as I entered the house of the *zemis*. All eyes turned in my direction. I tried to read my fate in the faces before me, but I cringed under the looks of disappointment and sorrow. So I had not been saved by the *zemis*. I must have lost my reasoning to think they were my friends. But why had they eaten my food if they were not?

Azzacca hurried to sit in the corner furthest from me, as if to let everyone know he wanted nothing to do with me. Bamako spoke.

'It now seems that your crime is not just against the spirits, but against the gods themselves.'

My heart beat a painful drum roll and my breath lodged in my throat. I knew the punishment for angering the gods. A Taino could be cut off from his people.

A dark cloud of doom wrapped me tight. I did not want to be sent away. Where would I go? What would I do?

I opened my mouth to beg for mercy, but Bamako silenced me with a wave of his hand.

'Have you visited the sacred caves which it is forbidden to visit without the priest?'

I glanced at Azzacca, but his gaze skittered away from mine. My lips tightened. So he had given away my secret. I was amazed and disgusted that he would break his word so easily. But I should not have been surprised. Anyone who could steal another's kill would not have any pricks of conscience about breaking his word.

Bamako held up a thin stick in his hand. He thrust it towards me.

'Do you recognize this?'

I took it and my forehead wrinkled. Then understanding woke and my heart sank. It was the handle of the arrow I had thrown away when Azzacca and I had gone hunting; the arrow which had broken off when I had pulled it from the iguana. They had no need to ask if I recognized it. There was my mark on the wood, clear for everyone to see. I hung my head, waiting for my sentence.

'I asked you a question.'

I looked reluctantly at the headless arrow and then at Bamako's stony face.

'It is mine,' I mumbled.

'We cannot hear you. Speak up, child.'

I cleared my throat and forced the words from my lips. 'It is my arrow.'

Bamako's brows rose, questioning. 'Did you lose it?'

'No, I threw it away. It was broken.' I could not bear the wait. Bamako was like a dog playing with a lizard before he ate it. I felt anger rise like undigested food in my throat, but Bamako's next words quenched it immediately.

'Have you been hunting the animals which belong to the spirits?'

My head jerked upwards in surprise. 'The animals of the spirits? I do not understand.'

'Where is the rest of that broken arrow?' My father's voice was weary, as if he already knew the answer.

'It broke off in the iguana.' My words tailed off as understanding dawned.

'Is this it?'

I took the arrowhead and turned it over in my hand. There was my mark etched into the bone. 'It is my mark,' I said. 'But how . . . ?' I stopped. In my mind was a picture of the feast for the visitors. I saw again Karaya handing something to Baba; Baba looking at it, then staring at me in surprise.

'So not only do you visit the sacred caves without a priest, but you kill the sacred animals which sleep in the cave. The animals every hunter knows it is forbidden to kill.'

'I did not know,' I whispered.

Bamako whirled on Azzacca. 'You did not tell her it is unlawful to hunt by the sacred caves?'

Azzacca squirmed and shot a look of hatred in my direction, but it did not meet my eyes. I could not believe he had kept this knowledge from me.

'I could not tell her about the caves, behique. She had already gone off on her own and the iguana was already dead when I found her.'

'Then why did you pretend you had made the kill?'

I looked gratefully at my father. He had not deserted me, after all.

'I was as shocked as you all are by what she had done, behique. I knew the gods would punish her, but she is my little cousin. I did not want her to suffer.'

My jaw dropped. Surely he could not be serious. That was such a bold untruth that he could not expect anyone to believe him. He went on.

'I thought if I took the blame for the kill I could draw the wrath of the gods away from Maruka. I see now it was a foolish thought. The gods cannot be tricked.'

I almost laughed aloud. Azzacca should take over

from my father at the *areitos*, I thought. His acting would enliven any storytelling session. Why had I not noticed it before? He could not expect to fool anyone with this act.

'That was a noble thing to do, Azzacca,' Bamako said, and as I watched, open-mouthed, the two council members nearest to Azzacca patted him consolingly on the back.

'But we must return to the problem we have.' Bamako turned to me. 'You not only killed an animal reserved for the spirits, but you were willing to let another take the blame in your place.'

I opened my mouth to protest, but I was too choked with the injustice of it. I felt the tears straining at the dam behind my eyes and did not trust my voice not to break if I spoke. My friend Bijirita had been right. I should have owned up and told my father about Azzacca's deception from the start.

It was my father who came to my rescue.

'But you forget, behique. Maruka did not know the animals were sacred. She has never been in the council of hunters, so could not have learned the laws governing the killing of the animals around the sacred caves.'

'That is what comes of allowing a female to hunt.'

My father nodded to the man who had spoken. 'I confess the fault is mine. But you know it was impossible to separate the girl from her brother, even in birth. If I have done wrong, let the gods punish me.'

Bamako rose. 'Now we know why the spirits refused to eat the iguana at the feast. They recognized it as one of their own. Even as the meat reached their stomachs it spoke to them. The gods have—'

'Forgive me, council.'

Everyone turned towards the door. Who would dare to interrupt the business of the council in this way? I groaned inwardly as I saw Karaya standing in the doorway. My family was being disgraced more and more as the day aged.

'What is it?' Bamako made no attempt to hide his irritation.

Karaya looked straight at Baba. 'Cacique Caonabo is here, noble lord. And he has brought all his warriors with him.'

35
Crisis

Cacique Caonabo was chief cacique on Kiskeya. His home was the subject of many stories and songs among the people on Kiskeya. To be visited by him was a great honour. But to be visited by his whole army?

My father and all the elders rose as one. They trooped out of the house without giving me another glance. When the last of them had left, I followed.

The scene before us as we entered the ball court was enough to stop the breath in my throat.

Cacique Caonabo sat on a chair that flashed fire as the sun kissed the gold with which it was decorated. The plumes of parrot feathers did not just sit on his head like my father's did, but they fell in a green and blue waterfall down his back.

He turned, and I felt the force of his power in the

piercing look which swept the council and came to rest on my father. On either side of him two lines of warriors stood tall, their spears held ready.

I frowned. His face was grave. Why was he visiting now? He had only been to see my father once before, when we had first arrived on Kiskeya. All the caciques had come to welcome us and explain the division of the land to my father.

I could see Baba was also bursting to find out the reason for the visit, but good manners prevented him from asking. 'The Great Lord honours us with his presence,' he said. 'You must be weary from your journey. Will you rest? Will you eat?'

I wanted to help Karaya and the other women to serve the food for Cacique Caonabo and his men, but no one had forgotten that I was in disgrace. I was not asked to help, and I wandered around, feeling useless.

Karaya took pity on me at last and thrust a large bowl of roasted sweet potatoes into my hands.

'Take this to the council house. Then come and help me carry the pepperpot to the visitors. Bajacu was supposed to help but she has not returned from gathering peppers. I do not know what is keeping her.'

I silently thanked Bajacu for being late. I smiled gratefully at Karaya, took the bowl, and scuttled towards the house of the *zemis*. The warriors sat on the ground in front of the house, talking in low voices.

As I entered I heard Baba's voice, but he stopped talking to frown at me. Bamako and a few of the elders looked at me as if I had committed another crime, but in the presence of their visitor, they said nothing.

The axe might not have fallen on my neck but it was still hanging over my head. Instead of going back to Karaya as she had asked I turned away from the compound and made my way towards the forest. I did not know what I was going to do or even where I was going, but I knew I needed to be alone.

Without thinking I found myself by the sea. I stood looking out to where the sky bent to lap the water and I longed to be back on Iyanola; back to the time before the Kalinago attacked; to when my mother and Caicihu were with me. It seemed to me that my life had only got worse since that meeting with the Kalinago.

A bitter anger against them filled my whole body till I shook with it. If they had not attacked us, Baba would not have taken us to Kiskeya. If he had not taken us here, we would not have met the covered men; I would not have had to make a canoe, I would not have found the sacred caves. If I had not found them I would not have entered and brought the wrath of the gods down on my head. I would not have put the whole clan in danger from the *zemis'* anger and I would not have killed anyone. Because of the killing I was in danger of going north to the place where bad people wandered in darkness forever.

There was only one way to get rid of the ill fortune which had followed me since Iyanola. One way to make sure I travelled south to Coyaba when I died.

I had to finish my canoe as quickly as I could. I had not paid enough attention to it recently. I turned to go back to the compound for my axe and carving tools. Now, when everyone was busy with the visitors, when no one wanted to have anything to do with me, I would not be missed.

I had only taken ten steps when I heard it. A woman crying as if someone had carved a piece from her heart.

I shuddered. It was a sound that cooled the blood in my veins. I listened until I found the place where the noise came from, and ran towards it.

She was trying to walk but the cuts on her legs were too painful. Angry, red weals criss-crossed her body and when she lifted her frightened eyes as I burst through the shrubs I could see they were swollen and black. She swayed and a cry of horror burst from my mouth as I ran to hold her up.

'Who has done this to you?'

'The pale . . . he . . . he . . .'

She could not continue. Her voice broke and dissolved into tears.

'Come, I will take you home. Karaya and Baba will know what to do.'

My canoe would have to wait again.

Baba and the visitors were returning from the house of the *zemis* as we entered the square.

Some of the women, led by Karaya, ran towards us with cries of horror, but my father reached us first.

'Bajacu! What happened?'

Bajacu hung her head and did not speak. Baba gently handed her to the women. 'Clean her up,' he said softly. Then he looked to Bamako.

'Will you make some healing medicine for her?'

Only when Bamako had gone did my father turn to me.

'Who did this?'

'She said it was one of the covered men, Baba.'

Cacique Caonabo stood beside Baba.

'Are you still determined not to fight?'

My father's face was a battleground for fear, anger and despair. He was silent for an age. Cacique Caonabo was patient. At last my father sighed and shook his head. Chief Caonabo beckoned for his ceremonial chair. When he was seated, and lifted on to the shoulders of his four bearers, he turned again to my father.

'I respect your desire to live in peace with all men,

my friend. But sometimes peace comes dressed in war's headdress. However, if you will not fight, then promise you will not interfere. Say nothing to anyone.'

'You have my word.' My father spoke as if the sky had fallen and rested on his head, but a dark look visited his eyes. A look I had never seen on his face before.

Cacique Caonabo gestured to his bearers and they strode towards the sea where his canoes waited. He turned. 'One more thing,' he said. 'Let all people stay inside tonight. They must not come out.'

Then he was gone.

36

Retribution

I was having a dark dream. I was in a place where no light entered. I could smell smoke: smoke from burning wood and burning flesh. Men's screams filled my ears. I did not want to be there. I struggled to wake. My eyes flew open, but the screams continued. There was shouting, the sound of running feet. And the smell of smoke was stronger than ever.

I jerked upright and the hammock swayed under me. Then realization awoke. I was not dreaming. This was real.

I slipped from the hammock and headed towards the door. Still groggy from sleep, I thought the Kalinago were attacking; that the village was on fire. Dread stamped across my mind, and my heart raced painfully. I reached the doorway of the *caney* and gulped in the night air. It was spiced with smoke and death.

I lifted a foot to step outside.

'Get back to your hammock.'

'Baba!'

In the dark I had not seen him sitting on his *duho* by the door.

'Did you not hear me say everyone should stay inside tonight?'

'I am sorry, Baba. My memory failed me.'

He patted the ground and I went to squat beside him.

'What is happening?'

He sighed. 'Revenge,' he said. 'That is what is happening.'

I frowned. 'Revenge for what? Is this because of Bajacu?' I was wide awake now.

'Bajacu was not the only one who was harmed by the pale strangers.' Baba sighed. 'They have dishonoured one of Caonabo's wives. He is honour-bound to take revenge.'

I sucked in my breath.

'And did Cacique Caonabo ask you to fight with him?'

Baba did not answer.

'Why did you say no, Baba?'

I already knew the answer. It was for the same

reason that we had fled from Iyanola. My father was a coward. Shame cocooned me and I was glad of the dark which hid it from Baba.

'I promised to look after the pale cacique's men. I could not break my promise and bear arms against them.'

'But they beat Bajacu! Surely you do not have to protect them now!'

'My promise was not to the ones who stayed behind. They behaved abominably, but that is because they are leaderless. If their cacique was here these things would not have happened.'

I thought none of the Taino would behave as the strangers had, even with Baba absent, but I said nothing.

Baba got up from his stool, yawned and stretched. 'Now let us get some sleep.'

His arm was a dark shadow, motioning me towards my hammock. His false yawn did not fool me. I knew he was as wide awake as I was. I knew that, like me, he would lie awake all night, wondering what we would see when we left the *caney* at sunrise.

When I opened my eyes, I could see from the shadow of the tree in the square that the sun was high in the sky. I must have fallen asleep just as morning's finger touched the face of the earth.

I leaped from the hammock and glanced towards

Baba's. It was empty. As was the rest of the *caney*. Why had no one woken me?

I rushed outside. The compound was deserted. Everyone could not be washing at the same time, surely? I turned to run to the river and stopped. A thin string of smoke rose towards the sky. I ran, forgetting about my morning wash.

The Taino had gathered in front of the pale men's village, or rather what used to be their village. It was now a giant pile of ashes smouldering feebly in the cool morning air.

I clamped my hand over my mouth in horror. Here and there the charred remains of the pale men could be seen. Some had escaped the fire, but they had not escaped the axes and arrows of Cacique Caonabo's warriors. All gazed at the sky with eyeless sockets. We all knew what that meant.

When a medicine man was wicked and used his medicine to harm people, the Taino would send him to Coyaba. His body would be mutilated and his eyes taken out, so that he could not use his magic to return from Coyaba to harm anyone.

Cacique Caonabo and his men had done the same to the pale men. They had been sent back to Coyaba, where they came from, and they would not be returning.

Had I been wrong? What Cacique Caonabo had done was not usually done to ordinary men. Could they have been evil spirits after all?

215

37

Respite

Time hurried into the past, and life returned to what it had been before. Almost. For days afterwards we went about with hushed voices and fearful looks, expecting some great punishment from Yucahu for the destruction of his messengers.

I had another worry rubbing at my mind. What was to be done about me? Neither Baba nor Bamako mentioned my punishment and I began to think they had forgotten.

Then one afternoon I was summoned to the house of the *zemis*. Only a few of the elders were there.

'It appears that Yucahu was displeased with the conduct of his messengers,' Bamako said. 'He has recalled them to Coyaba in disgrace and you are not to be punished for the one who died.'

I glanced at Baba. His face told nothing of his thoughts.

'However,' Bamako continued, and my heart sank, 'you have entered the sacred caves and killed an animal set aside for the gods. They are not pleased about that. You must make good what you have done.'

I hung my head, waiting. I could not think how I would be expected to 'make good' what had already been done. Was I supposed to 'unvisit' the cave and 'unkill' the iguana? What did Bamako mean?

'The gods have considered that your dog was destroyed by the spirit, or else your punishment would have been greater. They have decreed that you are to fish and hunt no longer. From now on you will plant and tend the crops, weave, cook and make pottery like the other Taino women.'

'No!' The cry was torn from my lips. Not to hunt or fish? I might as well be exiled.

'Maruka, the gods have spoken. You cannot question their judgement.' My father's voice was without expression.

'But, Baba—'

'There is more,' Bamako continued. 'You are to get rid of all your hunting and fishing weapons. You must bury them in the midden with the other refuse from the village.'

I started to protest again but he silenced me with a movement of his hand.

217

'And you are never to go near the sacred caves again.'

I stood at the top of the midden with my axe, my bow and arrows and my spear. No one had said anything to me as I walked through the square with them. No one except Nito. She had come up to me, and spoken with halting words.

'Shall I come with you, Maruka?'

I shook my head, unable to speak. There was a knot in my stomach, which did not seek companionship.

The walk to the midden was over too quickly. I peered down at the broken pottery, bones, dirt and discarded tools. I looked at my weapons which I had taken such care to make. They did not belong here. Every few days the rubbish was covered with earth, and I could not bear the thought of my weapons being buried forever.

Rocks jutted out from the sides of the pit and under one of these there was a shelf. I walked round the lip of the pit to see if the ledge was high enough to hold my weapons. It was, but I would have to climb halfway down the side to get to it, and the stench from the midden almost took my senses.

It was not easy to find footholds or handholds in the rock and I had to make three journeys to store all I had, but I did it. The ledge went further into the earth than I had thought, and by the time I had pushed them in as far as I could, they were completely hidden. Afterwards I slumped on the ground above, gasping for breath.

When I recovered, I stood on the edge of the midden and peered again into the shelf; I walked around and examined it from every angle. I could see nothing and I sighed with relief. They were safe.

My steps were much lighter on the way back. Perhaps they were too light. Baba came up to me as I entered the village and his look was searching.

'Have you done as the council asked?'

'Yes, Baba.'

'Are the weapons in the midden?'

'They are.'

'All of them?'

'All, Baba.'

He nodded and left me alone. I tried to arrange my face into a suitably miserable expression, but it was hard when I felt so light-hearted. I had not lost my weapons and I had not disobeyed the gods or the council. One day, I did not know how or when, they would be mine again.

And then I remembered. My canoe was inside the sacred cave, and I had been forbidden to go anywhere near it. How was I to rescue my boat without bringing down the wrath of the gods on my head? Suddenly I did not have to pretend to be miserable. I walked towards our *caney* as if Kiskeya itself was resting on my shoulder.

38
Plans

It was unbearable to watch the men and boys going off to hunt and fish while I stayed behind with the women. I escaped as often as I could, and I found refuge in carving and making bowls and pots for the fire, and for use in the ceremonies. Here I could at least use some of the skills I had learned from Caicihu.

Time crawled by and it was the Festival of Maize once again. I worked beside my mothers and the other women, digging cassava, sweet potatoes, yams and taro for the feast that would follow the ball game and the dancing.

The harvest was plentiful and now that we did not have to feed the pale men, it looked as if there would be plenty for the Taino to replace the food we had had to give away.

I pulled the maize from the stalks and stuffed them into baskets which were already full. The sun stamped fiery palms against my skin and I longed for the cool of the river.

I looked over to where Karaya was busy wrestling a large yam from the ground, her digging stick jabbing at the earth like a hungry woodpecker attacking a tree trunk. A thought occurred to me.

'Karaya.'

'Mmm?'

'We are *nitaino*, yes?'

'What kind of question is that? Have you lived ten and two dry seasons and you do not yet know who you are?'

I shook my head and lowered my voice so that none of the others could hear. 'What I mean is, are we not more – more privileged than the *naborias*?'

Karaya raised her head to look questioningly in my direction. She did not stop her digging.

'We certainly have more responsibility.'

'Then why do we have to work in the fields like everyone else? I heard that Cacique Caonabo and his family have their *conucos* tended for them.'

Karaya sighed.

'Maruka, you know your father would not ask any of his people to do something he was not prepared to do himself.'

I looked out over the fields still to be reaped, and

I thought of the festival when we would offer thanks to the gods for the great harvest. Last time we were preparing for the Feast of Maize, I was planning to go back to rescue my mother. But before the feast the pale men had come and turned our lives upside down.

This time there would be no pale men and I had no reason not to go. The longer I left it, the harder it would be to save her. She might become used to her new home.

I had to fetch my weapons first, but that would not be difficult.

There in the field, under the burning sun, I started planning my journey. Karaya looked over and nodded. Perhaps she thought her words were responsible for the smile on my lips and the new spurt of energy in my reaping. If only she knew.

39

A Theft

I raced through the trees with the bag of dried fish, cassava bread and fruits bouncing on my back. My axe beat against my legs like a stick on a drum. My bow hung round my shoulders and across my chest, and my arrows peeked from their pouch on my hips.

Where the land kissed the sea, I paused to gaze at the watery road I was about to travel. I looked back the way I had come. How long would it be before I could return? How long before I saw Baba, Karaya and Nito again? I felt the tears gathering behind my eyelids. I blinked and turned again towards the forest. There was no time to waste. I had to be away from Kiskeya before I was missed.

My steps slowed as I approached the sacred caves.

It had been a long time since I was last here, and so much had happened.

I stopped, a frown folding my forehead, as a thought crawled into my mind. It was a thought that had bothered me many times since that day I had been on trial in the council.

Why had the elders not said anything about my canoe? They could not have missed my mark on the side. They would have known I had made it. Why had I not been punished for that?

I shrugged and continued up the hill. Perhaps, one day, when I returned, I would ask Baba about it.

I stopped at the opening to the cave and my forehead creased in dismay and frustration. There was a pair of crossed sticks across the doorway. The cave was locked and I could not enter. And to make sure nobody mistook the sticks for anything other than a lock, there was a tangle of branches and twigs across the cave mouth.

What was I to do? I bit my lip and scratched the back of my ankle with my toe. I needed to get my canoe. Without it I could not go back to Iyanola.

Since the first time the *zemis* had eaten my offering I had not been afraid to enter the cave. But the *zemis* had told the behique I should not hunt or fish again. They had been angry with me for killing their game. It had been a long time since I had done that wicked thing. Had they forgotten? I hesitated. I could not ignore the powerful spell that guarded the entrance, even if the *zemis* were my friends. I sat on the ground cross-legged, praying to Atebeyra.

'Please, I need your help. I must go to rescue my mother. Give me a sign that you will not be angry with me.'

I sat like that for a while. Nothing happened. I looked anxiously out to sea. I could not wait much longer. Soon the sun would turn around and start his journey home. Someone in the village would notice I was missing.

'Please, Atebeyra. Do not fail me now.'

A movement caught the corner of my eye. I turned to see a *hutia* in the low branch of the soursop tree to the left of me. It stopped snuffling and stared, its eyes bright and fearless. I kept completely still, hardly breathing. Surely Atebeyra had sent it to help me. *Hutias* did not like the day, when people were around. They fed at night and in the early morning before most people were awake. It was unusual to see one at this time. It had to be a sign.

It jumped from the branch, stared at me once more, and headed towards the cave. I held my breath.

When it was nearly at the entrance it suddenly turned and headed for the second, smaller cave. Disappointment filled my throat like a piece of undercooked corn bread. It was not a sign from Atebeyra, after all.

The *hutia* stopped, stared at me once more and disappeared into the small cave. I stood up, stretching the stiffness from my legs and shoulders. I would have to go back to the village.

I lifted my bow from the ground where I had laid it and a thought lodged itself in my mind. What if I was supposed to *follow* the *hutia*? The more I thought about it, the more I felt certain that was what I should do.

It was dark inside the cave and the smell of animal droppings and urine assaulted my nostrils. I stood still to catch my breath and for my eyes to adjust to the dark. Then I looked around. There was nothing. No *hutia*, no other animals. The cave was empty. I stood still, listening for scratching or snuffling. A *hutia* could not disappear into nothingness. I examined the walls, the floor, the roof.

I knelt down and tried to track the *hutia* as a hunter should. It was difficult in the poor light, but I could see that the tracks nearest the opening were heading towards the back of the cave, so I followed them.

I had reached the wall at the back before I saw it – a hole that reached from the floor of the cave to just above my knee. I lay on my stomach and peered inside.

I wondered where the hole led. I knew the *hutia* must have gone into it, and now I had a strong feeling that I should follow. I took a deep breath and crawled through the hole.

I was in a tunnel. The ground sloped downwards and I had to cling to the walls to stop myself from falling. I could barely see the ground. The roof was low, and I had to bend my head to prevent it banging into the rock.

My heart was pounding and I was not sure now that I was supposed to be here. My breath was harsh in the darkness and it seemed I had been travelling for an age, crawling, one knee in front of the other. Still the tunnel went on. My shoulders ached from being hunched so long.

I stopped. Perhaps I should turn around again. The tunnel did not seem to be going anywhere and the longer I spent in the dark, the more I felt as if something terrible was in the tunnel with me. If only I had a light.

As if the thought had given birth, I noticed that it was lighter in front of me than it had been. I could now make out the green moss on the walls. I touched the walls with my fingertips. They were damp. And it was slime, not moss. The ground under my feet was also wet. I did not like this . . .

The slope had evened out so that it was almost flat and I shuffled forward. It was getting lighter, and my heart lifted as I found I could stand upright.

I was almost running when I entered a large open space and my mouth dropped open in surprise. I was standing in a room in the rock. The ceiling was carved with pictures of people making houses, building canoes, planting cassava – doing the things the Taino did every day. But the walls also told the story of people being killed by demons. My gaze followed the pictures around the wall as they curved over an opening which led away from the room I was in. The drawings then continued to the end of the wall, where it suddenly opened out to the sky. There were pictures of other men, men who had bulging foreheads and upturned fruit bowls on their heads. Men who had long sticks which spat fire.

I let out the breath I had been holding. This was the story of my people. The elders must have been drawing the pictures, telling our story every day since we arrived in Kiskeya.

I traced the pictures round the wall until I was standing in front of the opening that led away from the room. It was higher than the one I had come through, and I could stand in it without having to bend. I wondered where it led.

I thought of the passage I had just come through and I did not like the idea of going back the way I had come. I looked towards the sea. The beach below was hidden by cliffs which rose on both sides. To get to it I would have to clamber down the steep rocks and then climb the cliffs to get out. I guessed these were the cliffs I could see from the forest path, but I had never been round them before.

I turned again to the new passage. Perhaps it was a way out.

My feet made no sound on the damp earth and the silence was so complete that I was almost afraid to breathe. The carvings were in this passage as well, but now they were carvings of the *zemis*, and I felt their sightless gazes following me as I crawled forward. As long as I could see the *zemis*, I had contact with the outside. Someone else had been there before me so I was not going into an unknown place.

The ground was climbing as it had done in the other passage, but the ceiling remained high, and I was glad I did not have to stoop. The floor was not as smooth here as in the other tunnel, but littered with rocks and sharp stones, which made it hard to walk on. Soon it was too dark to see the walls clearly and I could not tell if the drawings were still there. The musty smell of stagnant water assaulted my nostrils.

It became sticky and hot. This passage was obviously leading nowhere. I could not see anything and I was sure I had been going for much longer than I had in the other tunnel. I turned to retrace my steps.

I had only gone a few steps back when I heard it. The sound of water swirling and gurgling over rocks.

I stopped, listening; my heart pounded like ceremonial drums. Something tickled my toes in the darkness. Something wet. I now knew the reason for the damp walls and floor. At high tide the passages were flooded. And it was high tide now.

I ran. The air leaped from my mouth in frightened gusts. Behind me, the water grumbled across the rocks, swishing and slurping like a hungry demon. I stumbled and clambered up the passage, praying to Atebeyra to save me.

There was light up ahead. I sprinted towards it, ignoring the pain of the stones biting into my feet. I burst into a large cave and doubled over, holding my side. The stitch was a needle jabbing into my flesh.

When I managed to catch my breath, I looked around me and my eyes widened. I should have guessed, of course. I was inside the large sacred cave, and I had not broken the lock at the door. Surely Atebeyra had been guiding me.

I almost laughed aloud with happiness. Now I just had to wait until the tide went out and I could take my canoe down to the sea and be on my way. I frowned. I would have to come up the hill again to get my things from outside the cave. I could not leave without the food which would appease the water spirits and feed me on my journey. But that was not much of a problem. First I would get the canoe and then I could plan the rest of my journey.

I went over to the wall where I had left my boat and stopped. My knees got into each other's way and my chest tightened into a ball. I felt light-headed, about to faint. I bent and moved a burial urn, as if a canoe could be hidden behind it. I could not fool myself. My canoe had gone. In the place where it had rested, a knife lay on a bed of dried leaves. I lifted it. The handle was carved with the fearful face of a demon. I dropped it as I would live coals.

I bowed my head, covered my face with my hands and felt the hot tears seep through my fingers. Nothing could be worse than this.

Or so I thought.

My head jerked upwards at the sound behind me. The voice was full of anger and disbelief.

'What are you doing in here?'

40

Surprise

I spun round, blinking hard. In the light coming from the opening I made out a shape standing at the far end of the cave.

'Well?'

I groaned. Of all the people who could have found me, Bamako was the one I would have least wished for. He strode over and, grabbing hold of my arm, propelled me towards the entrance of the cave.

I blinked in the bright sunlight. The thoughts chased each other around my head but could find no way of getting out of this.

I had been lucky last time, but I could not see how I could be spared now. I thought of the disappointment which would carve lines in my father's face and my spirit quailed in me.

Bamako stopped in front of my bundle, which I had left on the ground.

'What is the meaning of this?'

I could not reply.

'I have asked you a question. What have you to say?'

'I am sorry, behique.' Even to my ears my voice sounded weak and terrified. Bamako's voice was slightly less harsh when he spoke again.

'Do you not understand what you have done? What this means?'

I nodded dumbly.

He turned towards the path. The path I had taken only a little while before.

'Come, follow me.'

I looked uncertainly at my things on the ground and bent to pick them up.

'Leave them.'

I stared at Bamako. A hunter's weapons were precious. I would not leave them.

I bent and picked up the bow and arrow and turned to follow Bamako. His face was twisted with fury.

I knew that when the gods were insulted, when the spirits were goaded, then the behiques became avenging spirits themselves. I was pushing Bamako too far.

'Have you got a stopper in your ear?'

He took the bow and arrows and one by one broke

them across his knee. He threw the broken pieces on to the bundle of food, turned and strode off down the track without another word.

I shook like a sapling in a high wind. I felt the trickle of cold sweat snaking down my spine. I stood watching Bamako walk away, unwilling to believe what he had just done.

For a long while I stood staring at the broken bow and arrows. It felt as if my heart had died. I must have done an unforgivable thing to deserve this treatment.

My mind travelled back to examine my actions. I had disobeyed the council by keeping my weapons when I had been told to get rid of them. I had entered the sacred caves when I had been forbidden to go near them. I had ignored Bamako when he had told me to leave my weapons on the ground.

My spirit sank, to lie lifeless on the ground. I had been a terrible Taino, and the wrath of the gods was bound to fall on my head.

I turned and shuffled after Bamako, head bowed. I would never again be able to meet the eyes of anyone in the tribe. I would not be able to escape exile this time.

With my head lowered, I did not see that Bamako had stopped. I bumped into him before I realized he was there. I drew back, cringing, and waited for his anger to erupt.

'I am sorry, behique,' I babbled. 'I did not see you.'

I closed my eyes and waited. But the angry words did not come. I opened one eye, then the other.

Bamako was standing like a *zemi*, his eyes fixed on the ocean. I followed his gaze and I too became like a statue.

'Go, child, tell the cacique.' His voice was hoarse. 'I cannot go as fast as you. Run like the wind.'

This time it was easy to obey him.

41

Unexpected Arrivals

Baba's face was a mask, stiff with shock.

'Are you certain of this?'

'I was not alone, Baba. The behique was with me. It was he who sent me to warn you.'

'And how many winged canoes did you say were there?'

'I had not time to number them all, but there were many more than before. Too many to number in haste.'

His mask cracked, folded into tiny valleys of worry on his forehead.

'This is not the way it was foretold. The people from the sky are not supposed to return, once they leave. This I have not prepared to meet.'

I did not have any words to answer him.

This time when the winged canoes came to rest on the ocean there were no Taino to welcome them.

'We will wait here in the village for the visitors,' Baba said, and his face was grim. I knew the reason he was afraid. It was the reason we were all afraid.

I sat with Baba, Karaya, Nito and the rest of our family in the *caney*. In my mind's eye, I saw again the string of canoes like a flock of terrible birds suddenly alighted on the water, swimming towards the shore.

We heard the sound of the pale men's booming sticks and Baba sighed.

'That is the sound of the pale cacique's summons. We had better obey.'

The white cacique strode across the sand to my father. His face flowered into a smile, and he caught hold of Baba's hand and pumped it repeatedly.

The other small canoes were coming in to land. I had thought we had already had the biggest surprise but I was wrong.

The first to leave the canoes were the pale men, tens and tens and tens of them. So many more than had been burned by Cacique Caonabo.

After them came a line of Taino. They leaped from the canoes and dashed towards us and we stood in stunned silence for a breath, unable to believe what our eyes told us. These were the very people – the women and girls – who had been taken by the Kalinago on Iyanola. Now here they were, running among us, trying to find friends and family they had not seen for several dry seasons.

I saw my father, face alight with hope, searching the faces, and I knew he looked for my mother. But I knew that Bibi was not there.

I went over to Baba as he was talking to one of the women. She was explaining about my mother to him.

'Two Kalinago tribes had banded together that day to attack our village. Your wife must have been taken by the other tribe, my lord. The pale cacique rescued us but we do not know what happened to the others. We did not see them after we were captured.'

Baba turned away, bitter disappointment in his face.

I went to comfort him. Perhaps I should tell him now what I knew. But a movement caught my gaze.

Two people, a male and a female, were coming from the canoes which followed. At first I did not know who they were. They looked like Taino, but they were covered from head to toe as the pale men were.

They too ran among us, calling out. I heard my name and looked towards the sound. My mouth opened in wonder, but it had no strength to make any sound. Bijirita stood before me, holding tightly to her mother's hand with a grin that introduced her ears to each other. She reached out an arm towards me and the crimson cloth which wrapped her from head to foot rustled as she moved.

I raised my hand, slowly, fingers spread in greeting. She looked so strange, dressed like a pale person.

'Biji! You are covered.' I felt foolish for saying what everyone could see, but I could think of nothing else to say.

'I know. We had to wear clothes. But underneath these,' she flicked at the cloths covering her lower body with a careless hand, 'I am still the same.'

Macu, who had been gazing at her daughter, finally spoke.

'What is the home of the dead like? Is it true the sun does not shine there?'

'I do not know. I have not been there. These,' she waved towards the pale cacique, 'are not spirits. They are men.'

So I had been right after all . . . Biji's face hardened into seriousness.

'Some of the others were not as lucky as Dita and I. They did not reach the land of the pale strangers, but left us for Coyaba while we still travelled the great waters.'

She named the ones who had not completed the journey. Four of the six Taino who had been taken from Kiskeya were now in Coyaba.

The pale cacique was looking around impatiently.

His gaze collided with Biji's and he beckoned her over.

'The Almirante needs me,' she said, and went to him. My eyes followed her.

The Almirante greeted her with a torrent of words. We watched his hands and listened to the words, but only Biji's face wore the look of understanding.

I could not stop gaping as his words came out of her mouth in our tongue. What magic had he done so that she could understand his noises? What had they done to her, in their country at the end of the sea?

But although I longed to know all this I could not ask Biji now. She turned to Baba.

'He wants to know how his men at the fort are. Why have they not come to greet him?'

My father sighed and, looking like a lizard being lowered into the pot, he turned to Biji, carefully avoiding the Almirante's eyes.

'It pains me to tell the gracious lord that his people are no more. They have all returned to the land of the dead.'

Biji caught her breath and was silent. So were the Taino standing around. The Almirante felt our unease and rattled off more words to Biji. She answered him in the same strange tongue. My eyes widened. I had been surprised that she could understand him; I had not expected her to be able to speak his language as well.

Her words had a strange effect on the Almirante. He gurgled, choked and the colour abandoned his face so that his skin looked like the belly of a dead manatee. He whispered more words.

'How did it happen?' Biji asked.

Baba struggled with the thoughts in his head. I guessed what he was thinking. He did not want to get Cacique Caonabo in trouble, but he could not lie. It was still not the way of the Taino to speak falsehood. When he spoke his words were slow, as if he had to force them from his lips.

'Your people dishonoured the Lord Caonabo, who was honour-bound to seek revenge.'

'You did nothing to stop him?'

A look of pain passed over Baba's face when he heard the words Biji related. Then his face hardened and the same look he had worn when Bajacu had been harmed visited his eyes.

'The Lord Caonabo is too powerful for us to fight. We could do nothing.'

I waited for Baba to say that Cacique Caonabo was also his friend, but he said nothing more.

The Almirante shouted something to a few of his men and strode off with them towards his burned village.

For a while, we all stood around, uncertain what to do. Then Baba took charge and called all the Taino together.

241

'Taino, we have visitors. They have travelled far and must be hungry.'

I watched the pale men as we sat down to eat in the square. Baba spoke to the visiting sub-caciques who had come for the Feast of Maize and they sent runners to their villages for more food. By now we knew the kind of food the pale men enjoyed, so we did not offer the snakes, lizards or dogs which the women had prepared for our feast and which they gave to the Taino who had come home. But the platters of fruit, fish, ducks, turtles, sweet potatoes, squashes, yams, maize and *casabi* were piled high and there was plenty to satisfy even the hungriest of the pale visitors.

I scurried between the fires, helping to cook and serve the food. I put my meeting with Bamako to the back of my mind. I knew the return of the pale cacique had prevented him from calling a council meeting about my crime, but no doubt I would have to answer for my actions later. Right now I was angry. Angry with the Kalinago who had taken my mother, and even though I knew it was unreasonable, I was angry with the Taino who had been rescued. Why had they been spared and not Bibi? She should have been with me now. She was the cacique's first wife and *my* mother.

I avoided the Taino who had been taken from Iyanola, unwilling to see the happiness in the faces of those who welcomed them back, and the disappointment on my father's face which he was not able to hide. Neither was he able to hide his unease. He kept looking anxiously in the direction of the pale men's destroyed village. Many of the Taino were doing the same, even as they tended to the guests.

Nito had been helping to serve the visitors, and she followed me as I took my bowl of food to find Biji. But when I sat down, she stood looking at us for a breath, then turned and walked away without saying a word.

Biji raised her brows, questioning, but I shrugged.

'I want to hear everything,' I said.

Biji laughed. 'I have been away a whole year. There is much to tell.'

'A year? What is that?'

'Ah, I have been away too long. I will have to learn to think like a Taino again. A year is from one dry season to the next.'

And then she told me things that made my eyes try to leave their sockets. Of the pale men's country, Espana, where there were houses as large as some Taino villages; of villages which were so large they spread more than a day's journey in any direction. Animals taller than a man; boxes which took people from place to place at speed; cold particles like feathers falling from the sky; and a cold so intense that it made your whole body rigid.

'I would not like to live in such a place!'

I glanced over to where a group of the pale visitors stood. They were different from the others. Their covering did not mould itself to their bodies but flowed down to the ground and was gathered with a string at the waist. I turned to Biji and nodded towards them.

'Who are they?'

Biji looked at them and frowned. 'They are like our behiques.'

I stared at the three men. They did not look like behiques.

'They wear no amulets.'

'They need only one. The two shiny sticks stuck one across the other with the *zemi* on it. That is a strong amulet. They do not need others.'

I gazed open-mouthed at the pale behiques, then looked around for Bamako. He was standing behind my father, his chest, neck, ears and head dressed with shells, gold, feathers, stones and *zemis* of the tribe – all to keep him safe from evil spirits. It was hard to believe the pale behiques' one amulet could do the same work as all Bamako's charms. I shrugged and turned back to Biji.

'And this Espana you went to, it was not Coyaba?'

She shook her head and gestured towards the pale strangers. 'They are men, and the place we visited is their country, just as Kiskeya is ours. It is many, many, many days' canoe journeys away, but it is not yet the end of the earth.'

'And are there only men in this country?' I had

always wondered why there were no females among the visitors.

'There are women.' Biji pursed her lips. 'But they are not strong. I think the journey would have been too hard for them. I think that is why the men left them behind.'

We ate in silence for a while, and I thought of Biji, talking so effortlessly with the Almirante.

'What made you learn to speak their language?' I asked.

Biji chewed and swallowed a mouthful of roasted snake before answering. 'The Almirante wanted us to be his mouth among the Taino when he returned.'

How long did it take you to learn?' I asked.

Biji gave an answer, but I did not hear what it was. Over her head I had seen something that made my mouth hang open. Coming out of the trees was a strange and terrible creature, a monster whose earth-brown coat glistened in the afternoon sunlight. The fringe of hair that covered its long neck rippled as it tossed its head. And what a head it had! It was shaped like a grasshopper's, but larger than the head of two people together. A white band in the middle of its face separated eyes that were like pools of dark water.

Its ears, pointed fans, twitched as if it was hearing unpleasant news. On its back it carried the Almirante. And it was coming straight towards us.

42

Strange Beasts

The Taino jumped up and ran.

I leaped to my feet with the others, intending to escape, but Biji held me back.

'Do not be afraid. It will not harm you.'

I stared at her. How could she be so calm when the monster was getting closer with every breath? I felt her hand tighten on my arm. A muscle twitched at the corner of her jaw and her look was wary as it followed the motion of the beast. She was not as calm as she tried to appear.

The monster stopped two men's length from us and danced on the spot, his long legs beating a drum beat on the ground. The Almirante's gaze pierced the backs of the fleeing Taino. A smile crept across his face and a thoughtful look entered his eyes as he turned and spoke to his men, who were trying without success to control their laughter.

The Almirante tugged at the rope which was fastened to the beast's neck and the animal turned and stamped back down the track.

I had never seen a beast as big and neither had any of the Taino.

When they were sure it had gone, they drifted back to the square, talking in hushed voices, as if afraid that any noise might bring the monster back again.

Baba hurried over to us and clutched Biji's arm.

'I can see you have met this creature before,' he said. 'What is it?'

'It is called a horse.' Biji shook her head and a shame-faced smile widened her mouth for a breath. 'When we first saw it in the pale men's country, we too ran screaming from it. The Espanoles there laughed at us, especially the children. Horses are not dangerous, but I have never found the courage to go near them.'

Baba frowned. 'Did you travel with it all the way from the land across the sea?'

Biji nodded. 'There are others. Come, I will show you.'

The pale men whom Biji called Espanoles were leading many more of the horse animals across the beach, and they were not alone. Dogs almost as high as a man bounded around the people who held their ropes, dragging them across the sand. Loud, harsh sounds burst from them, hurting our ears and cooling the blood in our veins.

We had never seen dogs as large as that, had never heard dogs make such noises. Then there were the curious pink animals with tails as twisted as the liana plants that entwined the forest trees. Strange gruff sounds came from them as they pushed their long noses into the sand. Behind them, other creatures, almost as high as the horses but wider, lumbered over the ground. Two sharp spears grew from their heads and their skin rippled as they moved. The noise was as if demons had broken free from the underworld, and the smell was so powerful that I almost lost my senses.

I guessed that my eyes were the size of moons as I turned to Biji. I spread my hands, seeking answers to the questions I had no words to ask. She pointed to the animals at the back.

'Those are cows. Their flesh is good to eat.'

She nodded towards the pink creatures.

'Pigs. They are the ones with the bad smell. The horses you have met, and the dogs are mastiffs. Do not go near them, they are dangerous.'

The pale men stared down at us from the backs of the horses. Their gazes dismissed most of the Taino, but rested long on Baba, Karaya and me. At first I thought they were interested in us because they recognized we were *nitaino*, but then I noticed their gaze did not touch our faces, but stayed on the gold necklaces and earrings we wore as a mark of our position.

A shiver touched my spine. The pale men had looked at our ornaments in the same way the first time. And none of us had forgotten the result of their hunger for gold. This time there were a lot more of them, many more hungers to feed. How would the Taino be able to satisfy them?

43
Change

Over the next few days, the Espanoles rebuilt their village, a little distance from our settlement. We were amazed that they had chosen that spot. Baba went to the Almirante and tried to get him to change his mind. He took Biji with him to unfold his meaning, so there could be no mistake, and I went with them.

'My noble lord, this is not a good place for building,' Baba told him. 'In the rainy season this land is flooded. Even now it is swampy and teems with biting insects. My lord should choose another place.'

Baba was just doing what Cacique Caonabo and the other caciques had done for us when we had come to Kiskeya. Even as we stood with him the Almirante was slapping his neck and face, trying to escape the tiny insects whose bites were like spear points entering the flesh. If we had not painted ourselves with *roucou*, we would have been eaten as well.

The Almirante smiled politely at my father, thanked him for his concern and gave orders for his men to work faster.

Baba watched him in silence for a while, then turned and went back the way he had come.

'It seems the visitors do not need our help,' he said. 'Perhaps their magic is strong enough to keep them from sickness in this place.'

Baba was wrong.

The sickness started with one of the men who were building the new village. I had gone with Karaya to take food to the workers. Although the Almirante was displeased with Baba, his displeasure did not hinder him from accepting Taino hospitality. We were feeding the visitors every day.

The man was sitting on the ground and the sweat poured from his face like the water down the mountains in the rainy season. His clothes clung to him as if they wanted to change places with his skin and he shivered in the heat of the midday sun.

Karaya ran over to the man and placed her palm against his forehead. Then she whirled round and snatched the baskets from me. She dropped them on the ground, almost spilling the food, and spun me to face the village.

'Run, Maruka. Get the behique. Tell him it is the fever. He will know what to do.'

I had been avoiding Bamako, daily expecting a summons to account for my visit to the cave, but none had come. Each day I grew more anxious, wondering why he was keeping me in suspense. But now I could think only of the man whose skin was on fire. I barely had time to say 'fever' before Bamako was diving into his *bohio* and we were speeding back towards the pale men's place.

The sick man had his eyes closed and was moaning when we arrived. As soon as Bamako knelt in front of him his eyes flew open. His gaze walked over Bamako's ceremonial decorations to the pouch he was opening, and fear rushed into his face.

He pushed at Bamako, but there was no strength in his arms. He shouted something and two men ran at us from the side of the half-finished building. They waved their arms in the air as if they were scaring chickens from the vegetable plot, and chattered like disturbed parrots in the forest. I wished I had thought of asking Biji to come back with us. We could not understand the words they spoke, but before long we understood their meaning.

We stepped back and watched as the pale men lifted the sick one and took him towards the Almirante's house. Bamako shook his head.

'They are taking the evil spirit into the house. Why

would they do that?' He shook his head once more, then turned to walk back to his *bohio*. It was clear to us that we were not wanted there, so Karaya and I followed Bamako, leaving the baskets of food on the ground.

The next day I was going through the door of the *caney* when Nito woke up.

'Are you going to wash now, Maruka?'

I smiled. 'Would you like to come?'

She was out of the hammock before I had finished speaking, her face alight with anticipation. I felt a stab of regret. Since Biji had returned I had not spent as much time with Nito as I used to and she was obviously feeling left out. I made a promise to myself that I would include her in what we did from then on.

Her pleasure lasted until we reached my bathing place. Biji was already there, floating in the place where the sea said hello to the river. She turned her head when she heard us, stood up and waved.

Nito was in front of me. She stopped so suddenly that I almost tripped over her.

'Is something wrong, Nito?' I asked.

She stared at Biji then turned back towards the compound.

'I have to go back.'

And before I could say anything else, she was running up the track.

'Nito, what is it?'

It was as if she had not heard my shout. I half turned to follow her, but Biji was calling to me.

'Maruka, come quickly. There is something I have to tell you.'

With a last look after Nito, I ran towards Biji and dived in, shivering as the cold water bit into my skin, raising tiny hills on my flesh.

I shook my head so that droplets of water sprayed the air, catching the rays of the sun and making jewels which disappeared as they hit the sea.

'So what do you have to tell me?'

'That sick man, the one you told me about yesterday. He has gone to Coyaba.'

My eyes spread wide and the breath caught in my throat.

'I went with my mother to take the visitors' first meal, as it was the turn of our families to do so. We saw them putting him in a hole in the ground. But it was strange.'

'How?' I asked.

'Well, they did not give him any food to eat on the way to Coyaba. No plates, nothing. Not even a dog to help him hunt. They have strange ways.'

I nodded, but my mind was exploring other thoughts. It was lucky that Bamako had purified Karaya and me when we got home. Otherwise the evil spirits might have sent us to Coyaba as well.

44

Separation

Many of the pale men went to Coyaba before that season was over. The pale medicine men did not know how to get rid of the evil spirit which made them ill. Perhaps the spirit did not understand their language and when the pale behiques told it to go, it could not obey. So the pale men kept dying. And they were not the only ones.

With the pale men had come strange sicknesses which we could do nothing to cure. Bamako and the other behiques were hoarse from saying prayers for the dead Taino.

The deaths of his people must have been a hard blow for the Almirante. He became almost frantic for gold. He must have thought if he had more gold his people would be protected.

As each day slipped away I became more tense, waiting for Bamako to say something. It was as if our meeting in the cave had never happened. He could not have said anything to Baba either, because my father's attitude towards me had not changed. I was now almost wishing to be called to the council. At least then I might know what had become of my canoe.

The chance to rescue my mother had been lost with the disappearance of my boat. The thought of making another one was daunting, but I did not see what else I could do. I did not want to be shut out of Coyaba. As I walked through the forest I examined the ceiba trees, looking for a suitable one. I would have to start again.

One day the Almirante came to Baba and asked for Biji. We understood that he had something to say to us which he needed her to put into our tongue.

'The Almirante has decided that there is not enough gold being found,' Biji said. 'He needs much more. From now on every Taino, men, women and children, will bring him half a calabash of gold each seven days.'

But we had given all we could give. We had no more. *Then we must find more*, the Almirante said.

I stared, aghast, at Biji when she unravelled the Almirante's words to us. Where would we get as much gold as he demanded? It was not possible.

The men in the council turned to Baba.

'We have to do something, Great Lord,' Bamako said.

My father was silent, biting his lip as he sifted the thoughts in his head. Then he looked hard at Bamako. 'Yes,' he said. 'We must do something.'

He gave orders in sharp, short words and soon all the Taino men were ranged in front of him, each one with his *coa* in his hand. The digging sticks had been sharpened in preparation for action.

'Follow me.' Baba turned and marched towards the settlement of the Espanoles. My heart, like a hunted coney, raced as if it would spring from its cage. I wanted to go with the men, to see what Baba intended to do, but a look from Karaya told me I should put all thoughts of following them out of my head. I would have to wait for Biji to let me know what had happened.

The men had only been gone for a little while when they returned and we could see from their slumped shoulders and glum faces that the meeting had not gone as they had planned.

I looked hopefully at Baba, but he entered the *caney* without even glancing at me. I had taken three steps to follow him when Biji raced into the square.

She beckoned to me and we slipped under the trees and took the path down towards the beach. Out of the corner of my eye I saw a movement. I turned. Nito stared at me and then turned and walked away without a word. I vowed to speak to her as soon as Biji had told me about Baba's trip to the Almirante.

I clutched Biji's arm to stop her before we reached the beach. I could wait no longer.

'Biji, tell me. Did they fight?'

Biji frowned. 'Fight? Why?'

'They took their *coas* with them. I thought they were preparing to fight.'

Biji laughed. 'And did they wear their *zemis* in their foreheads as if they were going to war?'

My words slowed into thoughtfulness. 'No, they did not.'

'There, you see. Your father went to offer his services.' And Biji told me everything from the beginning, when Baba walked into the Almirante's compound with his men.

The Almirante was in his house, but Baba stood outside until he came out.

'Most noble lord,' my father said. 'We have come about the gold.'

An eager light sparked behind the Almirante's eyes.

'Have you brought me more?'

Baba shook his head. 'What the noble lord asks is too much for us. There is not enough gold in all of Kiskeya for us to supply what you demand. We can give you something better than gold.'

The Almirante's brows rose in disbelief.

258

'The most noble lord must eat,' my father continued. 'His people must eat. Instead of giving you gold, I and my people will plant and provide enough food to feed your people here and in your own country. See,' he gestured towards his men. 'We have our *coas*. We are all ready to work in the fields.'

The Almirante looked long at Baba, then shook his head. 'Food we can plant ourselves. Get me gold.'

Then he turned and walked back into his house, leaving Baba and his many men standing in the sun.

The Almirante left to travel to the other islands in search of gold. He asked directions from my father to go to Cubanakan, and left someone called the Gobernador in his place. The pale men chopped the land into giant squares. Each square was corralled by fences which they told the Taino to make, and we thought they must be planning to pen many animals. But it was not just animals that the pale men fenced. These were pens for crops.

The Gobernador came to the village with his men, all carrying their death-spitting sticks, and pointed to the men and women. He counted the people by heads and told them to stand in groups. Some groups were three tens, some four tens, some five or six tens. The groups he gave to his men. The Taino were presents for his people.

Biji was ordered to explain to the Taino what was expected of them. The men would go to dig for gold in the mines. The women would be required to tend the penned crops for the Espanoles.

They did not choose people from the *caney* and I was ashamed at the relief I felt. Baba hung his head throughout the counting, unable to look at the Taino who were being taken away.

A few of the men were slow to follow the others. The Espanole to whom they had been given rode back down the line of marching Taino to the stragglers.

'Do you not wish to come with me?' he asked. 'Would you rather remain here?'

They nodded, hardly believing they would be allowed to stay.

'Then stay,' he said, and pulled his shiny stick from its case.

Baba buried them in the midden where we had buried those who had been carried to Coyaba by the pale men's diseases.

Baba's friend Cacique Hatuey came to visit one day and we talked with him about the pale men's greed for gold. He took a piece of gold from the basket he had brought with him.

'Do you see this?' he said. 'This is the pale men's god whom they worship and adore. They will do anything for him. It is in order to get this god from us so that they can worship him that they kill and maim our people.'

He set the gold on the ground in front of him. 'If you agree,' he said, 'we will make an *areito* in honour of this god. Perhaps we will please him and he will order the Espanoles to leave us alone.'

Baba agreed. We danced until the sweat poured in waterfalls from our bodies and our feet screamed for rest. Baba and Cacique Hatuey sang praise songs to the god. Then Hatuey bent and picked the piece of gold from the ground.

'If we keep this god here, the pale men will come and kill us for it. We must get rid of it.'

We followed him to the river and watched as the gold sank to the bottom.

45
Thelord

The Padre, the pale men's behique, waddled, puffing and panting, into the village. Baba had gone to have his second bath but Bamako was in the square with a group of six men, including two other behiques, mending fishing nets. The Padre approached them and I left the maize I was husking to see what he wanted.

His podgy hand was clasped around the handle of a basket and I wondered if he had come for more food. The pale men seemed to have a hole in their stomachs through which the food fell; they were always hungry. But today the pale behique did not want anything from us. Instead, he had come with presents for the Taino.

He reached into his basket and brought out a *zemi* like the one he and the other Padres wore. The *zemi* dangled, white as bleached bones, on a silver string and, fastened to a pair of crossed silver sticks by his hands and feet, he hung his head upon his chest. Either he was ashamed or he was in much pain.

I wondered why the pale men had carved their *zemi* as if he hung from a tree. Among the Taino, it is an abomination to be hanged. But we had noticed that the pale men did not think as we did.

Naked, except for a loincloth, the *zemi* looked more like a Taino than one of the visitors, and I felt my mind reaching out to him, wanting to ease his pain, to take him down from where he hung. The Padre explained that the *zemi* was the image of the Christian god. He wanted us all to become Christians like the Espanoles.

The Padre placed the string round Bamako's neck. It nestled beside the *zemis* of Yucahu and Opiyelguaobiran, but the Padre was not happy. He wanted Bamako to wear only the *zemi* of the pale men. Bamako's face wore a look that said he would not be without his *zemis* for anything the pale behique could give him. He took the Padre's *zemi* from his neck and handed it back without a word.

The Padre stared at Bamako as if he thought our behique had lost his mind. Then he shrugged and turned his back on Bamako, who then turned and left the ball court.

The other men did not share Bamako's misgivings.

Each of the six held a white *zemi* when the Padre had gone, and we crowded round to look at the strange carvings. I reached out with the others to stroke the one held by Yamarex, one of the other behiques, and it was smooth as the polished stones we collected from the riverbed for our necklaces. Smooth and cold.

Yamarex turned to me as I stroked it and pressed it into my hand.

'What shall we do with this *zemi* of the pale men, Maruka? Shall we see if it will speak to us?'

They had all heard that Atebeyra spoke to me and, although most of them thought I had just been having bad dreams, they joked only in part.

I looked at their expectant faces and then at the *zemi*, bone-white against the copper of my skin. The *zemis* of the pale men were powerful, Biji had said, and I felt excitement stir in my stomach. Now we could have some of this power, if we could find out how to use it. Yucahu and Atebeyra had left. Our prayers were left unanswered and the pale men remained, even though we fasted and chanted for many days.

An idea crept into my head.

'This *zemi* has very powerful magic,' I said. 'You can see how he protects the strangers. We should plant it in our cassava ground as we do with our own. Then our crops will be plentiful.' I thought if it worked on our crops it would probably answer our other prayers as well.

'That is good, Maruka,' Yamarex said. He looked around at the others. 'Do we all agree with the cacique's daughter?'

So we filed down to the cassava field and planted the white *zemis* in the centre of the crops. Then we left them to work their magic.

A few days later the Padre came again to the village. Baba invited him to our *caney*. He swayed in through the door and collapsed on to Yucahu's *duho*. Father said nothing. I opened my mouth to tell him it was not allowed for anyone to sit on the *zemi*'s sacred stool but Father motioned me to be quiet.

Baba sent me to fetch Yamarex and Biji to tell us the Padre's words.

I found Biji, then I ran over to Yamarex's *bohio*. He was smoking inside. Normally I would not interrupt a behique in his smoke, but my father wanted him.

When we returned, the Padre was eating a guava from the bowl of fruit my mothers had put before him. He spoke through Biji.

'Ah! Yamarex,' he said. He looked at Yamarex's bare chest and his forehead wrinkled. His lips closed over his teeth, blotting out his smile.

'Where is the crucifix I gave you?' he asked. 'You are not wearing it.'

Yamarex shook his head when Biji told him the Padre's words, and a broad smile lit his face.

265

'We have buried them,' he said proudly. 'In our cassava field.'

A red dye climbed under the Padre's skin, up his neck and over his face. His mouth opened and closed silently so that he looked like a fish plucked from the sea. I knew it was an honour to have his *zemis* in our cassava, but I did not think it would mean so much to him.

After a minute he brought back his voice from the place where it had been hiding.

'You did what?' His words were like the crack a blowpipe makes when you fire a dart at a parakeet. 'You buried Thelord?'

The smile disappeared from Yamarex's face. I moved the weight of my body from one foot to the other. I was not sure now that the Padre was pleased. He got up hastily, knocking over the *duho*. A gasp flew round the *caney* but no one moved.

46

Talking to the Pale Men's *Zemi*

I stumbled into the field where we had buried the white *zemis*. The earth flew into my face, mingling with my tears as I scrabbled in the cassava mound, but I did not care. It was my fault that the men were going to be punished. It had been my idea to bury the *zemis*. I should have been the one to be tied up in the silver ropes. Why did I always think I knew the answer to everything? Why had I not kept quiet when the men asked for my advice? I was only a child. Why could I not remember that? And where was that *zemi*?

I found it at last. It had been in the mound for a few days and the field had been baked by the sun, but it seemed untouched; as white and cold as when we had first put it in. I held it next to my chest as I had seen the pale behiques do. 'Please, Thelord,' I whispered, 'we did not mean to dishonour you. Please speak to your people and explain to them that we meant no harm. They will not listen to us. Thelord, if you will do this I will bring you *casabi* every day. I will put you in the house of the *zemis* and we will pray to you. Please save our people.'

47

Vengeance

It was a hot day in the middle of the dry season, and it was even hotter for the men who were about to be roasted.

We had all been ordered by the Gobernador to be there.

'Everyone is to be at the fort at midday,' he had said, gesturing towards the sky. Even though he had people to give meaning to his words, he still needed to draw pictures in the air. We watched his red hands and listened to Biji.

The Gobernador pointed at the Taino men bound to the pole. His finger jabbed the air, as if he would make a hole in the sunlight.

'Let this be a lesson to all of you!' Biji repeated his words in our tongue. 'We do not dishonour

Thelord. Any dishonour to Thelord will be punished.'

The Padre waddled up to the men on the pole. He pointed to the wood stacked high around him. He made noises in his throat.

Yamarex stared straight in front of him and did not answer.

The Padre beckoned to Biji, who shuffled to stand beside him. He repeated the question and she told Yamarex the meaning of the words. It was hard to hear her voice. She spoke as if she had swallowed a whole potato and it had lodged in her throat. Her eyes sparkled with unshed tears.

'Before the fire is lit, will you repent? Say you are sorry?'

Yamarex looked at the Padre.

'What will happen if I do?'

The Padre grabbed the meaning from Biji's lips.

'If you repent you will go to heaven when you die.'

'And are there Christians in heaven?'

'Yes, that is where Christians go when they die.'

Yamarex looked away.

'Then I do not want to go to heaven.'

They lit the fires then. I looked at the Gobernador. He was staring at the men like a salivating dog. I turned and slowly inched my way to the edge of the crowd of Taino. They all had their heads bowed. No

270

one looked at me. At the back of the crowd, away from the Gobernador's eyes, I ran.

I ran as fast as I could with the tears blinding my eyes, but I could not outrun the screams and the smell of burning flesh.

48

Lessons

I scrubbed myself with the digo root; rubbed until the skin was sore and blistered, but I could not get rid of the smell. I was still scrubbing when Biji joined me. She stepped from her coverings and waded into the water. We clung to each other, unable to stop the shaking in our limbs; unable to stop the tears.

When at last I found the strength to speak, I dragged myself from the water and sat with Biji on the bank of the river.

'You have to do it now,' I said.

'Do what?' Her voice was flat and lifeless.

'You must teach me the language of the pale men.'

Biji spat. 'I will no longer taint my tongue by speaking their words. From now on, I will speak only Taino.'

I shook my head. 'They would kill you. Besides, that is not the way to defeat them. We must know their thoughts.'

Biji considered my words.

'They will want you to speak for them to the Taino,' she warned. 'Sometimes it will be painful.'

'They will not know I understand their tongue,' I said. 'Not unless you tell them.'

She stared at me and something in my face brought a tiny smile to tease the corners of her lips.

'When do you want to start?'

'Right now. As soon as I get Nito. She must learn as well.'

'Then let us fetch her.'

Biji stepped over her coverings on the ground. She did not even glance at them. Our faces set, we strode up the path to the village.

49

Desecration

A few days later, I was going past the *zemi* house when I saw something glistening in the sunlight. I bent to pick it up and turned it over in my hand. What was a piece of gold doing on the ground? I made to walk away, intending to give it to Baba, and as I did my glance skidded through the opening and into the house.

I clamped my hand over my mouth to stifle the cry that fought to escape. The floor was littered with the *zemis*. They had all fallen from their sacred stools, and lay face down in the dirt, except for the *zemi* of Yucahu who was gazing sightlessly at the ceiling. This time I could not prevent the cry of disbelief. The gold from the sockets of the *zemi*'s eyes was gone. Yucahu was blind.

The horror of it drew me as an iguana's watering eyes draw flies. Somewhere in the shadowed corners of my mind a voice whispered a warning, but it was too faint for me to hear. I had to put the *zemis* back in their rightful places. They should not be lying on the ground like broken water pots. They belonged on their sacred stools.

Only when I had picked Atebeyra up from the floor did I realize there was nowhere for her to sit. There was nowhere for any of the *zemis* to sit. All the *duhos* were gone.

I stared at Atebeyra and numbness crept from the bottom of my stomach and spread through my body. The *zemi* stared back at me from unseeing eyes. I ran to the *zemi* of Huracan. He too had been stripped of gold.

I had to get out of there. How could the gods have allowed this abuse?

I turned towards the door and stopped. Standing in the doorway, staring silently at me, were my father and the whole Taino council. Even though my eyes were blind with tears, I could not mistake the horror in their faces.

50
Sightless *Zemis*

I realized how it must look. I was standing in the centre of the *zemi* house with the idols scattered around me and the *zemi* of Atebeyra cradled in my arms.

I stared dumbly at the council and clutched the *zemi* tighter to my chest.

'What have you done?' Bamako's arm swept an arc around the room and the amulets of bone and shell jangled in bewildered indignation in front of him.

At last I found my voice. 'I did not do this, behique. I saw the *zemis* on the ground and came in to put them back on their stools. Only . . .'

'You should not be here, child. You are not allowed here,' Baba said, but his voice sounded as if the thought had travelled days to get to his lips and was weary from the journey. He looked past me to a dark corner of his mind.

Bamako bent and picked up the *zemi* of Huracan. He stared at the empty eye-sockets and a sound halfway between a whimper and a moan struggled from his throat.

As if it were a signal, the rest of the council woke from the spell which had held them motionless and dragged themselves around the house, picking up the fallen *zemis* and putting them on their feet.

'It is as you saw in your dream, child,' Bamako said flatly. 'The pale men have destroyed the *zemis*. There is no more life in them.'

'But why, behique? Why would they do this?'

Baba bent and picked up a small piece of gold from the floor. 'For this,' he said, holding it in the palm of his hand. 'For their god.'

51
Warning

Since I had begun to learn the meanings of the pale men's words, I took every chance to be near them so that I could find out their thoughts. When it was our turn to feed them, I volunteered to take the food. But their thoughts only caused me pain. I learned that they thought of the Taino as little better than animals. I understood now why Biji had considered her knowledge a curse.

I was beginning to regret letting Nito share the lessons, even though I saw how eager she was to learn. I shuddered to think of the things she overheard. I could tell how they affected her. Her laughter stilled, though she said nothing to either Biji or me.

And then one day when the sun was resting before starting his homeward journey, I took a basket of food to the Gobernador's house. It was food that was scarce, now that the Taino were too busy mining gold and tending the pale men's fields, but we had no choice.

The Gobernador had another man with him and they were discussing a cacique they were unhappy with. They were always complaining about the caciques so I was only half listening while I laid the fruit out on the table, but my attention was snared when I heard the plans they were making for him.

'He's a friend of the Almirante's,' the Gobernador said. 'That is the only reason I have not had him hanged before.'

'But the Almirante is not here now,' the other man said.

'Precisely. It seems a waste of good labour to kill him, but unless he is out of the way, his people will never be completely submissive. They keep running to the hills. That old woman we caught this morning was one of his.'

'So what do you intend to do?'

The Gobernador fell quiet.

'Tomorrow I will take him,' he said at last. 'When I have him in chains I will decide what to do with him.'

He got up and walked across the room. 'A pity. He could have been quite useful in getting to the other chiefs. He helped the Almirante build the first fort, you know, though he's not been acting so friendly lately.'

The basket clattered to the floor and my heart hung suspended halfway between my mouth and my chest. I was trembling with shock and fear. He was talking about Baba.

I snatched the basket from the floor and turned towards the door. I had to warn my father.

'Here! You!'

I stood like a *zemi*, clutching the basket, hardly daring to breathe. I heard the floor moaning in protest as the Gobernador strode towards me and it took all my will to keep my feet from running. I straightened and turned towards him. I forced myself to meet his gaze with a look of innocence. His eyes were cold and grey as the sea before a storm. I tried hard to disguise my hatred. The art of deceit was new to me, but it was not impossible to learn.

The Gobernador peered into my face, then, satisfied that I had not understood his words, he waved me away.

'Go.'

I did not need to be told twice.

52

Cacique Mabonex

'I will go with you, Baba.'

'You should stay here with your mothers.' But I could see he did not dislike the thought of my company and I pressed harder.

'Azzacca will be here, and you will need someone to tell the meanings of your words if you should meet the pale men on the way.'

He nodded.

'Very well. You may go with me. But we leave before the sun wakes, so do not be late in your hammock. Perhaps it is best you are not found here when the pale men find me missing. They are bound to suspect you warned me.'

*

Cacique Mabonex greeted us with all the honour due to my father and after we had eaten the food his wives had prepared for us, Baba and the elders went into the council house to speak.

It had been a long journey and my feet ached. I went to the *caney* where one of the cacique's wives had strung a hammock for me. Although it was not yet time for the afternoon sleep, I felt myself drifting out of wakefulness.

Then my eyes were wide open and I was looking at the sea. I frowned. Cacique Mabonex did not live near the sea.

The winged canoe of the pale men was sitting on the water and the baby canoes were travelling towards it. The baby canoes were filled with the Taino and in the first of them sat my father and me.

I jerked upright and the hammock swung beneath me. My palms were wet and my heart beat a painful rhythm. I had not had one of my waking dreams for some time, but each one had come true. I had to find Baba. We had to get away.

Fear brought trembling to my knees and I slipped as I climbed out of the hammock, but I picked myself up and hurried out into the square.

The women were sitting in groups, feeding babies, husking corn, grating cassava, weaving cotton and mending their fishing nets.

The men were making spears, sharpening axes, lying

in hammocks slung between the trees. The children played in the doorways of the *bohios*, teased the dogs and chased the tame ducks around the square.

It was a normal Taino village, as yet untouched by the pale men's poison. Time seemed to stop and in this normal atmosphere, my dream seemed only that – a dream. My steps slowed. Then I saw them.

I turned back towards the *caney* and the blood stopped in my veins. Rushing out of the trees, smoke pouring from their nostrils, were a number of horses. On their backs sat the pale men, their shiny sticks held ready, their eyes filled with death.

The Taino ran screaming into their *bohios*. They hastily dropped a stick in each doorway to lock the door. I wanted to tell them the pale men did not have any respect for locked doors, but I stood motionless and speechless, with a feeling of doom seeping into my body like spilt water into dry sand.

The first horse clattered to a halt in front of me. The Gobernador himself sat on his back. I wanted to run and hide, but I stood and stared into the deep black eyes of the horse.

'Where is he?'

I stood, as if struck dumb. Baba and the men had heard the screams and now came out of the council house to find out what the noise was about.

'Seize him!'

Before I knew what was happening Baba was on

the back of the horse, behind the Gobernador, and the beast was turning back towards the forest.

'Baba!' I ran after the horse, as if I could stop it. He looked back.

'Maruka! Run! Hide!'

The horse stopped, pulled up by the ropes the Gobernador held. His pale gaze travelled from my feet to my face.

'So you are Maruka,' he said. He motioned to one of his men and I was lifted up and settled behind the man. I was faint with terror. What did he mean? Had he heard of me before?

'I promised someone you would come to no harm,' the Gobernador continued. He laughed but his laughter was without enjoyment. 'And I always keep my promise.'

He motioned towards one of his men and made a wide arc with his arms; an arc that covered Cacique Mabonex's village.

'Burn them,' he ordered.

53

Captives

Perhaps we should have struggled as we were pushed and pulled on to the winged canoe, but we did not. I wanted to fight. I wanted to hit out at our captors and run to the safety of the forest. But the pale men waved their shiny digging sticks before our faces. We knew that if we resisted they would kill us. We chose to live.

My father and I were separated from the other captives and taken into the belly of the canoe.

The room we stood in was hardly large enough for us both. The canoe was tossing about on the water and it was difficult to stand.

Baba looked at me and his eyes were moist. 'I am sorry, Flower,' he said. 'I am so sorry that I have brought you to this.'

I fell to my knees before him.

'Baba, it is I who need to say sorry. It is because I have been wicked that this misfortune has come upon us.'

He gripped my shoulders and drew me to him. 'You must not blame yourself.' His voice was firm. 'You had to kill the Kalinago to save your life. That is forgivable. The death of the pale man was an accident. Yucahu knows that. And these devils deserve to die!'

'But that is not what I speak of, Baba. What I have done is much worse.'

His expression was serious as he tilted my face so that our eyes spoke to each other.

I gulped. Telling him was going to be harder than I had imagined. But I could not let Baba blame himself when I had caused the calamity that had fallen on our people.

'I have done something terrible.' I swallowed and continued. 'I broke one of the taboos of the tribe and did something it is forbidden for a female to do. I have displeased the gods and now they are punishing us all.'

Baba sighed and a smile of relief chased the dark look from his face.

'Maruka, Flower, the gods are not angry because you have hunted. If they were, they would have punished us a long time ago. Whatever Azzacca says, you are not to blame for this.'

I scowled. I saw again in my mind's eye the

Gobernador standing beside Azzacca as Baba and I were pushed on to the winged canoe. I heard his mocking words. 'Do not worry, your people will be in safe hands.'

'Azzacca is a traitor,' I said. 'We should not speak his name.'

A cloud walked across Baba's face. 'I do not understand how he could betray us, his own family.'

My lips curled. 'It is clear to me why he did it. He wanted to be cacique.'

'But he would have been.' Baba shook his head. 'There has to be another reason.'

'You are too trusting, Baba. Azzacca could not wait. He was hungry for power. Now he has eaten it, I hope it sits heavy in his stomach.'

Again his face wore its sombre look.

'No. We must not blame Azzacca, it is I who am at fault. I should have let the people know what I know. Then they would have been prepared. We could have sought shelter with any of the other caciques. Instead, I tried to do it all myself, and this,' his gesture took in the cramped room, 'this is the result.'

'Baba, I do not understand.'

'Of course you do not.' He paused. 'I knew before I left Iyanola. The Lord of the Sky told us as we smoked *cohoba* that covered men would come. That they would dominate and kill. When I saw them, I knew it was the time of the prophecy.'

'But – then why did the *zemis* tell you to welcome the covered men?'

Baba hung his head and was silent. When he spoke I had to lean towards him to hear his words.

'I have not heard the voice of the *zemis* since the pale strangers arrived. That night we emptied our stomachs as usual. I smoked *cohoba* before them as I have always done. But the *zemis* were dumb. They told me nothing.'

My breath rushed through my nostrils like the whisper of a storm.

'You lied to the Taino?'

Baba shook his head and laughed harshly. 'I had not yet met the pale men. If you remember, I did not say, "The gods have spoken." I said, "In the morning we will welcome our visitors."'

'But you knew we would assume the gods had spoken.'

'Perhaps. But I thought it best at the time. I thought – I hoped that if we befriended the enemy, he would not destroy us. You have heard it said, keep your friends by your side and your enemy in your bosom. I was naive. I had never met an enemy like this one.'

'So, in the council, you knew my dream about the pale men destroying the *zemis* was true?'

'As true as the ones about your grandmother and grandfather.'

My eyes widened. 'You knew about those dreams?'

Baba smiled sadly. 'When your grandmother died, your mother was shocked that you had foreseen it. But she kept her own council, afraid that you might be taken from her.'

'That is why she told me to say nothing to anyone. But then she told you?'

'Not until your grandfather also died, as you had seen in your vision. She was too terrified to keep it to herself. I knew then that Atebeyra had been speaking to you. I decided to watch you. If you were given more visions, we would have to consult the *zemis* about your future.'

'You – you would send me away?'

Baba reached out a hand to stroke my cheek. 'Only so that you could be trained as Caicihu would have been trained. Those whom the gods choose to speak to are always leaders.'

A sigh flitted from his lips like a trapped butterfly let loose.

'I was shocked by your dream about the pale men. I wanted to protect you. I had to convince the council you spoke without thought. If they knew you had the power – well, you were not yet ready.'

My thoughts held a meeting in my mind and gave me their decision.

'So this disaster was coming anyway. It was not because I made a canoe?'

I was talking to myself and only when I saw Baba's

start of surprise did I know I had spoken the words aloud.

'You made a canoe?'

He had told me his secret. I had to tell him mine. Even now, perhaps we could find a way to save my mother.

'I am sorry, Baba. It was only a small canoe.'

'But why did you want to build a canoe?' His voice was soft and hesitant as if he was afraid to hear my answer.

'I wanted to go and rescue my mother.'

He closed his eyes and nodded gravely.

Suddenly he seized my hand and pulled me towards the opening of the room.

'Come. I will show you something.'

I followed him up the steps to the top part of the boat. His hand was gripping mine as if he feared I would disappear into the air if he let go.

It was difficult to stay upright. The boat was flying across the water, its wings swollen with the wind. Now I was close to them I could see that the wings were large pieces of thick cloth. The pale men must have worked many dry seasons to make them.

But Baba showed no interest in the wings which moaned and cracked above our heads. He ignored the men hanging to the ropes like spiders in a web. He pulled me to the side and gestured towards the ocean below. His arm made a wide arc, taking in the edges of the sea where it spoke with the sky.

The ocean was empty. There was only a blur in the distance which I thought was Kiskeya.

'Where are we?'

I looked at my father, perplexed. 'We are on the ocean, Baba.'

'Yes, yes. But where on the ocean? Do we go towards where the sun sleeps or where it wakes?'

I looked towards the sky. The sun was directly above us. I could not tell where we were going. I looked again at the dark blur that was Kiskeya. I did not know which side of the island we travelled on.

I looked at Baba and he nodded as if my confusion satisfied him.

'We are still in sight of Kiskeya and already you are lost. So how long do you suppose you would have lasted in a small canoe on your own?'

I looked back towards the islands and my eyes widened. There was something bobbing on the water. I thought it was a manatee, but then I realized I was wrong. I turned, a smug smile on my face.

'I would have asked directions.'

My father threw back his head, but his crack of laughter had no pleasure.

'Yes, there are many talking fish in the sea. They would be willing to show you the way.'

'I do not speak of fish. Others also use the ocean, Baba.'

His gaze followed my pointing finger and he frowned.

'What is a loose canoe doing this far from land?'

A wind sprang up and drove the winged canoe across the water. I stumbled and bumped into Baba. We clutched at each other, struggling to stay upright.

'What are you doing up here?'

A pair of hands grabbed us and shoved us back the way we had come. I felt a wave of relief wash over me. I thought we were going to be thrown into the sea.

'We cannot have the merchandise being lost at sea now, can we? You will fetch a pretty price in the markets of Castile.'

The Espanole's voice rang in my ear long after he had left us in the little room in the boat's belly.

Baba saw the look on my face and clutched my shoulders. 'What did he say?'

I could not speak. How could I tell him what I had just learned?

'Maruka, tell me.'

'We are to be sold as slaves.'

Baba's body seemed to have been squeezed of life and he slumped on to the stool.

'It is as the prophecy says. With the coming of the pale strangers our people will be enslaved.' His eyes looked down the long road into the past and his voice deepened so that it was not his but someone else's who spoke through him.

'*And the people who sing shall be scattered throughout the world. None will escape the years of misery which walk with the rule of greed. Men will be turned into slaves. The sun will hide his face in sorrow and the world will shrink in humiliation.*'

The words ceased and slowly Baba's gaze returned to the present.

'We must get you out of here,' he said.

'And you, Baba. We will both get away.'

54

Escape

That night I told my father what I had told no one. How I stood on the hill on Iyanola and did nothing while my mother was being stolen, hands tied behind her back. How she called out to me for help and I stood, helpless with fear, and watched her disappear.

'There was nothing you could have done,' my father said softly. 'You were only a child.' His face crumpled, all hope finally gone.

I dashed the tears from my eyes and sniffed.

'But now you see why I have to rescue her. My name was the last she called before she went. I am bound to help her. Besides, I have killed two people. I will not enter Coyaba unless I do this.'

Baba was thoughtful. 'You will need help. You do not know the words of protection . . .'

'Then tell them to me.'

He looked long into my face as if he wanted to see my soul in my eyes. Then he sighed. 'Very well,' he said. 'I will tell you what to do.'

The next day we stopped near some islands and some of the men lowered the baby canoes and paddled ashore. I wondered what they expected to find on the islands. It was clear to me that the place was deserted. But I was wrong. They returned in high spirits with barrels of water and baskets of fresh fruit, dried fish and *casabi*. The captain helped to bring the men and their cargo aboard.

'Did you have any trouble?'

The men sniggered. 'It was just like the last time, captain,' one said. 'The savages took to their heels as soon as they saw us. But they very kindly left us all their worldly goods.'

The captain joined in the laughter. 'I hope you left them a token of thanks.'

'That we did, captain.' The one who had answered before covered his lips so the captain could not hear and whispered to his companion in the small canoe. 'Right in the middle of their bean field.'

If the people knew what demons these men were, they would have left them the poisonous juice of the cassava instead of fresh water and food.

'Maruka, this might be our chance.'

I jumped. I had not heard Baba coming up behind me.

'Even if we managed to get all the Taino to help, we could not overpower the pale men, Baba. Their weapons are too deadly.'

'I did not speak of all the Taino, Flower. Only you.'

I stared at him, appalled. 'I will not leave you.'

'It will be easier for one person than for two to escape.'

'No.'

He sighed. 'Maruka, can you not see? I have seen many dry seasons. It will be harder for me to out-swim the canoes. But you are young and swift. I will keep the pale men's attention from you while you escape. We are not far from Iyanola here. The air smells familiar.'

I was shaking my head as he spoke, hardly listening to his words. 'Baba, do not ask me to leave you. I cannot lose you as I lost Bibi.'

He pounced on my words like a hunting dog on a *hutia*. 'And your mother waits for you. Or have you forgotten?'

I had not forgotten. His words gave me the nudge I needed. I measured the distance to the nearest island. The baby canoes had taken a long time to get there. It would be hard to swim that far without being recaptured.

I turned back towards Baba. 'I cannot save

her without you. I – I do not know the words well enough . . .'

'Maruka, you are fishing in dry riverbeds.'

'And you are asking me to choose between my parents.' I was torn. I wanted to rescue Bibi; needed to rescue her. But I did not want to lose Baba. Not now, when I was just beginning to understand him. It was as if I had not spoken.

'I have told you all you need to know. If Bamako was here . . .'

'Bamako hates me. He would not help.'

Baba made a sound of irritation with his tongue against his teeth. 'Bamako only wants what is best for you and the Taino. You must trust him. If he seems harsh, it is because he knows the thoughts of the spirits and wants to protect you from their anger.'

I thought of arguing, but then I remembered how Bamako had kept quiet about my visit to the caves. Could my father be right? Had I misjudged Bamako? There was no time to give that idea more thought. Baba was looking anxiously towards the island.

'Now you must go,' he urged. 'The canoe is moving and soon the opportunity will be lost.'

He was right. The land was farther away than it had been before. While we had been speaking, the small canoes had been unloaded and were now being stowed. A wind had sprung up and the vessel was running before it. If I was going, it would have to be now.

I turned to Baba and knew I could not hide my despair. Would I ever see him again?

He pushed me towards the edge of the boat.

'Go!'

Then he was gone; striding towards where the men had just finished tying up the small canoes. My gaze followed him, drinking in his form, storing him in my memory for the days which were not yet born. I turned towards the ocean, stretched my hands towards the sky in a silent prayer to Atebeyra for protection, blinked hard once, twice, and leaped.

55

In the Water

I heard the surprised shout of the man clinging to the large wing before I hit the water. Then I was under the sea, salt water in my ears, my eyes, my nostrils. I swam underwater until my lungs were screaming for air. Then I pushed against the cold wet, and kicked as though I was untangling my feet from ropes.

I gasped, drinking a huge lungful of air.

'Swim, Flower! Swim!'

The sound of my father's voice was a prompt that gave wings to my arms and legs. I kept my eyes on the island, praying for it to come closer, but it seemed to stay as far from me as it had been when I was on the canoe. I prayed to Atebeyra and Huracan for protection from the water spirits. I prayed to the sea to take me safely to the island.

But my arms and legs were tiring. I willed my body to move, but my strength was gone. I was slowing. I heard a sound behind me and threw a quick glance over my shoulder. A canoe was almost on top of me. I struck out for the shore, fear lending life to my limbs. But not even the best swimmer in the whole of Atebeyra's kingdom could out-swim a canoe.

A hand clutched my leg. I kicked out and heard a surprised yell. Now there were two hands pinning my arms to my sides. I struggled, clutching at the neck of my captor. I was sinking and taking him into the depths with me.

A blow to the side of my head briefly lit the water with tens and tens of stars. Then I fell into the arms of darkness.

56
Bats

My eyelids struggled to escape from the tiredness that held them closed. I stretched and felt hard ground underneath my palms. I moved my hand, exploring, eyes still closed. Dry leaves rustled beneath my fingers.

I jerked upright and surprise pulled my eyelids open. I picked out the deeper shadows of rock in the dark; rocks that rose straight on each side to curve into a roof overhead. I was in a cave. I smelt the mustiness of damp earth and animal droppings, heard a gurgle nearby – the sound of a stream, and the muffled flutterings of cave dwellers. They were probably bats nesting in the denser darkness. I shivered.

A shadow drifted in front of me and a face leaned in towards me.

I opened my mouth, but before the scream could escape, a hand clamped hard over my mouth. Another hand closed over my chest and fastened my arms against my sides. The figure jerked me backwards, held me tight against him, so that I was unable to move.

Someone was beating a drum inside my head. My heartbeats were painful in my chest.

Then I heard another sound. The heavy steps of covered feet. The hands which imprisoned me tensed and tightened even more. The footsteps came closer.

Voices floated into the cave. Voices of the pale men.

'Have you seen anything?'

'Nothing.'

'They must have gone into those mountains.'

'They could not get that far so quickly. I know these savages. They'll be waiting in ambush to cut our throats.'

The words drifted off with the fading sound of the boots. I squirmed, trying to get loose, but my captor's hands only tightened more.

I raised my foot to kick him, but he seemed to be able to read my mind and stamped on my toes.

'Be still!' The whisper was full of menace. He spoke Taino, but he wasn't Taino. The words were thick and slow.

I stopped then, terrified. I heard the sound of the

pale men returning. They were the worst hunters in all of Atebeyra's kingdom.

'I can't believe they could make those hills that quickly.'

'But we've looked everywhere.'

The second man's voice was seasoned with impatience. 'The Almirante won't be pleased if we lose the girl. She was a gift for the Queen.'

'Well there's nothing – wait, what's this? Wasn't this what the girl was wearing?'

'I could hardly miss it. She wasn't wearing anything else.'

The other man said something I did not understand and they both laughed.

I wanted to move my hands, to touch my *zemi* and assure myself it was still around my neck. But I knew it was what the pale men were talking about. I could not feel the cool clay against my chest or the cord around my neck.

I heard the footsteps, getting closer to our hiding place. They were not talking now but they were still noisier than even the youngest boy on his first hunting lesson. They were beating at the bushes with sticks, the thwacks loud in the otherwise still air.

The hands around my chest lifted me, but he did not remove his hand from my mouth. He moved, silently, taking me with him. He timed his movements to match the beating outside so that we could not be heard. He did not stop until we were in the darkest corner of the cave, pressed against the wall.

My gaze scoured the walls and picked out an area covered with bushes. The cave was brighter here. That must be the entrance. And it was opening, the bushes parting.

There was a shout from outside.

'What have we here?!'

A pale head appeared among the bushes. The eyes blinked, adjusting to the dark.

'Can you see anything?'

'Not yet. It's too dark.'

I heard the flutterings of the bats lower down in the cave. They were disturbed by the light coming in through the parted bushes. The pale man heard it too and his eyes swivelled towards the direction of the sound, behind us. His eyes narrowed. Soon they would adjust to the darkness and he would see us.

The squeak rose in my throat before I had time to think about it and change my mind. My captor gave a start of surprise. The man at the mouth of the cave jerked. His eyes widened and his mouth opened, but he had no chance to say anything before the cloud of frightened bats catapulted into him.

He stumbled from the cave, yelling, as wave after wave of bats emerged from the darkness.

I let the tension drain from my muscles. I was

lucky that a bat's warning cry was one I could make with my mouth closed.

It felt like ten dry seasons before we heard the sound of the pale men's footsteps retreating into the distance. The arms around me relaxed and the hand cautiously eased from my mouth.

My captor watched me warily for a moment, but when I did not move he crept out of the cave. His voice floated back to me.

'You may come out now.'

I did not move. I was shaking like a young sapling in a hurricane. He came back and stood over me, a puzzled frown folding the skin on his forehead. Then a smile carved a white bow on his face and he chuckled, making the bone in his nose dance.

'That was a good trick.'

He held up his hand, palm forward in greeting.

'My name is Maruka,' he said. 'What is yours?'

57

Kalinago

I stared in silence at the boy I had killed. The last time I had seen him, he had been lying lifeless on the rocks by the roaring waters. Now he was standing in front of me and he did not look dead. Were ghosts supposed to look as healthy as this? I wanted to examine the place where his navel should be. That way, I would know for certain if he was a spirit. But the cotton belt he wore to hold his axe covered his middle and I could not tell for sure.

He peered down at me and the grin slowly faded. 'You are shaking,' he said. 'Are you not well?'

I shook my head. Words had fled from me.

'Come, we must leave.'

Still I did not move. He could not see me properly with my face turned away from the little light coming through the cave entrance. Once I was in the open, I would not be able to hide from him. He would recognize me as the girl who had killed him, and then he would take his revenge.

He grabbed hold of my hand and pulled me out towards the mouth of the cave. I knew I should run, but my brain was numb from the shock of seeing him, and could not speak to my feet. In the harsh sunlight, I blinked to regain my sight. He turned and his gaze travelled from the roof of my head to my toes. I watched him, ready to run when the light of memory entered his eyes. I waited. And waited.

His inspection over, he grinned once more and set off towards the sound of the stream.

'We must hurry,' he said. Nothing more.

I did not understand. Was he playing games with me? Sometimes when Cico had caught a lizard, he played with it, letting it run a little distance before pouncing on it again. Perhaps that was what this ghost was doing, pretending he did not know me so that I would not be fearful. Then when I was relaxed and unwatchful, he would kill me.

And how had he found me? How did he know I was on the winged canoe? I thought of the lone canoe that I had seen on the ocean. That must have been him. He had been the one to take me from the water.

He turned to stare at me and frowned, folding the white skull painted on his forehead.

'Can you not go any faster?'

'My head hurts.'

He came back and peered at the swelling. 'I had to do this.'

He reached out to touch the sore spot but his hand fell to his side when I cringed from him.

'You were trying hard to drown us both and the pale devils were not far behind.'

'I will live,' I said.

'Then come. I will take you home.'

Surprise held me fastened to the spot. 'You will take me home?'

'Have I not just said so?'

I bit my lip. If he was willing to take me home, perhaps he had forgotten that I had killed him. And if he did not have any reason to harm me, perhaps I could persuade him to take me to rescue my mother. Baba had said that Iyanola was close, and I was not sure I would get another chance if I went straight back to Kiskeya. But could I trust him?

He searched my face and I was sure he could see my thoughts written clearly there, but all he said was 'Follow me.' Then he shook his head, turned and, with a few strides, disappeared into the bushes.

I stood, mouth open, blinking in the sunlight. I had heard about the way ghosts could disappear into the air, but this was the first time I had seen it.

I turned to run in the other direction. A hand clamped around my arm.

'Where are you going? The canoe is this way!'

I gasped. He stared at me.

'What is the matter, now?'

'Y-y-you disappeared. I did not – could not see you.'

His laugh was scornful.

'Do you call yourself a hunter and do not know how to hide yourself among the trees? Now move, we must make haste.'

This time he moved in full view and I followed, frowning. How did he know I was a hunter?

His canoe was lying, upturned, among the bushes underneath a palm tree. I wondered how the pale men had missed it.

He turned the canoe over and my eyes widened in disbelief. I ran towards the boat and knelt in the wet earth for a closer look. There it was, as plain as the twin peaks on the face of Iyanola. My mark on the inside of the canoe.

I whirled on him, anger and fear fighting inside me.

'You – you – this is my canoe!'

'Yes. I had to borrow it. I could not get home without it. But I left you my knife in exchange.'

'A knife! For my canoe which took three dry seasons to make?'

'It was a good knife. I was forced to make another to replace it.' He spoke as if I had insulted his mother.

I inspected my canoe. It had been smoothed even more inside and two planks had been put in it for seats. I had not been able to do that on my own and I folded my lips with displeasure. In my heart I knew it was a better canoe, but in my head I was furious. He had no right to change my boat without my permission.

I frowned. 'But how did you find me? How did you know I was on Kiskeya? What are you going to do to me? I warn you, I will not taste good. I am a runner. My flesh will be tough!'

'What are you talking about?' He stared at me and then took a hasty step backwards. 'Are you – have you been visited by spirits?'

I straightened my back and stood as tall as I could. 'My mind has not left me.'

'Good.' But his look was still wary. 'I will tell you how I came to your island. But not now. We must get away from here.'

I stared out to sea. The winged canoe of the pale men was disappearing into the distance, the wind driving it like a child chasing a flock of geese. A pain, sharp as a hunter's arrow, tore through my chest so that I had to bite my lip to keep from crying out. How could anyone help my father now?

'It is safe to go,' the ghost said.

310

He held the canoe steady in the water and I stepped into it, my spirit heavy with grief. It felt strange to be getting into my own boat at another person's invitation.

He leaped into the canoe and pushed away from the shore.

I did not like sitting with my back to him, so I got up, turned around and sat facing him.

'Keep still,' he said. 'Are you trying to drown us both?'

'I did not know ghosts could drown.'

I slammed my hand against my mouth. I had not meant to let him know I knew he was a ghost.

He stared at me for a breath, his black-ringed eyes wide. Then he threw back his head. Laughter leaped from his throat and the bone in his bottom lip jiggled a horrible dance that made my insides quail.

The canoe swerved and scraped against a rock.

'Be careful!'

'I am a good seaman. I will not let us overturn.'

'I do not worry about overturning. I would not like you to damage my canoe.'

He looked hard at me but all he said was, 'So you think I am a ghost?'

'Well, are you not?'

He shook his head and a smile danced around the corners of his mouth and eyes.

I frowned, my mind confused. 'So, you have never been – dead?'

'Never.'

What did this mean? I had *seen* him die. His eyes had been closed and when I had talked to him, he had not been able to answer. I was sure his spirit had left him. Perhaps this was his twin. But no, he had said his name was *Maruka*.

As if my thoughts had travelled to his mind, he spoke. 'I have told you who I am. Are you going to tell me your name?'

My mind was still trying to work out what had happened on Iyanola. I spoke without thinking.

'Maruka.'

'Yes?'

'My name is M—' I stopped, realizing what I was saying. 'My name is An—' but no, I could not tell him that either. My mind flew back to my mother shouting 'Anani, run!' He might remember that. I would have to search for a name that would mean nothing to him; one that I would have to use from now on since he had reclaimed his.

'Do you still think I am a ghost who will steal your name from you? I will show you.'

He laid the oars on the bottom of the canoe and stood, planting his feet on both sides to steady the boat. He loosened the belt that held his axe and revealed his navel. It was unmistakable. He was not dead.

'I am no ghost. I am Kalinago.'

'But the Kalinago – you – hate our people. Why would you help me?'

He was silent for a few breaths. 'We do not hate you,' he said at last.

'And it is because you love us so much that you raid our villages and kill and steal our people.' I poured as much scorn as I could gather into my words.

'It was necessary.'

'Necessary! How? There are enough fishes in the sea, enough birds in the air, enough animals in the forest. Why do you need to hunt people?' My chest was rising and falling with the fierce anger burning inside.

'We cannot marry fishes, birds and animals.'

I felt the anger escaping like air from a manatee's punctured lung.

'You kill our men because they will not marry you?'

He made a sound of disgust in his thoat. 'We kill your men because they would stop us taking their women as wives.'

'And that surprises you? What is wrong with your own women? Why do you not marry them?'

'When our people left the mainland, they were exploring, so they brought no women with them. Once they had settled on the islands, they needed companions. That is why we make raids on your villages.'

'So you are just like the pale men. They too came

to our land without women. They too kill our men and take our women by force.'

His eyes blazed in their pools of blackness. 'You speak foolishness to say that we are like them. I have seen what they do to your people. I have seen the Taino with ropes around their necks, hanging in long lines from poles like fish drying in the sun. I have seen them roasted in pits like iguanas.'

He spat into the water in disgust.

'It is dishonourable for men to behave like that. They are primitive beasts who have no respect for others, for the earth, for anything. Not even for themselves. A Kalinago would never do those things.'

I was silent. He had revived the images of the Taino suffering and there was an ache inside that left no room for words. I gazed out towards the horizon, but that only reminded me that my father and the other Taino were out there. I blinked and looked down at the bottom of the canoe, trying hard to take control of my feelings. I suspected this Kalinago boy would not have time for tears. I rubbed my foot against the wood which, though smoother than when I had last seen it, still had the axe-marks in places.

'It is not finished.'

His brows rose in a question. I pointed to the rough places on the floor and sides of the boat.

'My canoe is not finished. You should not have taken it on the water when it was not finished.'

He stared at me as if he could not believe what I had just said. 'If I had not taken it on the water you would now be on your way to the pale men's land.'

I hung my head. He was right.

He saw my dejected expression and the sternness melted from his face.

'Do not be sad. You are not on the winged canoe any more.'

'I am not. But my father is.'

'I am sorry I could not save him.'

'They brought back some of the Taino they took the first time. Perhaps they will bring him back one day . . .' But although my mouth spoke the words, my heart did not believe them.

The sun was far on its journey home when I saw the outline of an island in the distance. Maruka saw it at the same time and relief spread over his face. He nodded towards it.

'We will stop there for the night.'

He had paddled all the way and I could see how tired he was from the work. When I had offered to take a turn, his brows had climbed to talk with his fringe.

'Have you paddled a canoe before?'

When I remained silent he smiled. 'Then I will go on.'

Now I saw how the muscles in his neck and shoulders strained with each movement of the oar; how the perspiration dripped from his face and how his breath came in tired gasps as he pulled. How could I have thought I could rescue my mother alone? How could I have paddled all the way from Kiskeya? I had been such a fool. A dark feeling made its nest in the pit of my stomach.

By the time we reached the island I could have eaten a whole manatee by myself. I helped Maruka to pull the canoe from the water and wedge it between the trees. We did not want it washed away if the tide rose.

We found a raised bit of land which was hidden among the trees but not too far from the sea.

'You make the fire while I catch some fish for our meal,' Maruka said.

I frowned. 'Have you got a line?'

'No.'

'A net?'

He shook his head.

'Some poison bark then?'

Again he shook his head.

'Then how will you catch fish?'

He stood looking at me for a breath, then turned towards the sea.

'Come, I will show you.'

He took the knife from the pouch at his waist and, as we came to the water's edge, he cut a long straight sapling from the young guava trees growing there. He stripped it of its leaves and branches until he held a bare straight pole. With his knife he sharpened one end until it was like any bone-tipped spear.

He stood waist-deep in the sea, still as a *zemi*, his gaze fixed on the water.

'That is a clever way to catch fish,' I said after a while. 'Are you expecting them to die of boredom?'

'Shhh!' He did not move. Then in one rapid motion he jabbed the spear into the water. When he lifted it, a large parrot fish was struggling at the tip, its blue and yellow scales making rainbows in the sunlight.

He used his knife to scale and clean the two fishes he had caught while I made the fire. I borrowed his knife to cut two leaves from a taro plant and, after softening them over the flames, I wrapped the fish in them. I scraped the hot ashes from a corner of the fire with a piece of stick and buried the fish parcels before heaping more hot coals on top. The taro roots I put on top of the hot coals to roast.

'That is a good way to catch fish,' I said later as I licked the last of the tender flesh from my fingers. He looked at me across the dancing flames and grinned.

'So the Taino do not fish like that?'

I shook my head. 'I do not know why. It is so simple. Almost as simple as the calabash.'

'What is this calabash fishing?'

I laughed at the picture his words made in my

mind. 'They are not for fishing. We use them to catch geese.'

His brows climbed up his forehead and I explained. 'We float the calabashes on the river until the birds are used to them. Then we scoop out the inside of some large gourds, make eyeholes in them and put them on our heads. We swim out to the geese and they think it is just another calabash so they do not fly away. We grab their legs and pull them underwater before they know we are there.'

'Why do the birds not grow wise to your tricks?'

'Because the ones that are caught cannot get out of the pot to warn the others.'

We chuckled together.

'Perhaps I will try that one day,' he said. But now it is time to sleep.'

I studied the two beds of leaves and grasses we had made while the fish cooked.

He pointed to the one furthest from the fire. 'I will take that one.'

I lay on the bed near the fire, feeling the warm flames caressing my skin, hearing the lullaby of the waves lapping the shore. Soon I could hear his even breathing. And then I heard nothing.

58

Awakening

I was woken by the kiss of the sun on my eyelids. My eyes flew open and I jerked upright. I glanced over to where Maruka lay snoring gently, his face covered by one arm.

For a breath I thought of tiptoeing away to the canoe and taking off without him. He was Kalinago and the Kalinago were enemies of the Taino. What if he was only pretending to take me back home?

I took a step towards the place we had hidden the canoe and my gaze travelled to the great country of water in front of me. I could not journey across it on my own. Even if I was strong enough to pull the oar, I had had no practice. I would probably still be spinning around in the shallows when Maruka awoke.

I turned to examine the land behind us. The

trees were the same as those on Kiskeya; ferny-leaved poincianas with their scarlet and orange blossoms and seedpods like flattened spears; tall palms with fat bunches of yellow-green coconuts marching towards the edge of the sea; trumpet trees offered their red bunches of flowers to the sky; and bamboos whispered secrets to the forest. I could have been on the beach on Kiskeya. A longing for my home, for Nito and Biji, and Baba, took hold, squeezing my insides into a knot of pain. How long would it take us to get to Kiskeya? The wind would not help us as it did with the pale men's canoe. We did not have their wings for the wind to fill.

I paused in my thinking. What if we attached wings to *my* canoe? Would Huracan fill our wings and drive us home faster?

I shook my head and, with another look at Maruka, I turned back towards the sea. Even if I could attach a wing to the canoe, I had nothing to make a wing from. It would take many days to weave a piece of cloth that big.

But there is a kind of thought which sneaks into the brain and sticks there as a bird sticks to the gum that baits the trap. That was the kind of thought I had about my winged canoe. It bedded itself quietly in a corner of my mind as I waded into the water and swam for a while, enjoying the cool wet against my skin.

I looked towards the beach to see if Maruka was awake and realized with surprise that I was much further out than I had thought. I could see much more of the island than I had seen before.

It was only slightly larger than our village in Kiskeya. It would not take long to explore.

I swam back, making for a spot to the left of where I had entered the water. The beach here was better than where we had camped; not pebbles but soft, golden sand.

I ambled across the sand, feeling it squish between my toes. The warm sun kissed my skin dry. It was not possible to hurry on a morning like this.

A movement to my right stopped me and I gazed as if under a spell. The animal lumbering towards me was a female green turtle, about the length of Nito. The sun caught the yellow spots in her dark brown shell, so that she looked as if she wore gold ornaments. She was returning to the sea after laying her eggs.

I held my breath. She would provide food for the Taino for many days, but I did not like to think of killing her. We would not have time to dry the meat and I was not sure we could carry it all in the canoe even if we did. She lifted her head and gazed short-sightedly in my direction, then, with a dismissive toss of her head, continued on her way.

She was so slow on the sand, but when she was in the water her flippers spread and the clumsiness fled before the grace and ease of her movements. I sighed and turned to the place from which she had come.

It was easy to spot where the eggs were buried. The ground around the small mound was damp from the disturbance. I took ten of them and covered the rest again. They tasted warm and sweet. I ate five, turned to take the others to Maruka for his first meal, and stopped. I blinked and stared. Over to the right, almost hidden by the trees, were the twin peaks I had lived beside for almost ten dry seasons. The twin peaks of Iyanola.

Maruka came running when he heard my shouts, his axe held ready for a fight.

'What has happened!'

'Iyanola!' I was having difficulty forming words with the excitement.

'What?'

I pointed.

'Over there! It is Iyanola. Iyanola is over there!' I was laughing without control.

'I know.'

That stopped the words, and the laughter.

'You know?'

'Of course. I . . .' He stopped and his eyes grew wary. 'Why does that please you so much?'

'I lived there once. I have to go back.'

'You want to revisit the place where you lived? But you have no family on the island now.'

'There is something I have to do. I have to go there before we go home.'

'What is it you must do?'

What could I say? Your people captured my mother. I have to release her, but first I have to collect some things from Iyanola. He would not be rushing to help me if I told him that.

'I cannot tell you,' I said quietly.

'Then I cannot help you.'

'Very well. I will take my canoe and go on my own. You may remain if you wish.'

I ran, expecting him to follow me, but I heard no footsteps and when I paused to look behind me, he was calmly entering the water to have his bath. He probably thought I could not do it. I would show him. I might not be able to get all the way to Kiskeya, but Iyanola was only a short distance away. I could reach there easily on my own.

The canoe was heavier than I remembered and I realized the seats must be thicker than I had thought. I struggled to hold it steady in the water so that I could climb in. It was so much easier when someone else held the boat still. But at last I was seated.

I took up the oar and the boat rocked from side to side. I clutched the side and held my breath while it steadied, and dipped the oar cautiously into the water. The boat rocked some more, but did not move forward. I had not used enough force.

I dug deeper with the next stroke but this time I must have used too much force. The canoe spun in a crazy circle and I almost fell out. By the time I righted the canoe my temper was simmering. Why could Maruka not have agreed to take me to Iyanola? It would not have taken him long and it was not as if he was in a hurry to reach Kiskeya. He was just selfish.

I glanced over to where he was swimming, a little distance away. He was acting as if I did not exist. I raised my shoulders and grasped the oar tighter. I would paddle this canoe to Iyanola or die trying. I would show him I did not need him.

I was still in the shallows, I could see the sand at the bottom of the sea. I pushed the oar into the sand and leaned hard against it. The canoe shot forward, but forgot to take me with it. I found myself in the water, still clutching the oar. The boat was on its way to Iyanola without me.

I dropped the oar and swam after the boat. As I grabbed the front, Maruka caught hold of the back. How had he reached it so quickly? Surely it was not possible for anyone to swim that fast?

He shook his head, spraying droplets of water over me. I pushed the wet hair from my face and peered inside the canoe as though I expected to find something in it. I could not meet his gaze.

'I think it is still in the water where you left it.'

I had to look up then. 'What?'

'The oar. Is that not what you are searching for?' Laughter danced in his eyes though his lips remained closed.

'There is no need to make fun of me.'

I must have looked as miserable as I felt because the laughter left his eyes. 'I will take you to Iyanola, but only after I have eaten. I cannot paddle on an empty stomach.' He started swimming towards the shore, pushing the canoe before him. I remembered the turtle eggs I had been saving for him. I must have dropped them in the excitement of seeing Iyanola. Once we had beached the canoe and found the oar, I sat on the sand and let the sun dry my body and hair.

'There are turtle eggs over there,' I said, pointing to where I had found them. 'I saw the turtle which laid them but she was too big for us to eat by ourselves.'

He looked as if I had suggested he eat mouse droppings or something as disgusting.

'Surely you do not eat turtles?'

'Why not?'

'Do you not know they will make you stupid? I suppose you eat hens as well?'

'And I suppose you think hens make you stupid too? We have been eating hens and turtles all our lives and they have not made us stupid.'

I saw his face and knew what he was thinking.

'We are not stupid,' I said hotly.

He shrugged. 'The Kalinago are not the ones who befriended the pale men, gave them everything and became their slaves.'

I glared at him. Was he suggesting we had invited the pale men to mistreat us? Did he think we willingly made slaves of ourselves?

'And we are not the ones who feast on people. At least we are able to tell the difference between friends and food.'

His eyes blazed at me and he raised his hand. I cringed, waiting for the blow to fall, but nothing happened. When I looked up, he was disappearing into the trees.

Where had he gone? Was he leaving? Had I gone too far? I bit my lip and scratched the back of my left heel with my right toe. If he left me, how would I get back to Kiskeya? How would I get to Iyanola? I had a boat but could not travel on water.

After a while I decided I could not sit doing nothing any longer. I went to stand in front of my canoe, trying to work out the best way to teach myself to paddle.

'Are you planning another trip?'

I spun round. Maruka had a pigeon and three lizards in one hand and his axe in the other. He threw the animals he had killed on the ground.

'For the first meal,' he said. 'Then we leave.'

59

The Rescue

I felt my heart fluttering in anticipation as we neared Iyanola. My eyes searched for familiar landmarks, but the island was not as it had been when we left. Without the Taino to slash and burn the bush to make fields and build canoes and houses, the forest had taken over.

I searched for the place where Caicihu and I had swum and dived during our morning baths. The large boulder from which we had jumped was barely noticeable among the new-grown bushes and trees.

The track which had led up to the village and which used to be plainly seen from the beach was completely hidden by shrubs. I stood up to see if I could glimpse the tops of any houses.

'Be careful, you will have us in the water if you move about like that.'

I sat down and turned to Maruka. 'It is so different. Not as I remembered it.'

He nodded. 'Change arrives too quickly when you are not there to welcome it.'

'It is not just the change. It is . . .' I searched my mind for my meaning. 'It is the loneliness. The island is lonely. It misses us, I think.'

'Perhaps it will be happy again, now that you have returned.'

I shook my head. 'It knows I cannot stay.'

Together we dragged the canoe up the beach away from the high tide mark. I looked around, trying to find out where I was. Without the path and the familiar trees I could not see where to start.

I looked towards the sky. I would have to plan my journey as I would on the ocean, using the sun and its position in the sky.

We found the remains of the path a little while later and Maruka hacked at the bushes with his axe. Once I had seen it, it was easier to head for the village.

Most of the houses were still standing, even though there was nobody to care for them. Some had trees growing up through the smoke holes. As we approached, an iguana waddled out of one *bohio*, stared at us and crawled away to hide amongst a pile of rocks. I heard the rustle of life from inside our old *caney*. I stood at the door, looking at the roof, part of which was now open to the sky. I did not enter, but left the animals undisturbed inside. I stooped and scooped a handful of earth from just inside the doorway, and thanked the spirits of the earth.

I turned towards the ball court. The hard earth which had been trampled flat by so many Taino feet was now a wilderness. But the guanabana tree was still there, its branches low with fruit.

I ignored the fruit and picked the three leaves my father had told me to pick, thanking the spirits of the tree as I did so.

Maruka had been leaning against one of the pillars around the ball court, watching me. I went over to him and laid the soil and leaves in a heap beside him.

'I have to visit our old *conuco*. Will you watch these until I return?'

He did not move. 'There will be no food left in those fields after all this time.' He nodded towards the guanabana tree. 'If you are hungry it would be wiser to pick one of those.'

It was his way of asking what I was doing. I thought about how he had brought me here when I had refused to tell him why I needed to come. Of how he had said nothing more after I had angered him. I thought of the way he had helped me to make the fire for the morning meal after he had brought the

329

bird and lizards for us to eat. Perhaps I should trust him. It would be easier to free Bibi with his help.

I told him about my mother's capture, watching his face closely all the time. If there was a spark of recognition I would stop. But his face remained without expression until I told him about my plan to rescue Bibi.

'Have you lost your senses? You cannot do this. You will be destroyed.'

'I have to do it.'

'Why? It may already be too late. It has been a long time. Your mother may no longer want to be rescued.'

'That is why I need the cassava and potatoes from the *conuco*. She will remember planting them and they will be payment for her release.'

'But why put yourself in danger?'

'She is my mother!' My words were heated by the fire of indignation.

My speech slowed as I told him the other reason I had to do it.

'Besides, I have taken the life of a man. It is a dreadful thing for a Taino to do. I might not be admitted to Coyaba when I leave this world, unless I make amends. If I do not, I may never see my family again when I die.'

His eyes narrowed. 'This man you killed. Was he Taino?'

'No, he was one of the pale men.'

A sound of disgust rose from his throat.

'You will not be punished for that. You will be rewarded.'

I shook my head though a smile eased its way to my lips at the violence in his voice. 'It is permitted to defend ourselves during war, or if we are attacked. But when I killed him, we were not at war.'

Maruka's look said he did not understand the ways of the Taino, but he nodded at the leaves and soil.

'If you are determined to do this foolish thing, I will help you. But we will wait until nightfall. Her jailors will not expect us at night.'

I stared at him in disbelief. 'Have you lost your wits? It will be more dangerous at night! I am not going on the water after nightfall.' It was just the kind of action Caicihu would have suggested, and my heart ached for my brother. We should have been doing this together, he and I.

Maruka's look was scornful. 'The Kalinago always attack at night. Where is your spirit of adventure?'

'Being kept from suicide by my spirit of good sense. I will not go on the water after dark. That is the time when the homeless ones walk.'

He sighed. 'In that case you had better get that *cohoba*.'

*

We sat in the canoe with the things I had gathered on the floor of the boat. Maruka stared at me. In spite of his words earlier, I could see he was as tense as I was. His skin shone with the oil I had rubbed into it.

He had not liked using the vomit stick, but I managed to convince him we could not ask the gods for protection unless we first emptied our bodies. Persuading him to scrub away his body paints with the digo root and wear the Taino ceremonial marks had been even more difficult.

'Who would be afraid of these markings? Your enemies will laugh at you.'

'We are not trying to frighten anyone. Not all battles are won by force.'

There was another struggle when it was time to pray to the *zemis* for protection. He would not pray to Huracan, but insisted that Maboya was the most fearsome god alive and we should ask him for safe travel rather than the gods who would continue to be good to us anyway. He did not understand.

In the end we prayed separately to our own gods, before we set out. But we had smoked the *cohoba* and tabaco together before we prayed, drawing the sacred smoke into our nostrils from the pipe we had made from the hollow stem of a trumpet tree leaf.

Now we sat in the canoe, and in my mind I practised the words Baba had taught me. I looked towards the land and saw the hill where I had stood and watched my mother, hands tied behind her, calling my name.

I scooped up the earth I had collected from the mouth of the abandoned *caney* and sprinkled it on the surface of the water. I whispered the words which Baba had told me to say. The words that would help my mother remember; that would call her to us.

For a few breaths I panicked. Should I have called my mother first or should I have fed the water spirits? I could not remember. If I angered them, Maruka and I could be dragged down into the deep.

I snatched the cassava and sweet potato I had collected from the old *conuco*. I watched them sink and then threw in the guanabana leaves.

'Spirits of the water, we offer you food.'

I took the earrings from my ears and dropped them over the side.

'We give you gold.'

With shaking fingers I unhooked the *zemis* from around my neck.

'In the name of Atebeyra, goddess of the earth, Huracan, god of the water, Yucahu, the supreme one—'

'And Maboya, god of the night.' I whirled round to see Maruka holding his *zemi* over the side of the boat as I was holding mine. His words were not part of the ones I had rehearsed with Baba. What if he spoiled the spell? What if he had angered the water spirits and turned them against us?

I opened my mouth to shout at him to put away his *zemi*, but I did not say the words. A wind had sprung up and the boat was bobbing on the small waves like an empty bean pod on the river.

Alarm was a bushfire inside me. Though Maruka tried to look unconcerned, his fingers had tightened round the string of the dangling *zemi* and his eyes had widened a fraction.

I gabbled the rest of the words, clutching the *zemis* tightly as I lowered them into the water.

'In the name of the *zemis*, I ask that you accept our gifts and release my mother. Here, in this place where she . . . died, I leave you these offerings in exchange for her spirit. Let her go to Coyaba in peace.'

The wind died as suddenly as it had woken. The waves flattened themselves and the sea was calm again. Then a ripple broke the surface and spread in a widening arc towards the land.

A sound like the sigh of the wind whispered around our heads and disappeared. I heard again my mother's voice, as clearly as I had that day. The wind had carried away a part of her words then, but I had heard enough to know she asked for my help.

'Anani, please save . . .'

I heard them again. But there was no wind today.

The last whisper of breeze had faded and I heard Bibi's words clearer than I had that day.

'Anani, please save . . . *yourself*!'

I gasped and clutched my chest, gulping mouthfuls of air to ease the breathlessness that suddenly overcame me. My mother had not been asking for help. She had been helping me! I understood now what I had not before.

I saw myself standing on the hill, screaming for Bibi, but unable to move. Saw the boat that held my mother turning back to the land. I heard Bibi shouting, 'Anani, please save . . . *yourself*!' Then I saw Bibi throwing herself backwards, hands tied, into the water, capsizing the boat as she went over.

I saw the Kalinago struggling to right the long canoe, recapturing the Taino girls and women who were trying to swim for shore; saw them searching in vain for Bibi. And I saw them climb back into the boat and leave without her.

I felt a touch on my arm. Maruka's face was concerned.

'Are you all right?'

I looked at him but did not see him. One thought circled my brain. Bibi had given her life to save me.

'It is over,' Maruka said. 'She is free now. The water spirits no longer hold her captive.'

I nodded. Finally, I had rescued my mother's spirit. Now a dreadful tiredness invaded my body so that my eyelids drooped and my head felt too heavy for my shoulders. I did not have the energy to move my tongue into speech.

'We should go.'

This time I could not even manage a nod. He took up the oar and turned the boat back towards the land.

'We will stay on Iyanola tonight and leave for home when the sun wakes.'

He could have suggested we walk to Kiskeya that night and I would not have had the strength to say no. When we reached the shore, I tried to get out of the canoe. My knees buckled and I would have fallen if Maruka had not held me.

His face swam in front of my eyes and, each time I tried to look at it, it moved away. I frowned, squinted to see it better, but my own head felt light now, as if it was flying away from my body.

60

Surprise Arrival

When I woke, the sun had already washed and left its house. Maruka was nowhere in sight. I searched the bushes with rising alarm. Surely he could not have deserted me? But my rapid breathing slowed when I saw the canoe nesting between two coconut palms. He could not be far away if the boat was still here.

'Your spirit has returned then?'

I whirled round. He was standing where the forest greeted the beach. His body had been scrubbed of the red *roucou* and white clay and he was painted like a Kalinago once again.

He came towards me and I saw that he had a large crab in his hand.

'I thought the water demons had taken your spirit

forever. But when I heard your snores I knew they had only borrowed you for a while.'

'I do not snore.'

He made a noise of amusement in his throat and squatted beside me.

'How do you feel?'

'Rested.'

'So you are ready to continue our journey?'

'Not before I have washed and eaten. I see you have caught a crab.'

He rose and nodded towards the forest. 'They are like fallen fruit on the ground. I have already eaten. This one is for you. I shall put it on to cook while you wash.'

I nodded, but as I turned towards the sea my forehead was wrinkled with uncertainty. The pale men had taught me to be distrustful, but perhaps it was time to unlearn that lesson.

The decision taken, I felt the tension seeping away and when I had bathed, I ran to find him, a broad smile on my face. His brows rose in enquiry and I shrugged. The pungent smell of roasting crab brought water to my mouth.

'Smells good.'

I sank on to the sand and reached for the crab. The meat was tender and sweet and I licked the juices from my fingers. My stomach welcomed the food with contented rumbles. I felt Maruka watching me eat and looked up. He spoke first.

'Has the time arrived yet?'

I paused, the crab suspended halfway between the embers and my mouth.

'The time for what?'

'For you to trust me with your name?'

I weighed the thoughts in my mind. Now that I had decided to trust him, there was no reason to keep my name from him.

'Anani. My name is Anani.'

He repeated the name, rolling it with his tongue.

'It is a good name,' he said. 'Water Flower. It sits well with you.'

I inclined my head in thanks. 'Now that we are hiding nothing from each other, is it time for you to tell me how you came to be on Kiskeya? And why were you following the winged canoe?'

His lashes lidded his eyes so that I could not see into them. I felt a twinge of unease. What did he conceal in his thoughts?

But almost at once his eyes were uncovered and a smile lightened their depths.

'I was fishing one day, two dry seasons ago. I had followed the fish into deep water and when I saw I was close to Guanahani I thought I would camp there for the night. It was while I was making a fire to cure the fish that I saw something I had never seen before. Giant canoes which moved without oars. And their noses were pointed to the island.'

339

I remembered my first glimpse of the pale men's canoes and shivered.

'I hid and watched. I saw them capture some of the Lucayans and when they left I followed to see what they would do with them.'

'Were you not afraid that you would be taken as well?'

His lips curled. 'I am Kalinago. A Kalinago does not keep company with fear. When we reached Kiskeya, I went ashore in the night and hid. I watched you welcome the strangers. I was planning to return home when the storm arrived. My canoe was lost and I could not leave.'

'So you waited to steal mine.' My brows furrowed. 'But why did you wait so long to steal it? You could have taken it at any time.'

'I did not want anyone to know I was there. When you came to shelter from the storm in the cave where I was hiding—'

I gasped. 'It was you in the sacred cave?'

'It was the first place I could find before the storm broke. It was dry and warm and I did not even have to hunt since you brought me food every day.'

I was speechless with shock for a few breaths. When I spoke my voice came out thick with fury, disbelief and confusion.

'You ate the food I left for the spirits!'

He shrugged. 'It would have been wasted if I had not had it.'

A feeling of sadness and disappointment put an end to the hot words that tried to tumble from my lips. The *zemis* had not liked my food after all. They had not been my friends. Now I understood why we had been overcome by the pale men. The *zemis* had not been protecting us.

'I was looking for shells to make new tools when I saw your men heading for the cave. I knew you would not want them to see the canoe, so I ran back and dragged it down to the cliff by the back entrance. I took it down to the beach and hid it in a small cave there until I had finished it.'

My eyes narrowed. 'The council visited the cave last dry season. It could not have taken you that long to finish the boat, so why did you not leave before?'

His lashes veiled his eyes again and I knew the words he was forming were those he wanted me to hear and not those which carried the truth. My distrust had returned with the knowledge that he had been spying on me and had eaten the food of the *zemis*. But how had he escaped from Iyanola? I burned to know but could not ask him without revealing that it was I who had left him for dead. He opened his mouth then seemed to change his mind about speaking and closed it again. He rose and dusted the sand from his body.

'It is time to go.'

We had not been long on the water when the island approached. I was puzzled when he directed the canoe towards it.

'Why are we stopping here?'

'You will see.' He was trying to disguise his excitement, but I caught it in the tension of his shoulders as he paddled towards the island, and in the way his eyes sparkled in the black circles he had painted around them. My uneasiness was now fully awake. He jumped from the boat almost before we had brought it into the shallows and hurriedly wedged it between two trees. Then he hunted along the beach.

'If you tell me what you are looking for I might be able to help you.'

He pounced on something among the stones and held it up with a triumphant smile. 'No need. I have found it!'

It was the large shell of a conch. Its pearly pinkness glowed softly as he put it to his lips. A long low moan sped from it and went floating over the tops of the trees. My heart stopped. Who was Maruka calling to? And what was he saying? The sounds were not the ones I was used to from the *guamos* of the Taino.

His message sent, he grabbed my hand and headed

towards the trees. I felt my curiosity flowering in spite of my doubts, so though my mind held a warning, my feet followed where he led.

We were suddenly in a clearing and I felt my breath lodge in my throat. Before us was a village of *caneys*. What kind of place was this where only caciques lived? I had no time to think about it. Maruka raised the shell to his lips again and its wail woke the houses. They poured out of the doorways and swarmed towards us. My eyes popped, my mouth fell open and my heart died inside me.

61

Caterpillar at a Chicken's Feast

My knees knocked against each other, however much I tried to stand up straight. My teeth chattered like parrots in a guangu tree and I clamped them together so hard that my jaw ached. I could not let them see how frightened I was.

I prayed that they would think my wide-eyed look was of amazement rather than uncaged terror.

I stared at the people ranged around me and met their curious gazes in silence.

After the first glance, the men ignored me, turning to greet Maruka. But the women and children continued to inspect me. I felt like a goose in a pen being considered for the pot. One of the men stepped forward. The strings of bones around his ankles and neck rattled as he moved, and the bone threaded through his nostrils shone white against the black of his face paint. A band of white across the upper part of his face was broken by the black rings around his eyes, so that he seemed to peer out from two deep pits.

I trembled as he came near, certain that my time to visit Coyaba had come. I should have tried to escape from Maruka on the way here. How could I have let him lead me to this place? Why had I believed him when he had promised to take me home? I knew the Kalinago could not be trusted. I had known it from birth.

The man spoke in a strange tongue. I glanced sharply at Maruka as words without meaning tumbled from his lips in answer. Had he learned my language so that he could trap me?

I thought of running now, but discarded the idea at once. My knees were shaking so badly that I would not have gone two steps before I was caught. I could not hope to fight my way out with the whole Kalinago tribe around.

An old woman who looked as if she should have long been resting with the ancestors hobbled from among the group of women.

She took Maruka's face in her wrinkled hands and brought it close to hers. She stared at him and I wondered how she could see through the milky whiteness that covered her eyes.

'So you have returned.' She spoke Taino as Maruka had done. A thick Taino, but Taino that I understood. Her voice was like the wind whispering through the bamboo groves.

'Thank Maboya that no harm came to you while you were from us. And you have been given a prize for your bravery.' Her strange eyes swivelled in my direction, then back to Maruka's face. 'From now on you will no longer be Wakanik the vanquished, but you will be Wakanik the conqueror.'

She continued to speak, but I did not hear the words. Why had she called him Wakanik? His name was *Maruka*. Perhaps she had lost control of her senses. I peered at her, then glanced at Maruka. He was listening to her, his head slightly bowed in respect. He was not treating her as if she had mislaid her wits.

She stretched out her hand and another woman sprang forward to give her a bowl. She took a sip from the dark liquid it held. She parted her blackened lips and hissed like a steaming volcano. Through the toothless gums, a spray of liquid flew and covered Maruka's left cheek. Another sip, another hiss and his right cheek was sprayed.

'Blessings,' she wheezed. 'Blessings.' She turned to shuffle back to the women.

I searched their faces, hoping to recognize some of the Taino women and girls who had been stolen from Iyanola, but there was no one who looked familiar.

The man who had stepped forward first stood, silent, beside Maruka, but when I glanced at him, I saw what looked like pride peeking out of the dark-rimmed eyes. I noticed how his lips under the black coating tilted a little to the side as if he was thinking of smiling, exactly the way Maruka's did. His eyes, too, were wide and piercing like Maruka's. This had to be his father.

He said something to Maruka, who beamed with pleasure and replied with the same strange words. I shook my head in confusion. Why did this man speak a different tongue from the woman?

I wanted to ask Maruka what was going on but my courage had deserted me. He did not seem to be the same person I had fished, hunted and shared meals with on the way here. The one who had helped me say goodbye to my mother.

'She must be prepared,' the old woman said.

Suddenly I was being dragged away by a group of women who had surged forward. I tried to resist, but the women were determined and my feet, without my permission, followed where they led.

I looked back at Maruka. He was the only one I knew in this strange place and although he had brought me here by trickery, lied to me about his name, and about many other things, I did not want to leave him.

He was being led away by the man who had come

to stand beside him. I willed him to look back at me, to tell me it would be all right, but he walked away without a glance in my direction. It was as if I no longer existed in his thoughts.

Despair came like a flash flood, threatening to drown me. We were moving towards the bush. What were they planning to do with me? What was I to be prepared for? The stories I had heard about the Kalinago surfaced in my mind. I could think of only one explanation.

I struggled, but the arms around me were like granite bands which I could not break. I searched for the old woman who had blessed Maruka. Perhaps I could reason with her in Taino, persuade her to let me go. She was nowhere in sight. I turned in desperation to one of the women on my right. Perhaps she spoke my tongue as the old woman did.

'Where are you taking me?'

She laughed and a knowing look visited her eyes.

'We are taking you to the water. You have to be prepared.'

The other women holding me giggled and I felt my heart somersault inside.

We came to a stream and the women stopped. One looked around and pulled a digo plant from the bank. She washed the earth from the root, then picked up a rock from the ground and her eyes measured my body.

I flinched. Surely they were not going to kill me with a rock! I fought with more energy than I knew I had. I would not accept death without a struggle.

The women holding me yelled as I managed to loose one hand and strike out at my captors. Another three women ran up and my brief revolt was over.

'I would not expect a Taino to be so afraid of water,' one woman said.

I noticed then that the woman with the rock was using it to beat the digo root against another rock. The stone was for crushing the digo root, not for smashing my head. I felt slightly foolish. They were not going to kill me – yet. There was still a chance I could escape.

I realized what the women were doing. As they scrubbed me with the digo plant and splashed the cool water over my body I wondered if they always took such care in cleaning their food.

'I have already had my morning bath,' I said.

The woman who had crushed the digo root smiled.

'Your morning bath cannot cleanse you for the ceremony,' she said.

'You have a special ceremony for eating people?'

She stared at me, her brows creased. Then, as my words pierced her mind, she threw back her head and laughed, a tinkling sound that was not unpleasant.

'Forget what you have heard. The Kalinago do not feast on young girls.'

'Are you saying the tales of Kalinago eating people are untrue?' She must have thought I had lived only one dry season to believe her!

Her hands paused in the act of rubbing digo into my left shoulder.

'It is not what it seems.'

She paused as if she was about to say something that she was not sure she should say. Then she shrugged.

'You will see for yourself that the men only take a small piece of those they defeat. It is so that the enemies' spirits can become a part of them. Each enemy whose flesh is tasted is another man's strength added to the Kalinago.'

I was horrified. 'It is worse than I have heard. You eat a man's spirit?'

She shook her head. 'Do you not see? The spirit of the man lives on in the Kalinago. So he is not gone forever.'

'I will not let you eat me.'

She laughed again. 'Only warriors taste flesh. And only warriors are tasted. A Kalinago male would not want the spirit of a girl inside him.'

I frowned. 'Then I do not understand. What ceremony do you prepare me for?'

She sent a knowing look towards the other women.

'You are to be mated to Wakanik. That is why he went to find you. We are preparing you for your betrothal.'

Someone had brought a bowl of food for me but it remained untouched on the floor where she had left it. I sat in a daze while the women rubbed *roucou* into my skin and drew patterns with white clay and soot over my face and body.

The shock of the women's words had left me without speech and I let them bathe me and take me to a *caney*, where the preparations continued.

'My son has chosen well.'

It was the woman who had told me about the ceremony. I turned my head to look at her and it felt like I had a massive pumpkin on my body which my neck could barely support. She was smiling and I was surprised to see a look of kindness in her eyes.

I shivered. I was still a child. I was not ready.

'I cannot be your son's mate.'

She nodded and understanding softened her face. I felt my spirits rising. Perhaps she would help me.

She gestured towards the other three women in the *caney*.

'We all felt the same once,' Maruka's mother said. 'When we were taken from our people to become Kalinago wives, we felt as if our lives were ending. But we have come to accept this life. You will see it is not as bad as you imagine.'

My eyes widened. 'You . . . you were captured?'

She nodded. 'My people live on Guanahani. We are Lucayan.'

The flame of hope flared inside. 'So you understand. I cannot be mated yet. I have not yet had my age-ceremony.'

She frowned and her eyes skimmed my body. 'How many dry seasons have you lived?'

'I have just come to the end of ten and two dry seasons.'

'Then why have you not had your age-ceremony?'

I opened my mouth to tell her how I had been taken captive by the pale men before the ceremony could take place, but there was a sound just outside and I looked up to see Maruka, who they called Wakanik, standing in the doorway.

'What is it, my son?'

'Uanhui would like to speak to Anani,' he said.

His mother frowned. 'But she is not ready, and there is something else to be done before the ceremony.'

Maruka glanced at me and his eyes widened for a breath. He looked at his mother and shook his head.

'There is no time for the ceremony now. We are preparing for war.'

62

Kalinago Council

First came a flood of relief that I was not to be betrothed after all. Then came alarm and concern that the Kalinago were preparing for war. Which poor people were they about to destroy this time? But these thoughts were quickly buried by a burning anger against the boy who had tricked me into coming here with him.

I whirled on Maruka as soon as we left the house.

'You traitorous son of a snake. You twisted viper! You spawn of a toad! You promised to take me home. I should have known a Kalinago's word is not worth the breath that speaks it.'

His look was scornful. 'Save your words. I said I would take you home. I did not say I would take you to *your* home.'

'You . . . you knew I would think you spoke of Kiskeya.'

'Then it is your thinking which is at fault.'

'And I suppose I also imagined you said your name was Maruka when what you meant was *Wakanik*.' I laced my words with as much disdain as I could.

He shrugged. 'My name is Wakanik *and* Maruka. Maruka is my travel name.'

I stopped, forcing him to stop too. 'A travel name? I have never heard of such a thing.'

His brows rose. 'And I am to be blamed for your ignorance? No Kalinago would travel with his real name.'

'Why not?'

He spoke as if to a young child. 'Because, if we did, an evil spirit might hear our name and use it to harm us.' He paused. A grin spread across his face, and I saw again the boy with whom I had shared so much on our journey there. 'Or a sly Taino girl might steal it and try to send us *nameless* to the land of the dead.'

I gasped. 'You knew who I was all along?'

'From the moment I saw you on the beach in Kiskeya, welcoming the pale strangers to your home.'

I stared at him. 'But how did you escape from Iyanola? I thought you were dead.'

He shook his head. 'The knock on the head had taken my memory. For days afterwards I did not know who or where I was. I saw the smoke from your cooking fires and headed for them, but I had broken my leg and arm. I could only crawl a little each day before the blackness claimed me. It must have been days before I came to your village.'

I had my hand over my mouth, aghast at what he was saying, forgetting for a moment that he was my enemy. 'You must have suffered so much pain!'

'The Kalinago are not strangers to pain. It is part of the ceremony which welcomes us to manhood. But my useless limbs were a hindrance.'

'Why did we not see you?'

'You had gone by the time I found your village, and it was another two days before my people returned. Once they realized I was not in any of the canoes which had returned from Iyanola, they came back, as I knew they would. Thank Maboya that Uanhui had come with them. She knew the herbs and potions to make me well again and she gave my memory back to me. Now we are expected in the council of war. We have kept them waiting long enough.'

I did not move. A seed of concern was growing in my thoughts.

'Why do you need me in your council of war?'

'Even though I have been there I do not know Kiskeya as well as you do. You will be able to guide us when we attack.'

'If you think I would guide you to attack my people again you must be—'

'Attack your people?' He put a hand to his head as

if he had given up trying to make me understand. 'We do not plan to attack your people.'

He spoke as if the idea was too outrageous to be considered. As if the Kalinago would never think of attacking the Taino.

'We go to fight the pale men!'

'Oh.' I felt my outrage expiring like a live coal in water. It took a while for his meaning to lodge itself in my brain. 'Why do you want to fight them? They are far from you. They do not harm you.'

'The pale men have raided our villages, stolen the women we captured. They have killed some of our men with their sticks which spit fire. They are our enemies. But we cannot fight them alone.'

'So now you need our help? Why should we help you?'

His look was scornful. 'You need us more than we need you. This enemy is stronger than both our tribes. But our elders say when spider webs unite they can tie up a raging iguana. Now come, the men are waiting for us in the *carbet*.'

'Wait!'

'What is it now?'

'What is your cacique's name? I must show my respect by giving him his title when I address him.'

His smile said I had asked a silly question. 'The Kalinago do not need leaders while they are at home. Leaders are chosen for fishing and fighting expeditions according to their ability. It is not yet known who will lead this trip.'

The *carbet* was a large *caney*. Hammocks hung from the roof posts, but the men were seated in a circle on the floor, holding axes as if about to fight. In the middle of the circle sat Uanhui, the old woman who had welcomed Wakanik.

I sat down where Wakanik indicated, beside his father, and he sat next to me.

'Welcome to the council of warriors, Anani,' the old woman said. 'Wakanik told us how you defeated him on the island of Iyanola, took his honour from him. We salute your bravery.' Surprise held my tongue captive. 'When he vowed to find you, bring you here and regain his honour, we did not believe he could do it on his own. But our son has proved us wrong. He searched all the islands until he found you.'

She warbled a ululation and the men shouted something in their language. I guessed it was in praise of Wakanik because he did not join in, but his eyes shone with pride.

So he had lied about how he came to be on Kiskeya too. He had not been following the pale men. He had been looking for me. From now on I would not swallow his words without the seasoning of disbelief.

Uanhui turned her attention back to the men. 'So it is decided. We travel to Kiskeya in five days with the

357

rising sun and Amaru will lead. He has taught his son well and excelled in the last war. He is a worthy leader.'

All the men turned to Wakanik's father and he inclined his head to show that he accepted the honour, but his dark eyes were as fierce as before and the blackened lips did not part in a smile.

Uanhui spoke again.

'The pale men came to our island without being invited. They stole the women the Kalinago worked so hard to find.'

There was a roar of anger from the men.

'They stole the young girls we were grooming as wives for our sons.' Another roar.

So these were the Kalinago the Almirante had rescued our people from. For a breath I did not know where my loyalties should be: with the pale men for rescuing my people or with the Kalinago for making war on the invaders. But my indecision lasted only a breath. The Taino that the pale men had rescued were now dead or enslaved. If they had been with the Kalinago they would still have had a life.

'From Guanahani to Kiskeya, Boriken to Hamaica and Cubanakan, they have taken the land and enslaved the people.'

The roars were getting louder, angrier. I glanced at Wakanik. His face was contorted with rage, just like the faces of the others. I did not recognize him.

'The pale men have taken the people's gold and

destroyed their gods. Soon they will turn their attention to the land of the Kalinago. They will enslave our children, kill our men and take our women as wives.'

The men jumped to their feet and chopped the air with their axes.

'Will the Kalinago wait for those sons of turtles to come?'

I looked up, expecting the roof to be lifted from the posts by the noise and the pounding of feet. Uanhui's voice became more strident as she goaded the men into a frenzy. I wondered if it would be considered rude if I covered my ears. They hurt so much from the noise that I expected something inside them to break.

Then as suddenly as she had started her tirade, Uanhui stopped. The men, though, were only just beginning. Still in the circle, they started to dance. I guessed it was a war dance by the way they chopped the air with their axes as if they were severing an enemy's head from his body. The cries rang in time to the pounding of their feet and the dipping and rising of their bodies. Without my permission, my mind was captured. Eyes wide, I watched as if under a spell. I watched the necklaces of bone bouncing around their necks, the anklets of bone, shell and feathers bouncing in time to the dance; the way the bones in their lips and noses flashed white as they moved their heads sharply to the right and left as if stalking an animal. But most of all, my gaze was drawn to the vicious chops of the axes, and I thanked Yucahu that the Kalinago were not preparing to fight the Taino.

A hand touched me on the shoulder and I started. I had not noticed Uanhui leaving the circle. Her white-glazed eyes stared down at me and I gazed into their milky depths, repelled and fascinated at once.

'You are to tell the men everything you know about the pale men,' she said. 'Where and when they eat, sleep, work, relieve themselves. Everything.'

Then she was gone, leaving me sitting on the ground inside the circle of yelling, war-hungry Kalinago.

63

Preparations

'You will not be allowed to take that.'

'I am not leaving my canoe.'

'It is too slow. You will travel with us in one of the war canoes.'

My face was set and I placed my hand protectively on my boat. I had been cleaning it, ready for the journey, when Wakanik had come to find me. I still thought of him as Maruka sometimes, even though I now knew his real name.

He glared at me. 'Must you always argue?'

I scowled at him. 'Must you always ask me to do impossible things? You know how long I took to make this boat. It brought you all the way from Kiskeya. How can you just abandon it now?'

He sighed. 'The long boats travel fast. There are at

361

least ten men five times over in each war canoe. Your little boat could not keep up.'

In my mind's eye I saw the pale men's boats and how the wind could send them skimming across the water. But when there was no wind, they lay on the surface like slugs on pumpkin leaves. What they needed was a canoe which did not just rely on the wind. One which could be used when the wind was resting. I turned to smile at Wakanik.

'If I can make it go as fast as the war canoes, then can I take it with me?'

His laughter was spiked with scorn. 'If you can make it go as fast as the war canoes I, Wakanik, will take you to Kiskeya in it.'

I tried to hide my smile but it was difficult.

'I have your word?'

'Have I not said? But you had better hurry with this magic you intend to perform. We leave with the sun in five days.' Then he was gone.

I went to find his mother. She shared my plan and soon a group of women were weaving cotton as if their lives depended on it. I joined them, for once enjoying the scrape of the spindle on my thigh, the pull of the thread through my fingers.

Uanhui hobbled over as we were fastening two pieces of the spun cloth together. When she found out what we were doing, she cackled, throwing back her head so we had a perfect view of her toothless gums.

362

'Did I not tell Wakanik a girl who tricked him as you did should be watched closely? What a match you and he will make!'

Still chuckling, she shuffled away, but her words had chased the pleasure from my mind. Did she still expect me to be mated to Wakanik? Did she think once I had returned to Kiskeya I would be coming back here? She must be losing her mind as well as her teeth.

Once we had sewn the cloths together, we took the material down to the canoe and I realized I had a problem. How was I going to attach the wing to the boat?

'If you had a hole in the boat you could put a stick into it and tie the cotton to the stick.' It was the woman who had bathed me with the digo root.

Wakanik's mother snorted. 'If there was a hole in the boat, Naniki, the water would get in and the boat would sink.'

'Perhaps not,' I said. Naniki had given me an idea. The women looked at me, puzzled. I explained and their doubtful expressions gave way to wide grins.

'You have been blessed with a large brain, Anani. I cannot wait to see the men's faces when they see this.'

64

Fighting the Kalinago Way

'You are to come with us.'

'Where?'

'To the training ground. Uanhui has decided you are to be taught how to fight like a Kalinago.'

The training ground was a clearing among the trees and I was surprised to see a number of women and girls lined up with the men and boys. Wakanik looked round to see why I had stopped and read the surprise on my face.

'What is it?'

'The women fight with the men?'

'The men are not always home. The women must be able to defend themselves if they are attacked.'

It seemed a good idea to me. If the Taino had thought like that, my mother might still be alive.

Wakanik's father and three of the other men were standing before the line of warriors. He signalled to us to join the group and then spoke.

'The pale men are well armed. Their fire-spitting sticks can kill from a long distance. We will need to use our arrows much more than our axes and spears. So let us perfect our shooting.'

For the rest of the morning we worked without stopping. Wakanik's father, Amaru, and the three men with him, each took a number of people to work with. Wakanik and I were in the group with Amaru.

The shooting target was a leaf at the top of a large kapok tree. At least I would not disgrace myself. I had shot arrows much farther than that while hunting. I smiled inwardly, thankful that I had learned to shoot with Caicihu. But the thought of Caicihu reminded me of him being carried on the men's shoulders with a Kalinago arrow in his back. One of these men might have killed him. The thought brought shivers to my joints so that my hand trembled as I raised the bow.

The first of my three arrows went sailing off a long way below the target. There were murmurs of sympathy from the women and sighs of resignation from the men. They probably thought that they would have to spend most of the morning teaching me to shoot. My anger at what they had done to Caicihu still simmered. I breathed deeply. The breath cooled my rage so that it hardened into determination.

I squinted at the yellow leaf. The arrow sped, swift as thought, and pierced the centre. The leaf fell to earth, still fastened to the tip of the arrow.

There was a hush. I felt the eyes of everyone trained on me. Then the women stamped their feet and yelled. The men watched me in silence, but something like the child of respect had visited their eyes.

Amaru nodded at my last arrow and pointed to another yellow leaf. It was almost at the top of the tree.

I armed the bow, keeping my eyes on the leaf so that it filled my vision and I saw nothing else. I raised the arrow slowly, trained my sight along it until the tip was centred on the leaf, pulled and released it. The leaf said goodbye to the tree as the other had done.

My success with the bow and arrow was shadowed by my uselessness with the axe and spear. With the bow and arrow I could pretend the leaves on the trees were birds; food for the Taino. It was not as easy to forget that the wooden post was supposed to be a man.

I approached it with fierceness enough, but each time I lifted my arm to strike, the picture of a face swam before my mind's eye, and the Taino reverence for life asserted itself. The strike was without force; unlikely to dent the skin, much less kill a man.

Amaru was losing patience. 'You will be killed before you can blink twice if you approach a pale man

366

like that. You are trying to kill him, not asking him to marry you.'

I felt the shame mask my face as the women tittered. Wakanik came up to me.

'Think of your father,' he said.

I did. The blood rushed to my head, washed there by a wave of anger and despair. The axe connected with the post and it split in two.

'That is better,' Amaru said into the silence.

I stepped back so that one of the women could take her turn. Now I knew how to overcome my worries about killing them, I was ready for the pale men.

65
Homeward

My canoe sped across the water, the wind in the wing pushing it faster than I could have dreamed. I stood holding the two poles to which the wings were fastened, moving the wing from side to side as the wind changed. We had learned that it was best if we did not guide the canoe straight into the wind, but let it fill the wing from the side.

Wakanik saw my smile and grinned. He looked back and saw that the long canoes were far behind. He whooped and dipped the oar even harder into water.

'If the wind goes with us like this all the way, we will be in Kiskeya long before the others.'

'That will teach them to laugh at my boat.'

'It is a lesson they will not forget in a hurry.' His grin disappeared. 'And neither will I. I am sorry I mocked with the rest of the men. I should have known better.'

I shifted uneasily. I was not used to his praise. I pulled my gaze from his and sent it back to the other canoes. One of the men was waving his oar at us and I forgot my awkwardness.

'I think they want us to stop.'

He glanced behind him and a smile played across his face. 'They do not like to be left behind. Shall we ignore them?'

I shook my head as I folded the wing to bring the canoe to a crawl. 'They might have something important to say.'

The lead canoe came alongside us and Wakanik's father spoke to us.

'The Taino did not lie,' he said. 'Her canoe goes like the wind. You will go ahead of us to Kiskeya and prepare the Taino there for war. The more people we have to fight with us, the surer our victory will be.'

He did not speak to me, but he inclined his head in my direction. Wakanik's brows rose and a smile tickled the corners of his mouth, but he said nothing.

His father motioned to the men in his boat and waved us on. Wakanik turned to me.

'Put the wing on the canoe, Anani,' he said. 'Let us go . . . like the wind.'

66
Arrival

It was early evening when we arrived. The Taino should have been in the square, having their *areito*. The cacique should have been telling the stories that taught us our history. There should have been laughter and song, dancing, and the squeals of Taino children. Instead, the village was as silent as the people who journeyed to Coyaba. The square was empty and the *bohios* were quiet.

I headed for the *caney*. My heart ached at the sight of the unswept streets, the *bohios* with their thatch needing repair, the dead communal fire. It was hard to believe anyone lived here and my heart raced with the thought that suddenly visited me. Had the Taino all gone away? If so, how would I find them? I ran towards the *caney* with Wakanik close at my heels, but my steps slowed at the door, fearful of what I would find inside.

I turned to Wakanik. 'I think it is best if you wait here.'

He nodded and, taking a deep breath, I stepped inside.

67

Reunion

'Maruka! Are you a spirit?'

I laughed, though tears were threatening to bathe my face. 'Karaya, look at my navel. I am no ghost.'

'But when . . . how did you get here? I thought you had gone to the pale men's land.'

'They tried to take me there but, as you can see, they did not succeed.'

She peered behind me. 'And your father? Is he with you?'

She saw the answer in my face, and hers crumpled.

'I am sorry, Karaya. I could not save him.'

She folded me in her arms and I felt the warm moistness of her tears on my shoulders. Her bones dug into my flesh and my heart ached for her. Like all the Taino, Karaya was no longer getting enough to eat. I blinked rapidly to clear the tears from my eyes, and looked around the *caney*. A few of my younger brothers and sisters huddled in a corner, their eyes wide with fear and confusion. They had probably been told they would never see me again. I scanned the faces but the one I searched for was not there.

I drew back from Karaya. 'Where is Nito?'

A cloud darkened her eyes. My heart leaped painfully in its cage. 'What has happened? Nito is well?'

She took a time to answer and I held my breath, willing her to speak but fearing to hear her words.

'Perhaps now you have returned from the dead you might be able to bring her back as well.'

My heart stopped. 'Where is she?'

'In your cave by the river. But Maruka,' she stopped me as I turned to run from the *caney*, 'I must warn you, she is not as she was when you left.'

My voice was thick with apprehension. 'How do you mean?'

'Nito does not speak any more.'

'I do not understand, Karaya. Is something wrong with her tongue?'

Karaya was weeping openly now, so it was difficult to hear her words. 'Go to her. Please try to bring her back.'

I hastened towards the door of the *caney*. I had to

get to Nito. Wakanik was still standing by the door where I had left him. I had forgotten he was there. I turned back and almost bumped into Karaya. Before I could introduce Wakanik, she saw him and her scream brought the women running from their *bohios*. They took one look at his decorations and shrieked. I took hold of Wakanik and pushed him behind me. When they saw that I was not fearful of him, the women stopped their screams.

'Karaya! It is well. This Kalinago is with me. His name is Wakanik. He will not harm you. He has come to help us.'

As my words penetrated, Karaya held up her hand and the babble from the women stopped. Her gaze did not leave Wakanik. I could see she did not trust him not to attack if she did not watch him.

Wakanik did not like being sheltered behind a girl. I could tell by the way he gently but firmly shoved me aside to stand facing the women. There was a movement among the group as though they were preparing to flee. He held up his hands, palms turned outward to show he had no weapons. The women recognized the sign of peace and remained where they were, but their bodies were still poised for flight.

'It is as your daughter says,' he said. 'I have come to help you fight the pale strangers who rob and kill your people.'

Karaya laughed; a sound without mirth. 'What

can you do against fire-spitting sticks and death rods? Can you stop the pale men's horses from trampling you into the ground; their giant dogs from eating you while the life still beats in your veins? You are only a boy.'

A dangerous light flashed in his eyes but he did not speak to Karaya. Instead, he turned to the other women assembled before him.

'I am not alone. Even now the war canoes of the Kalinago are on their way here. They have sent us ahead to prepare you for the fight against the pale men.'

A ripple of fear went through the Taino when they heard about the war canoes. They did not trust the Kalinago and I could not blame them. It would be up to me to assure them that he spoke the truth.

'Women of the Taino —' my voice was urgent — 'this is my friend. You remember I was taken by the pale men in their winged canoe? I would have died if he had not rescued me. He is no longer our enemy. He is on our side.'

The women edged closer. I wanted to tell them more about the war plans of the Kalinago, but I also wanted to see Nito. When I saw that they were willing to listen to Wakanik, I edged away. I was going to find my sister.

68

More Reunions

The path to the beach where I had bathed only ten and five days before was getting overgrown. I was halfway down when I heard footsteps coming towards me. I slipped among the trees, blending into them.

As the footsteps neared I realized that they were not the steps of a pale man. They were too light. When the owner of the footsteps came into view my eyes widened.

He wore the parrot-feather headdress of the cacique, but his steps did not carry him with any of the dignity or pride belonging to a cacique. His shoulders were hunched as if he was preparing for a blow to his head, and he moved as if his feet were weighted with large rocks, making furrows in the leaves on the path.

I stepped from my hiding place and he yelled,

raising his arm to ward off the evil he thought had overtaken him.

'Stay away from me.' He raised the staff, which my father had been given as a present, like a shield in front of him. I should have been angry with him for what he had done, but he looked so broken that I could only find pity for him in my heart.

'It is me, Azzacca,' I said.

The staff descended slowly, but the wariness did not leave his eyes. 'How did you get here?'

'It is a lengthy tale, which I am happy to tell you later. But what has happened here? Why do you look as if you have been to Coyaba and back?'

'I am tired, that is all. I have been working in the mines all day.'

My brows climbed my forehead. 'The caciques have been forced into the mines as well?'

He shook his head. 'I go of my own will. Your father has taught me well. I could not let my people labour while I enjoyed a life of idleness.'

I frowned. This was not like Azzacca. I studied my cousin. Perhaps he would be a better cacique than I had thought he could ever be. Then I remembered he was only cacique because he was a traitor and my spirit hardened.

'If you had not been so hasty to betray your family you would have found the cacique's *duho* easier to sit on.'

His face was a picture of bewilderment. If I had not known him so well I would have believed he did not know what I was speaking of.

'The meaning of your words escapes me, Maruka.'

'Do not mistake me for a fool, Azzacca. I know how you sold Baba and me to the Gobernador.'

'I sold—?'

He did not finish. I had seen a movement behind him and my attention was now on the figure trembling on the path, mouth open in a silent scream.

69

Confession

I rushed to gather Nito in my arms, shocked to see how her eyes almost filled her face; how her skin seemed to want to get as far away as it could from her bones. She backed away. Her slightly swollen stomach heaved with anxiety and her head moved from side to side in denial.

Her voice was like the wind whispering across the dry leaves of the forest floor.

'Have you come to take me to Coyaba?'

'Nito, it is I. I have not died.'

Her top lip bulged where her tongue worried the gap in her teeth.

'Is that the truth?'

'Have I ever spoken twisted words to you?'

She shook her head, but she was still not convinced. I squatted before her and folded her to me.

'Nito, Nito!' I rocked her in my arms and our tears mingled.

'You have not come to punish me?'

Her head was lowered to the ground in shame and I raised her chin so that her eyes were forced to meet mine.

'Why would I want to punish you?'

'You do not know?'

At the shake of my head her gaze again fell to the ground.

'It was I who told the pale men where you and Baba had gone.'

'Nito, what are you saying? Why would you do that?' She must have been visited by a lying evil spirit. Her words did not make sense.

'I promised Atebeyra I would not speak again until she brought you home. If I had not spoken, you and Baba would not have been taken away.' Her eyes sparkled for a breath with the light that used to be always in them. 'Has Baba come back with you?'

While I searched for the words to tell her gently, she read my answer in my eyes. Her face caved in on itself. She allowed me to hold her and rock her while the sobs shook her bony frame.

After a while Azzacca spoke. 'We should go. It is almost time for the spirits to walk.'

*

While we travelled back to the village I learned the story of her deception from Nito. The pale men had come looking for Baba. Because none of the Taino men would tell them anything, the pale men started cutting out their tongues. Nito had screamed at them to leave the men alone. She had forgotten the pale men were not to know she spoke their language. The Gobernador had seized her.

'So you speak Espanol, do you, little parrot?' He had squatted in front of her and his silver fire-spitting stick caressed her cheek. 'Tell me, where is the cacique?'

It was a direct question. Nito was bound to answer. But she had been frightened for us.

'You will not harm them?' she had asked. 'My sister Maruka and my father. You will not harm them?'

He had smiled. 'They will come to no harm. I promise.'

To Nito that promise was as binding as the silver ropes the pale men used to tie the Taino. She told him what he wanted to know.

70

A Gathering

I stared at Nito. It was difficult to make sense of her words. Azzacca was not responsible for our capture.

My father and I had misjudged him. My gaze met his and I felt the footsteps of shame creeping over my face.

'I am sorry, cousin. I thought you had betrayed us.'

He grimaced. 'I made it easy for you to doubt me. I have been foolish. I believed the pale men were spirits long after it was clear that they were not.'

We walked the rest of the way to the village in silence. Nito clutched my hand as if fearful I would disappear if she let go.

We entered the square and my mouth fell open at the scene in front of me. Wakanik was sitting on the ground, surrounded by the women and the children who had come out to join their mothers. They were no longer afraid of him. How had he managed to gain their trust so soon?

We sank to the ground behind the women. Their gazes were fixed on Wakanik. They had not even noticed we were there. He was just coming to the end of his story about how we had escaped from the pale men. The women murmured in admiration.

'And now we must fight; we must chase them back to their own land.'

The women shifted uncomfortably and I could almost taste their fear. It was a great task we were asking of them, but it had to be done. But I was sent reeling by Wakanik's next words.

'Do not fear. Only the men will be required to fight.'

What was he saying? We could not hope to win a fight against the pale men unless *everybody* fought. We were at a disadvantage anyway. Why would we give ourselves even less chance by keeping the women from the war? I leaped to my feet.

'Of course the women must fight!' There were sounds of protest around me.

His jaw jutted in the way that said his mind was made up. 'Women do not take part in war.'

'But your women fight. I trained with them.'

'They train to defend themselves if attacked. Not to take part in war.'

'So the women coming here in the war canoes have just come for the ride?'

'They cook for the men on the journey. They do not go into battle.'

I could hear from the edge in Wakanik's voice that his patience was taking leave of him, but now that I had buried my misgivings, I was determined to wage war to avenge my father.

'So if the women do not fight,' I said, 'who will?' My hand swept across the assembly. 'You can see there are no men here. How will you train them while they work in the mines?'

'Perhaps I can help.'

I turned to Azzacca and knew my surprise was written on my face.

'How?' I asked.

'I work with the men in the mines. I can take messages to them. I can bring them here.'

Although I did not say anything, he saw the doubt in my face.

'I am the cacique. They will listen to me.' The shadow of the old Azzacca covered his face. The words held a touch of his former arrogance and I smiled, surprised to find I was glad to see a glimpse of the boy I had known. The broken, disillusioned look did not sit comfortably on him.

I looked around at the women, hoping at least one of them felt like me; that one person wanted to avenge the death or enslavement of a husband or brother, the death or abuse of a sister or daughter. But a lifetime of gentleness and abhorrence of violence could not be shrugged off in an evening.

Karaya got to her feet and came to place her arm around my shoulders. She peered into Nito's face and Nito's shy smile brought tears to her eyes.

'Thank you, Maruka,' she whispered.

I should have told her Maruka was no longer a name I could wear, but I could not speak. Disappointment was a closed door in my throat.

'I know you would like us to fight.' Karaya squeezed my shoulders and pulled me close to her. 'But these are Taino women. We will never be fighters, no matter how much training we have.'

I nodded. In spite of my words, deep down I knew she was right. The Taino women could not fight.

But I could. And if I had to, I would.

71
Handouts

My stomach was grumbling. It was past the time of the evening meal, but no fires were lit in the compound.

'Karaya, when do we eat?'

Karaya turned her head towards the wall of the *caney*. 'There is no food.'

'What do you mean? The *conucos* could not have been emptied in the short time I have been away.'

'It is true.' Nito's eyes were large dark pools in her face. I looked from Karaya to Nito and back again.

'The pale men have taken the *conucos*. The land is theirs now,' said Karaya sadly.

'I do not understand. The land belongs to all the people. How can the pale men have taken it?'

Perhaps they had not understood properly what the pale men had said.

'Where is Biji?' I realized I had not seen her or her mother among the women.

'Biji has been taken by one of the pale men to the other side of the island where they have their other village.'

'So if Biji was not here to put meaning to the pale men's words, you could have misunderstood them.'

Karaya laughed, a sound so without mirth it sent shivers skittering down my spine.

'We did not misinterpret their actions. Some of the Taino went to the *conucos* as usual to reap the cassava we had planted. The pale men caught them and cut off their hands and noses. That is the punishment, they said, for stealing.' A sob caught in her throat. 'How can someone steal what is already theirs?'

There was a knock on the post by the doorway of the *caney*. Karaya smiled and sniffed.

'Here is our meal. We are lucky he comes today. Sometimes he has to visit the other villages and then we must sleep with empty stomachs.'

A pale behique stood in the doorway, a basket in his hand. He squinted in the gloom of the *caney*. 'I have brought you some food,' said the Padre in his imperfect Taino.

I shook my head, trying to understand. How could

387

the Taino, who had fed so many tens of pale men, now be dependent on one pale behique for scraps?

Wakanik had been silent by my side while Karaya spoke. Now he reached for my hand and squeezed it. 'Soon,' he whispered. 'Soon.'

72

Kalinago Arrival

Although they had accepted Wakanik, the Taino were still unprepared for the army of Kalinago that descended on the village.

We heard the sound of the conch and Wakanik disappeared into the forest to lead the men to the village. In true Kalinago fashion, they had arrived at night. I offered to go with him to welcome them, but he shook his head and nodded to the fire where the coneys, snakes and lizards he and I had hunted were cooking. 'Make the food ready. They will be hungry.'

The night before, we had crept from the *caney* and I led him to the *conuco*. The rest of the Taino might be reluctant to reap from the fields the pale men had stolen, but I had no guilty feelings about harvesting what the Taino had planted. On the way back we had

389

managed to catch three *hutias* and they simmered in the pepperpot with the lizards and snakes.

All day, while the women had been working in the pale men's *conucos*, Karaya, Nito and I had grated and squeezed cassava and made *casabi*. Yams, sweet potatoes, chow-chows, pumpkins and maize made up the rest of the meal.

Once the visitors were fed, Azzacca spoke as cacique.

'The Taino welcome the Kalinago to Kiskeya. We have not always been friends, but now we can put enmity aside for the greater good of us both.'

He inclined his head to acknowledge the stamping of his listeners.

'This war will not be easy. Our men are weak from lack of food and overwork. But the thought of freedom has lent strength to their bones. They are ready to fight.'

He sat down to more stamping, and Amaru, leader of the Kalinago army, stood. His oiled skin glistened in the firelight. The dancing flames played with the ornaments he wore, lighting the empty eye-sockets of the skull on his belt and bouncing from the bones in his nose and neck.

'Taino, my son has told you of our quarrel with the pale men. It is true we have been enemies in the past. But now we have a common enemy. We must prepare well for this war.'

His gaze skimmed the assembled Taino. 'We know you have no stomach for war. But when a shark cannot find the fish to feed on, it has no choice but to make do with crabs. We will show you how to fight like Kalinago. Then you will be able to defend yourselves against the pale parasites.'

I wondered that the Taino were not put out by Amaru's words, but then I remembered how slow the Taino were to take offence. Had I been like that once? Slow to anger and trusting of everyone? I had a feeling that once, before Caicihu and Bibi died, I was like other Taino. But that was a long time in the past.

The Kalinago sat with Azzacca late into the night, making plans. Azzacca did not go to the mines the next day. He told the plans to Karaya and me.

'The Kalinago will show the Taino how to use the forest as a hiding place.' He turned to me. 'And you will take the women into the mountains.'

He pointed to the smoky hills above the village.

'There are caves there where the Taino can stay.'

'What about the men?' I asked.

'I will train them in the mines. The pale men never go underground. We will not be discovered.'

I frowned. 'But if you are training, there will be less gold mined. The Espanoles will become suspicious.'

'Do not worry. We will be careful. We fight the pale men in three days. On the third day the Taino will not go into the mines or the fields. The pale

391

men will come to find out why, and we will be waiting. In the meantime we need to dig holes in the streets.'

'Why?' Karaya asked.

'Traps for the horses. We will cover them with leaves. The horses will fall into the holes, making it easier to attack the pale men. Will you come to help?'

I followed him, wondering at the excitement in his eyes. The life had returned to them since the Kalinago had arrived. He was no longer the Azzacca, the child I had known and fought with. He was a true cacique.

73

Battle Cries

I checked that I had remembered everything. My axe
was in my belt, my bow on my shoulder, my arrows in
my pouch. Karaya was packing the cooking pots and
bowls into baskets. Azzacca burst through the door of
the *caney*.

'Leave those,' he yelled. 'Run. The pale men are
coming!'

But how? We were not ready. The sun had just
left its bed. How had the pale men missed the Taino
already? We had barely finished painting our bodies
with a dark dye that would help us to blend in with
the forest.

Karaya did not move. Her eyes were pools where
terror swam unhindered.

Azzacca grabbed the bowl she was holding and

hurled it into the corner, where it smashed. The sound was like a signal. Karaya snatched two of the young ones in her arms and made for the door, followed by the other women and children.

'Take the women to the hills, Maruka. Hurry!'

I felt Nito's hand slide into mine and as I leaped for the door I thought I should have told the Taino I was no longer to be known as Maruka. Why I thought that then I could not say.

Outside was chaos. Women and children ran like scattered hens in every direction. I slipped my hand from Nito's. 'Wait here!' I dived back inside the *caney* and collided with Azzacca coming out.

'Are you still here?'

'I need the *guamo*.'

He understood.

I lifted the shell from the wall where it hung and raised it to my lips as I ran from the *caney*. The first sound was a feeble wheeze. I took a deep breath and blew as if the island of Kiskeya was sinking into the sea.

The frenzy stopped and the women hurried towards me. And so we followed the drill the Kalinago had taught us and melted into the trees.

We moved fast, but not fast enough. The clatter of the horses' feet told us that the pale men were almost upon us. I whistled like a pitcherie.

At once the women and children threw themselves

to the ground and wriggled under bushes and behind trees as they had been taught. I pressed my body into the trunk of a kapok tree, becoming one with its spirit.

Just then a horse reared into the clearing, followed by tens more.

The men who sat on their backs had their shiny digging sticks by their sides. Their fire-spitting sticks rested on their laps.

I turned as the last of the horsemen passed. The women and children were crawling from their hiding places, each face telling of the fear we all shared.

I opened my mouth to tell them to hurry. My mouth remained open but no words came. A numbing cold was creeping through my joints. A picture flashed before my eyes and I cried out in despair.

'What is it, Maruka?' Karaya was by my side, holding me.

'I have to go back. You take the women up the mountain. I have to go.'

Before she could say anything else I was racing through the trees, back the way I had come. My heart on my tongue, I sprinted to the village.

74
War

The smoke from the pale men's weapons snaked into
my eyes, my nose, my throat. The screams of dying
Taino combined with the boom-boom-boom of the
fire-spitters to form a ghastly music. I knew they were
Taino screams. The Kalinago did not recognize pain
and showed no fear of death.

I did not know what I had expected. The noise
and the smells should have prepared me, but it was
still a shock to see the streets littered with the bodies
of Taino and Kalinago men. A few horses lay on the
ground where they had fallen into the pits we had
dug, their riders sprawled among the dead, Kalinago
arrows sprouting from their backs.

My bow was armed and ready. My eyes scanned
the rearing horses. Where was he?

And then he was there, a skull banging his leg as he ran. He raised his bow at the same time as the pale man behind him raised his fire stick. I lifted my bow and screamed a warning.

My arrow leaped from my hand at the same time as Wakanik's leaped from his, a breath before the fire stick spat and he fell.

'No!' I was screaming as I ran, arming my bow and sending arrows speeding among the pale men. I heard someone behind me shouting my name, but I did not stop. I had almost reached Wakanik when he sprang up and snatched an arrow from his pouch. I stopped, confused. In my waking dream he had not moved.

I heard my name again, closer this time. I spun round. Azzacca was running towards me, his axe raised. In front of him and almost on top of me was a pale man on his horse.

Azzacca buried his axe in the rump of the horse. The animal screamed, a sound that was like tens and tens of angry iguanas, and reared on its hind legs. The pale man fought to control his horse. He raised his shiny stick and brought it down in a sweeping arc.

The ground blossomed red where Azzacca fell.

The pale man turned and raised his stick once more. I heard the sound of an insect by my ear and the man was falling from his horse, an arrow in his neck.

The sound of the *guamo* rose above the clamour, ordering the men to take to the forest. A hand was dragging me towards the trees.

'Run!' Wakanik ordered.

I ran.

75

Into the Mountains

We sped through the forest as if the demons from the underworld were chasing us. The smell from the pale men's fire sticks filled our nostrils and throats so that we coughed and spluttered as if we had sniffed the Kalinago's pepper smoke.

We climbed the mountain like people possessed, our feet eating the ground. The pale men were not climbers. They did not like the mountains, and if we were above them, we could use the rocks at our feet as weapons.

Besides, we had learned the lessons from Wakanik well, and could melt into the forest like any Kalinago. The pale men would never find us.

On a rise above the forest we stopped. I looked out

over the treetops and the breath stopped in my throat. The village was on fire.

Wakanik came and stood beside me.

'Do not grieve, Maruka,' he said.

I whirled on him. He had never called me Maruka.

'I give you my name,' he said. 'From this day think of me only as Wakanik. If you had not warned me I would now be lying in the streets with the dead of Kiskeya.'

I thought of Azzacca and the tears trembled on my lashes. I blinked rapidly. I did not want to appear weak in front of Wakanik, but Azzacca's death hurt more than I would have thought possible. I was only beginning to know the new Azzacca and now he was gone. But I could not think of him now. There was too much to do. I searched the faces of the Taino who had escaped with us. It was the first time I had seen the men since I had left Kiskeya, and pity moved inside me. Beside the Kalinago, their condition was more shocking. Their ribs pushed against their skins and their eyes were sunken pricks of light. Bamako was there with them and my eyes widened in shock. Without his amulets he had lost his air of authority. He looked no different from any of the men.

I searched the faces of the Kalinago men, then I turned to Wakanik.

'Your father?' I asked quietly.

His jaw tightened but he showed no other sign of grief. 'He goes to rest with the ancestors.'

'I am sorry.'

His eyes sparkled with pride. 'Do not be. He died with honour. As did your cacique. Now you must go to build a new home for your people.'

My heart beat painfully. 'But you are coming with us, are you not . . . ?'

He shook his head. 'Not yet. There is much to be done. The Taino and Kalinago dead must be removed from the battlefield and helped on their journey.'

He turned as if he would go, but I needed to keep him there.

'You have given me your name,' I said. 'But I have nothing to give you in return.'

He looked at me for a long time and then he smiled.

'Go now. One day we will meet again. Then you may repay me.'

'But how will you know where we are?'

'I have found you before, and I will again.'

His face clouded as he turned to look at the smoke that marked the place where the Taino had lived.

'The Taino are not alone any more. The Kalinago will fight beside you. Just sound the conch when you need us. We will not be far away.'

I watched him turn and melt into the trees, followed by the Kalinago men. I swallowed hard and turned away from the empty place where he had stood.

The gazes of the Taino were trained on me. Bamako, at the head of the men, had the most piercing stare of them all. They were all looking for leadership, for guidance. With my father and Azzacca gone, there was no one else they could turn to. My other male cousins were still children. I felt the responsibility like an overloaded maize basket on my head.

I could not lead anyone. I had not even had my age-ceremony.

But if I did not lead them, who would?

I raised my head, pushed back my shoulders and addressed them as my father would.

'Taino, men of the good. Why do you stand about as if you have nowhere to go? The mountains of Kiskeya are waiting. Your women are waiting. The pale strangers may have won the battle on the plains, but from our mountain homes we can be a thorn in their flesh. They tried to destroy us, but we will not be destroyed. Guakia Taino Yahabo!'

Their answering shout shook the birds from the trees.

'Guakia Taino Yahabo. We the Taino are still here!'

Bamako stepped from the front of the men and came to stand beside me.

'Would the casika do the behique the honour of walking with him?'

I stared at him, unable to speak. A smile chased the fierceness from his face. He looked up towards the mountains, then back at me.

'We should not be standing here if we want to join the others before dark. I have much work ahead. An age-ceremony and an accession on the same day.' He shook his head ruefully. 'Only you, Maruka. Only you.'

He held out his hand.

'Your people and your *duho* await, casika.'

I put my hand in his and turned towards the mountains. The rest of the Taino fell in behind us and the evening sun peeped from behind a cloud and carved us a dappled path through the forest.

A Note from the Author

In 1492 Christopher Columbus set out to find a new route to the East. Though most of the people of his day thought the Earth was flat, he was convinced it was round and was determined to prove the East could be reached by sailing westwards. After many days on the ocean he saw land and thought he was in India, so he named the people he met Indians.

These people called themselves *Taino*, meaning 'men of the good' and, as Columbus noted in his journal, they were gentle, trusting and trustworthy people. In his *book of his First Navigation and Discovery of these Indies,* he wrote:

> *. . . they took and gave to us of all that they had with good will . . . Some of them wore pieces of gold*

hanging from the nose, which they very willingly exchanged for a hawk's bell of the sort we tie to a falcon's foot, and for little beads of glass, but there is so little of it that it is virtually nothing, which is true of all the little things we give them . . . Those who gave pieces of gold did so . . . as freely as those who gave a gourd of water.

What we know of the Europeans' first meeting with the early inhabitants of the Caribbean we learn from a number of letters written by Columbus and the officers who sailed with him. Because of this, we see the Taino only as the explorers saw them – as commodities for Spain.

But they are very meek and do not know what it is to wreak evil or murder or enslave others; and they are without weapons of war and are so timid that a hundred of them will flee from one of our men, however good-humoured his approach . . .

Therefore your Highnesses should resolve to make Christians of them, for I believe that once a start is made, a great multitude of peoples will have been converted to our Holy Faith in a short time and your Highnesses and all your peoples in Spain will acquire great new lordships and riches therby. For there is no doubt that there is a very great quantity of gold in these lands.

The customs and language of those early peoples were recorded by men like Fray Ramón Pané and Bartolomé de Las Casas, priests who accompanied Columbus on his later journeys. It is from the latter especially that we learn of the brutality of the visitors.

Because of the difficulties with communication at that time, there are inconsistencies in the spellings of certain words and names. I have chosen the most popular ones. Wherever possible, I have used the Taino names for places and objects.

Other peoples also lived in the Caribbean before Columbus arrived: the Kalina/Kalinago, the Macorix and Ciguayo. All these people had stories to tell. *The Tribe* is just one of those stories.

Valerie Bloom

STAR DANCER

BETH WEBB

The omens warn of great evil to come. But there is a promise too: a shower of stars will mark the birth of the Chosen One who shall stem the tide . . .

On the night of the dancing stars, the prophesied child is born somewhere in the land. The druids begin their search for the enchanted boy, unaware that a baby named Tegen is also drawing her first breath . . . a girl who grows up with magic in her steps.

It is only years later, when the oldest and most honoured druid is dying, that Tegen is finally declared the rightful Star Dancer. But can she defeat the dark and demonic forces that are hell-bent on destroying her?

STAR DANCER begins an enthralling
fantasy sequence set in a stunning
but harsh prehistoric landscape.

A selected list of poetry titles available from Macmillan Children's Books

The prices shown below are correct at the time of going to press.
However, Macmillan Publishers reserves the right to show new retail prices
on covers, which may differ from those previously advertised.

BETH WEBB
Star Dancer   978-0-330-44570-2   £5.99

LENE KAABERBØL
Silverhorse   978-1-4050-9047-6   £10.99

CAROLE WILKINSON
Dragonkeeper   978-0-330-44109-4   £5.99

PETER DICKINSON
The Tears of the Salamander   978-0-330-41540-8   £5.99

JULIE BERTAGNA
Exodus   978-0-330-39908-1   £5.99

All Pan Macmillan titles can be ordered from our website,
www.panmacmillan.com, or from your local bookshop
and are also available by post from:

Bookpost, PO Box 29, Douglas, Isle of Man IM99 1BQ
Credit cards accepted. For details:
Telephone: 01624 677237
Fax: 01624 670923
Email: bookshop@enterprise.net
www.bookpost.co.uk

Free postage and packing in the United Kingdom